Lost
Summer

Also by Alex McAulay
Bad Girls

Available from MTV Books

Lost Summer

alex mcaulay

POCKET BOOKS   MTV BOOKS
New York   London   Toronto   Sydney

POCKET BOOKS, a division of Simon & Schuster, Inc.
1230 Avenue of the Americas, New York, NY 10020

This book is a work of fiction. Names, characters, places and incidents are products of the author's imagination or are used fictitiously. Any resemblance to actual events or locales or persons, living or dead, is entirely coincidental.

Copyright © 2006 by Alex McAulay

MTV Music Television and all related titles, logos, and characters are trademarks of MTV Networks, a division of Viacom International Inc.

All rights reserved, including the right to reproduce this book or portions thereof in any form whatsoever. For information address Pocket Books, 1230 Avenue of the Americas, New York, NY 10020

ISBN-13: 978-1-4165-2573-8

This MTV Books/Pocket Books trade paperback edition August 2006

10   9   8   7   6   5   4   3   2   1

POCKET and colophon are registered trademarks of Simon & Schuster, Inc.

Manufactured in the United States of America

For information regarding special discounts for bulk purchases, please contact Simon & Schuster Special Sales at 1-800-456-6798 or business@simonandschuster.com

For Lisa

Lost
Summer

1
complicated

Caitlin Ross slammed the door to her bedroom, locked it, and stood there fuming. She was fighting with her mom again, which was a pretty typical scenario for the two of them. Since Caitlin's dad had left home a year ago, she and her mom had been at each other's throats. But in the last month, things had gone from bad to unbearable. Caitlin didn't know if she could stand it anymore, but she didn't know what else to do, short of stealing her mom's credit cards, hijacking the Mercedes, and running away for good.

Caitlin could hear her mother moving around angrily in the hallway outside her room, talking to herself. Caitlin crouched down to look under the door, trying to see if her mom was heading in her direction. It was too hard to tell, so she stood up and leaned against the wall.

They'd been fighting over the usual suspects again. The argument had started over Caitlin's clothes, but then spread like a virus to her hair and makeup, and then to the million other things her mom always nagged her about.

At least she isn't banging on the door trying to continue the fight, Caitlin thought. She took a deep breath through her nose, counted to six, and then exhaled through her mouth, like she'd learned in yoga. It didn't help her feel any better, so she walked over to her bed and knelt down to extract a small, silver flask from underneath the mattress. She pulled it out, opened it, and took a sip, which burned her lips and made her cough. *Vodka neat.* Like her boyfriend Ian once said, it tasted like crap, but made the pain of living hurt less. *Of course, he'd been drunk at the time . . .* She took another sip as she fumbled around for a pack of cigarettes. Usually she didn't smoke in the house, but today was an exception.

As she sat on her bed and lit the first cigarette with her chrome lighter, she heard her mom start calling for her again, implacable and relentless. *Ah fuck,* Caitlin thought, closing the flask and slipping it back into its hiding place. *Just when you thought it was safe to go back in the water . . .*

"Caitlin!" her mom yelled. Caitlin studiously ignored her, taking a long drag on the cigarette and breathing out slowly. Her mom started rattling the doorknob. "Open this door right now and talk to me!"

Fat fucking chance. "If I wanted to talk, I wouldn't have locked you out," Caitlin muttered to herself. She cranked the iPod connected to her stereo, and her mom got drowned out by the blaring sounds of the Killers. But under the pounding drums and churning guitars, she could still hear her mom banging on the door. Caitlin turned the music up even louder, feeling the bass in her chest.

Caitlin knew from experience that her mom would get tired and go away pretty soon. But she also knew that this would just be a brief détente, and the fight would continue at a later date. Her mom couldn't resist an argument; she was like a pit bull once she got started.

If only Dad were still around to help balance things out, Caitlin thought. Her dad had been her champion and kept her mom's chaotic tendencies reigned in. Yet the divorce was final, and her dad was living in a Manhattan penthouse with his new girlfriend, Sofie. She was a nineteen-year-old model from Paris whose vacantly beautiful face Caitlin sometimes saw on the covers of fashion magazines.

Caitlin tried not to think about it as she stared around her room because the emotions were too painful. Instead, she focused on her surroundings, and thought, *God my room is a mess—what the hell's wrong with me? I'm turning into a bigger slob than Luke.*

Luke was her eleven-year-old brother, five years younger than her, and his room generally looked like Osama bin Laden had sent a suicide bomber to visit it. Luke had three main passions in life: playing games on his Xbox, watching violent gangster and horror DVDs, and shooting at cars with his paintball gun. Other than that, he was kind of lazy and slobby, and didn't have many friends. He dressed mostly in black, had a scruffy haircut, and was about twenty pounds overweight. Caitlin felt sorry for him, but also a little embarrassed that he was her brother.

The Killers gave way to 50 Cent, which amused Caitlin because she knew her mom hated hip-hop more than anything, especially if it were laden with profanities. Not that her mom didn't swear all the time, which was fairly hypocritical of her. If anyone ever said anything to Caitlin about having a potty mouth, which sometimes happened, Caitlin always made sure to say she'd picked it up from her mom. That and her drinking, and occasional smoking. She drew the line at those bad habits, though. Unlike her mom, she didn't constantly pop Valiums, Percocets, and other pastel-colored pills like M&Ms. Her mom was taking so many pills these days, it was frequently impossible to deal with her at all.

Sick of looking at the mess, Caitlin got up and opened the blinds on her two huge picture windows, unveiling a panoramic view of the Pacific Ocean. Her spacious bedroom looked down over the La Jolla Cove far below. Sunlight sparkled on gentle waves under the vivid blue sky that seemed to stretch to infinity over the water. The house, which was nearly a mansion, was located up high on the crest of a steep hill.

Caitlin sometimes felt guilty about living in such a lavish home. It had seven bedrooms, four-and-a-half bathrooms, a huge pool, and a gleaming kitchen larger than some people's entire houses. In Southern California's inflated real-estate market, the house was worth over five million dollars: one for the house and four for the land. Her dad had given it up in the divorce, along with so many other things. Caitlin didn't blame him for the collapse of her parents' marriage, although she'd been devastated at first, thinking he'd abandoned her and Luke. With time, she'd gained some perspective. She still loved her dad and most of the time she just missed him a lot. *If only Mom hadn't driven him so crazy!*

As Caitlin looked out at the admittedly spectacular view, she mused that prettiness could be so boring. In fact, the more she'd looked at the idyllic scenery over the past year, the more depressed she'd felt. Maybe she was just letting her parents' divorce spoil everything, but recently it seemed like there was nothing interesting whatsoever about La Jolla. Not all of Southern California was exciting and glamorous, like it seemed on TV. La Jolla was mainly populated by old people with garish mansions, too much money, and yachts they never sailed.

It's hard to believe I loved this place so much once, when I was a little kid, Caitlin reflected. Things had certainly changed since then, when she'd imagined spending her entire life here on the coast. She'd since realized the town was like a cute guy with nothing upstairs: superficially attractive, but not a good long-term prospect.

Caitlin pushed back a strand of her dark, wavy hair and stubbed out her cigarette on the edge of her oak desk, where it left a round scar. She immediately regretted it and tried to rub it away, but failed. With a sigh, she went over to her bed and slumped on a pile of pillows, under her framed poster of *Donnie Darko.* For some reason, she loved that movie, even though all her friends hated it, and whenever anyone saw the poster for the first time, they'd ask, "What the fuck is that about, Caitlin?"

Caitlin knew the poster didn't square with the stereotypical image of a spoiled, rich, fashion-conscious SoCal princess. *And so what?* She wasn't that kind of person anyway, and had never been, despite appearances. Besides, she'd discovered that it was an asset to seem unpredictable—to her mom, her friends, her boyfriend, and pretty much everyone else in between.

50 Cent faded into an old Weezer song, and Caitlin tapped her fingers on her knee in time with the beat. Judging from the fact that she didn't hear any banging and screaming under the music anymore, she figured her mom had gone away. *Probably back downstairs to take some pills, and then call one of her friends*

to complain about me. She stared up at the ceiling, listening to the music, and felt like a pathetic refugee from one of those stupid *Gossip Girl* books she used to read.

Suddenly she sat up. *Shit!* All the drama with her mom had made her forget that she was supposed to call Ian at 3:00. She checked her watch and saw it was already 3:20. She was surprised and a little disappointed he hadn't called her. She took out her cellphone, which no longer displayed images because she'd spilled beer on it the week before, and turned the music down a little. Then she called Ian, lying back on her bed. Just as her call was about to go to voicemail, Ian picked up.

"Hey," he practically grunted, articulate as ever. Caitlin had never figured out why boys got so awkward on the phone. In Ian's case, he wasn't much easier to communicate with in person. He was only her second long-term boyfriend, and they'd barely been going out for three months. She wasn't sure they'd make it too much longer.

"It's me. Don't you miss your girlfriend?" Caitlin asked.

"Sure, I miss you," he said. "Weren't you s'posed to come over today, like at three?" He sounded distant, maybe even annoyed, but perhaps she was reading too much into it.

"Was I? I thought I was supposed to call you then . . ." Their plans were always getting mixed up. *I hope I didn't flake on him,* Caitlin thought. "Maybe I got things confused," she said, plowing ahead hopefully. "But anyway, I got in a big fight with my mom today. Huge. So I'm sorry I didn't call."

Ian didn't sound very interested in what she was saying. "It's okay, I guess."

In the background Caitlin could hear someone trying to tune an electric guitar, and failing. Ian was the bassist for an up-

and-coming band called Box of Flowers that sounded, for better or worse, a lot like Green Day. Even though he was only seventeen, they already had a demo deal with a major label, mostly because the singer's dad had connections. Caitlin had formulated vague plans to sing backup on some of their songs if the album ever got made, although she hadn't told Ian about this idea yet. She didn't know how he'd react, but she hoped she could think of a way to talk him and the rest of the guys into it.

Not that singing backup for Box of Flowers was much of anything, but her ultimate goal was to become a singer or an actress one day, even though she knew it was pretty unlikely that would ever happen. *Who doesn't want to be a singer or actor in Southern California?* she wondered glumly. If it didn't happen for her, then she'd probably go to law school instead. That would be much less exciting, but then maybe she could work in the entertainment industry as an attorney, like her dad. She just didn't want to end up like her mom, who didn't have a college degree and had always depended on men for money.

I want to be my own person and actually do something with my life, she thought, *not just be some rich brat from La Jolla who sponges off their parents forever. Besides, that'll probably be Luke's job.*

Ian's voice on the phone snapped her out of her reverie. "Still wanna come over?"

"Definitely." She sat up again and lit another cigarette, feeling like she was getting a headache. "I'll be there in fifteen minutes." Caitlin heard the kick of a bass drum. "Sounds like you guys haven't even started practice yet. Still setting up?"

"Yeah." Long pause. "We scored some weed, so things are progressing . . . slowly . . ."

Since talking to Ian was like pulling teeth even when he wasn't high, Caitlin said, "Listen, I gotta go, but I'll see you soon, okay?"

"Okay," he echoed.

"Love you." She hung up before he could say anything else—in case he wasn't going to say "I love you" back—and slipped the phone into the pocket of her jeans. Now she just had to find a way to sneak out of the house and into her car without getting into another blowup with her mom.

She sighed and put out her cigarette, this time in a half-empty bottle of San Pellegrino. It was only the second week of June. School had been out for just ten days. *Who knew the summer would already be so complicated?*

2

Caitlin grabbed her purse, slipped on a pair of mules, and finally dared to unlock the door and head into the wide hallway. Her mom was nowhere in sight. Caitlin crept down the hall, past all the useless antiques and the garish canvases hanging on the wall. Her mom had purchased an extensive art collection and hired a team of interior designers to redo the entire house after Caitlin's dad left. She had made out remarkably well in the divorce—getting the house, the Hummer, the Mercedes SL-600 Roadster, and almost three hundred grand a year in child support and living expenses. It was a nice deal, even though she didn't deserve it.

On her way out of the labyrinthine house, Caitlin stopped to go to one of the downstairs bathrooms. She stepped inside and locked the door, breathing a sigh of relief that she hadn't run into her mom yet. Her reflection in the large gilded mirror caught her eye, so she stopped to stare back at herself. She looked fine—mostly. She held a finger under her chin, trying to make her jawline look thinner. Ian always told her she looked like Keira Knightley, but she didn't believe him. *If only I could drop another five pounds,* she thought, glancing away. *Or ten.*

Her train of thought was broken when she opened the lid of the toilet and saw what was inside. "For God's sake," she muttered. She let the lid drop back down and got out of the bathroom fast, into the hall, just in time to see Luke emerge from behind a black leather couch in the distant living room, laughing. It was his new trick to gross her out—going to the bathroom without flushing. "You're disgusting!" she snapped, as she strode in his direction. "Why are you always so immature?"

"Like you're any more mature than I am," he called back. As she stepped into the living room, he raised his arm and she saw that he was clutching his paintball gun, a wide grin lingering on his face.

Caitlin didn't have time to deal with Luke today. "Don't fire that thing in the house or Mom's going to kill you. She's already pissed off."

"Mom's always pissed off." Luke pointed the gun at her. "Might as well shoot you anyway."

Caitlin sighed. "Luke, put it down. You know I hate guns." She started walking toward him again, knowing he wouldn't really do it. But he kept the barrel disturbingly steady. "You're such a brat."

"At least I'm not a shallow snob who dresses like a ho." He stuck out his tongue at her childishly. "Your clothes are so tight, you should go turn tricks on the street." Before she could even respond to the insult, he suddenly licked the barrel of the gun in an exaggerated gesture. *Revolting.* "I could be your pimp . . ."

"Where did you learn to talk like that?" she asked him, wanting to wring his neck. Caitlin should have been shocked by his language and tone, but she already knew her little brother was completely crazy. Twice he'd shot people through their open car windows with paintballs, and twice the police had brought him home. *He's going to end up in juvie if he doesn't start behaving himself,* she mused. He had all the makings of a total delinquent. "You're not Snoop Dogg or Jay-Z. You're not even Kanye West. You're eleven years old. You don't even have any friends. Pimps have friends, Luke. That's a prerequisite for the job."

A frown creased his brow. "I've got friends."

"Name one. I know you can't, because they don't exist."

He thought for a few moments, as Caitlin waited, her arms crossed. "My gun is my friend," he finally decreed, pointing it at her again, "and if you keep talking, I'm going to have to shoot you. Don't make me do it, because then you'll be useless to me as a ho. You won't be able to join my stable of bitches . . . and I want to keep my pimp hand strong."

Caitlin didn't know whether to laugh or throw up. *Isn't Luke too old for this? Or too young?* "Luke, you're beyond demented. And stop being sexist. I'm not a ho. That's a really offensive term, by the way—not that you care."

He squinted at her. "Look at your tank top. Your boobs are busting out of it."

"My boobs aren't any of your business, you little freak."

"Ho bag, ho bag," Luke chanted. "You better check your stats on Am I Slutty dot com."

Caitlin rolled her eyes. "You've made that dumb joke before. You're boring me. Work on your material."

He brandished his gun and did the world's lamest *Scarface* impression: "Say hello to my little friend!"

Someone's got to stop him from watching those kinds of

movies, Caitlin thought, as Luke struck ridiculous poses with his weapon. *Mom's really asleep at the wheel.* "You're going to end up like one of those Columbine kids, aren't you?" she muttered. "I just know it."

"All I need is a real gun, right?" He licked the barrel again.

Suddenly Caitlin was too grossed out to take it anymore. "Stop it, stop it," she said, as she covered her eyes because she couldn't watch. She knew he was just trying to tease and torture her. But she also knew he wouldn't push it too far because she was still taller than him and could kick his ass if she had to, or so she hoped.

Right then, her brother raised the gun and pointed it at the cathedral ceiling of the living room. Before she could stop him, he began to scream out lines from *Apocalypse Now,* one of his favorite war movies, which he misquoted from constantly. A split second later there was a sharp crack, and a large blotch of red paint appeared on the white plaster high above them. A few droplets rained down on an imported Syrian rug, staining the pale, handwoven fibers bright red.

"You've totally lost your mind," Caitlin observed sadly as Luke cackled and danced around the room, whooping with glee. "I'm taking off. Have fun dealing with Mom."

Caitlin was just turning to leave when she heard screaming heading in their direction. The gunshot had obviously attracted their mom's attention.

Luke immediately took off running into the kitchen with his gun. Caitlin was about to follow right behind him, but her mother burst through a doorway on the other side of the room before she could escape. From the strange look on her mom's face and her familiar glazed eyes, Caitlin could tell immediately that she'd taken some tranquilizers, probably a palmful of Valium.

"What's going on here?" her mom yelled. She was so out of it, she didn't notice the red paint right above her on the ceiling, or on the carpet, which Caitlin thought was bleakly funny. She could only conclude that Luke was going to get in big-time trouble for this. Her mom valued her rugs more than life itself.

"I'm heading out," Caitlin said, praying they wouldn't start fighting again. She tried to sound calm and collected, even though she felt anything but. "Just to warn you, Luke's gone psycho. He thinks he's either a pimp or a deranged Vietnam vet. Or both."

Caitlin's mom rubbed her bloodshot eyes. "Can't you keep a better eye on him for me?"

"I don't control Luke, Mom," Caitlin explained. "If anything, you're supposed to do that. You're the parent, right?"

"And you're the child, so don't talk back to me like that." Her mom waved her hand dismissively at her. "I'm not done with you anyway, little missy. Locking yourself in your room isn't going to make your problems go away. We haven't finished talking . . ." *Talking* being her mom's favorite synonym for *arguing*.

Caitlin knew better than to stay and risk more feuding. "I'm meeting Ian and the band at his place, and I'm already running late. We can talk about it when I get back."

"So you're still seeing that boy." Her mom tottered unsteadily on her feet, like she was about to fall over. Caitlin noticed that her mom's faint southern accent had become more pronounced, which only happened when she was extra loaded. Caitlin's mother had grown up poor in small-town Texas, but always tried to hide that fact, presumably so her wealthy West Coast friends wouldn't think she was a hayseed. Caitlin had even heard her mom lie before and say she'd grown up outside Del Mar, not that she fooled anyone.

"Ian is my boyfriend," Caitlin said slowly, like she was talking to an eight-year-old. "So of course I'm still seeing him." To Caitlin, it seemed like her mom had an irrational hatred of Ian, and she wasn't sure why. "We've been dating for three months now. You know that. What's the problem?"

Her mom's eyes swam into focus briefly, as she sat down on the couch. Light streamed in from the curved wall of floor-to-ceiling windows. Behind her mom, Caitlin could see the houses below them on the hill and the cerulean ocean beyond that. "The problem is, I asked you to stop seeing Ian. I don't like his parents . . . and I don't like him, either. He's just not the right kind of boy for you. You have to think about your reputation, Caitlin. Why are you disobeying me like this?"

Caitlin laughed, trying to defuse the growing tension, wondering how a house this large could feel so small. "Mom, are you nuts? I haven't 'obeyed' you in years. And unless this is Korea, I still get to choose my own boyfriends."

Her mom scowled. "You think you know everything, don't you?" Another drop of red paint fell down and went unnoticed. "Well, maybe you shouldn't be so sure of yourself. Especially when it comes to this summer."

"What does that mean?"

"Has it ever crossed your mind that I'm so sick of you and

your brother's behavior that I might have done something about it?"

"Honestly? No."

Her mother smiled, and it wasn't a happy smile. "Then you've underestimated me, Caitlin, like always." After a dramatic pause she added, "I was going to tell you this in a few days, at the last minute, like an intervention. But you might as well know now. I've had it with you and Luke—the situation has become intolerable. So we're going away this summer, Caitlin. To the Outer Banks of North Carolina."

"What?!" Caitlin didn't think she'd heard her mom correctly.

"North Carolina," her mom repeated. "For the whole summer. Maybe longer."

It was like a kick in the guts. To Caitlin's complete surprise, she found that she was almost too drained and horrified to scream at her mother, maybe because they'd already spent all day arguing. She wanted to start yelling again, but she just felt a crushing wave of despair wash over her.

Caitlin would have thought her mom was bluffing, but there was something steely and cold in her mom's eyes that let her know it was the truth. Her mom had tried something like this once before, two years ago, when she'd secretly arranged for Caitlin to go to a ten-week summer camp in Temecula. Her dad had intervened at the last second and saved her. Still, Caitlin was totally blindsided by this new act of betrayal.

"What are you talking about? Are you serious?" she asked. "Why didn't you tell me about this earlier?" Her mind started racing, trying to figure out a way around the problem.

"I knew you wouldn't understand, and I knew you and Luke

would fight me on it. This is my house, and I make the rules—
despite what you think. I didn't want to be undermined by both
of you. We're going to North Carolina for the summer, no matter what you do or say. All three of us. You, me, and your
brother. It's booked and arranged. We'll be living on the very
edge of the Outer Banks, on an island called Danbroke. I doubt
you've ever heard of it . . ."

Caitlin continued to register the news with shock and horror. "An island? Jesus. Why?"

"Because I think this town, and this house, have become an
unhealthy environment for you and Luke. You've become too
spoiled—"

"It's not La Jolla's fault. If anything, it's *your* fault! Taking
pills all day long has screwed up your mind." Her mom, of
course, always refused to acknowledge she had a drug problem
whenever Caitlin dared to bring it up.

"Nobody's perfect. You don't understand the stress I've been
coping with since your father left. You and Luke have just been
making everything worse—"

"Did it ever occur to you that I made plans for this summer? Plans involving my friends? I have a life here. You can't
just put me and Luke on a plane like hostages. I'm not some
little kid you can drag around anymore. I'm going to spend
the summer in La Jolla, where I belong, not on some shitty
island."

"It's just one summer, Caitlin. You'll have all the summers in
the world left to do what you want with—but this one is going
to be mine. We'll be living in a totally different environment.
No more shooting up the neighborhood for Luke. No more in-
appropriate boys and shopping sprees for you. I'm sick of it,

Caitlin. I'm sick of *all* of it. I refuse to have my two children grow up to be vicious, spoiled brats, understand?"

In her head, Caitlin was thinking the word "bitch" over and over again, like a mantra. "By doing this to us, and by keeping it secret, you're just going to make me and Luke detest you more than we already do. And why North Carolina, of all the lame-ass states? How could it be better for us than California?"

Her mom looked tired. "You and Luke are running wild. You're always out with boys I don't approve of—like Ian—doing God knows what, and Luke is completely out of control. I've talked to my therapist about what to do, and he fully approves of the trip. He thought North Carolina would be an excellent idea."

Caitlin felt her fists clenching. "You don't see a therapist anymore, Mom. You quit, remember?"

"I talked to him on the phone." She sounded sincere, but didn't make eye contact when she said it. Caitlin didn't know if that meant anything. *Could be a lie.*

"Is this the same therapist who prescribed all those pills for you in the first place?" Caitlin asked. Her mom didn't answer. "What does Dad think about your crazy plan? I bet he doesn't know anything about it."

Caitlin's mom smiled thinly. "You're wrong. He knows everything." She rubbed her forehead. "I even talked to him about it this morning. He thinks it's a good idea, too. He said Danbroke would be a good change of pace for you and Luke."

"You're lying," Caitlin said, certain her dad never would have agreed to this scheme. "No way." She knew that her mom and dad barely agreed about anything, except to get a divorce.

"It's true."

Caitlin took out her phone. "Then I'm going to call him right now and ask him about it."

To Caitlin's surprise, her mom nodded. "Good. Maybe it'll help you calm down and come to your senses."

Caitlin ignored her mom. "Just wait and see," she muttered. She could only imagine her dad would greet the news of the trip with the same dismay she felt. But she had to admit she also felt a tiny sliver of doubt that maybe somehow her mom had managed to convince her dad about North Carolina. *Surely Dad would have told me about it, though,* she thought. *He wouldn't just strand me in such a dire situation.*

The phone rang once, then twice, then clicked over into voicemail. *Shit.* Caitlin had been sure she'd be able to reach him. She left an urgent message and then hung up.

"Dad's going to be so pissed when he finds out," she told her mom.

Her mom leaned forward, hunching her shoulders. "Like I said, he already knows."

"You really thought you were going to get away with this? That Luke and I would go with you on some half-baked 'vacation' all the way across the country?"

"You don't have a choice. Everything's already set up—it's too late to change the plan now."

"Where are we going to stay? And why North Carolina?" It sounded so completely bizarre that Caitlin wondered if there were more to it than met the eye. "I get the feeling something really weird's going on . . ."

"There's nothing weird about a change of locale," her mom replied. "And for your information, we'll be staying at a resort hotel called the Pirate's Lodge."

Caitlin's heart dropped further. "I don't want to stay at some cheesy resort, especially one with such a stupid name. I want to stay right here."

Her mom shut her eyes. "We're leaving in four days. On Tuesday."

Caitlin thought she was going to pass out, because all the blood suddenly rushed from her head. She wondered if she'd heard it right. "Tuesday?!" she yelled. "Are you fucking kidding me?" *Could things get any worse?*

Her mom was about to say something more when Caitlin's phone suddenly rang. The ringtone was a song from Beck's last album, which sounded incongruously cheery blaring in the tense atmosphere of the living room. It was her dad calling back. *Thank God,* she thought. She opened the phone up and said, "Hello," as she glared daggers at her mom. Her mom still hadn't noticed the paint on the ceiling.

"Caitlin, what's going on?" she heard her dad's concerned, gravelly voice say on the other end.

Her words came all at once, as she began to tell him exactly what her mom was threatening to do to her and Luke.

Dad will fix things for me, she thought to herself as she talked, willing it to be true. *He always does, and today will be no exception.*

She could trust her dad, she just knew it.

3
fight or flight

Four days later, Caitlin was sitting in the first-class section of an airplane, next to Luke, on her way to North Carolina. She gazed out the window, a paperback copy of *Prep* in her lap, as her brother watched the unrated version of *Carlito's Way* for the millionth time on his portable DVD player. Whenever she glanced down at the screen, she either saw someone getting blown away by a shotgun or doing coke. She'd brought her iPod along, but didn't feel in the mood to listen to music. Somehow it seemed like nothing would be appropriate, considering her current predicament. Sitting across the aisle from her and Luke was her mom, basking in the glow of victory.

To Caitlin's utter shock, it turned out her dad had known about the plan to go to North Carolina. She'd thought her mom was lying. Her dad didn't approve of the plan, necessarily, but he was powerless to stop it. Caitlin understood that he just hadn't wanted to waste his energy fighting with her mom, and that knowledge made her feel sad. He had let her mom sabotage her summer, presumably out of laziness and preoccupation with

The Model. It was a bitter pill to swallow. Caitlin had almost broken down in tears that day on the phone when she realized her dad wasn't going to help her. *And he's supposed to be the good parent, the one who actually loves me,* she thought. Clearly, now that he'd left California, he had different priorities.

She didn't cry when she talked to her dad, though, because she didn't want to give her mom the satisfaction. Instead, she and her mom had another terrible fight, in which Caitlin had basically told her mom she loathed her and her addictions, and would rather run away than go to Danbroke. Caitlin had been quite serious about this plan, but unfortunately, her mom controlled all the money, and she ultimately realized that there was no choice but to go. *What the hell else can I do?* she'd thought. Her mom wouldn't let her stay with her best friend, Alison, or any of the other friends who'd offered to take her in. And on top of everything, her mom kept saying that if things went well on Danbroke, maybe they'd move there for good. Caitlin thought it was more of a threat than an actual possibility, but she couldn't be sure.

At first, Luke had put up just as much of a fight as Caitlin did, on principle. But then, unexpectedly, he'd caved. His change in attitude partly had to do with the fact that their mom had bribed him with the promise of a ten-thousand-dollar four-wheeler she'd buy him when they got to Danbroke. It didn't seem to occur to her mom that this would be completely unsafe for Luke, and for anyone unlucky enough to get in his way. Caitlin also realized Luke's sudden capitulation was because he didn't have any friends in La Jolla, so there'd be no one for him to miss. As long as he had his DVDs and no responsibilities, he'd be happy, no matter where he was living.

She looked over at him on the plane. Luke was lost in the world of the movie, as though his surroundings didn't matter, or even exist. In a strange way, Caitlin envied the way he didn't overtly care about anything, but she also felt pissed. Unlike Luke, she had tons of friends back in La Jolla, and a boyfriend. Even Ian, who was usually so laid-back about their relationship he was nearly comatose, had been shocked when Caitlin told him she was leaving in just a few days.

"For real?" he'd asked, thinking she was teasing him. All too soon, he'd realized she was serious. She'd spent her last night in town with him, Alison, and Alison's boyfriend Casey. They'd had dinner at José's on Prospect Street—one of the few places that didn't card—and then they'd gone down to one of the huts overlooking the ocean in Scripps Park, to drink more. After that, they'd walked down to the beach and lit a fire in one of the fire pits, huddling around it. It had been her big send-off for the summer, she supposed. Nobody had really known how to act, and she could tell they all felt bad for her, but were trying to cheer her up.

"I doubt I'll actually be gone for too long," she'd told them, praying that she was speaking the truth. "I'm sure when my mom figures out that there aren't any designer boutiques on Danbroke, or flaky doctors she can scam into giving her pre-scription pain pills, she'll drag us back to California as fast as she can."

That last night on the beach had been a tearful, drunken good-bye, with Alison pledging her friendship, and with she and Ian reaffirming that they wouldn't let Caitlin's trip ruin their relationship. Yet today on the airplane, fighting a hangover and a modicum of depression, Caitlin felt small and alone. She knew

Alison would always be her best friend, but would Ian wait around for her? Somehow she doubted it. He'd always been, in the lingo of the ultracheesy teen magazines she read at the hair salon, "Mr. Right Now" instead of "Mr. Right." Caitlin had known that and been fine with it, but now that she'd been ripped out of her environment so quickly, she was suddenly craving all the things she'd taken for granted.

She'd only brought two large suitcases with her, because that was all her mom had allowed. More of their clothes from home would be shipped to their new digs in the next week. Caitlin's mom had been remarkably vague about the place they'd be staying. Caitlin assumed it had to be one of those garish luxury resorts for retirees and wealthy European tourists—which in a way, wouldn't make it very different from La Jolla. These were the kinds of hotels her mom loved. However, the name "the Pirate's Lodge," didn't instill much confidence, because it sounded more like a cheap roadside dive than a five-star resort.

Caitlin couldn't believe they still had two more hours of flying time left—and that was only the first part of the journey. They would be landing in James Port, a small city in North Carolina near the coast, and from there, they'd be driving down the Outer Banks to Cape Hatteras. Caitlin's mom had chartered a car and a driver for that part of the journey. From Hatteras, they'd be taking a ferry to the island. Caitlin and Alison had Googled the Outer Banks together, and learned that Danbroke was a pretty desolate place, just a long strip of land in the thin chain of islands comprising the Outer Banks. A lot of it was designated as national seashore, and there was only one town on it—a town so small that it didn't have a name.

If I were a sixty-year-old retired guy who loved fishing and hunt-

ing, then Danbroke would be my idea of paradise, Caitlin had thought when reading about the island. *Unfortunately, I'm the complete opposite of that.* There were few mentions of the Pirate's Lodge online, and it didn't have a website. Caitlin did learn it was the oldest and the largest of the few hotels on the island, and that Sean Penn had stayed there once while filming a movie in 1988. Caitlin clung to this random trivia as a link to her life in California, and a sign that the hotel couldn't be too bad if a movie star had once spent some time there. She also figured it might make the hotel sound more glamorous when she told her other friends about it.

Caitlin missed her friends so much that it actually hurt, a dull ache on the left side of her chest. She thought about all the things she'd miss from back home and felt a surge of self-pity. What had promised to be the best summer ever was now a train wreck. She settled back in the wide leather seat, waiting for the flight to be over, and craving a cigarette.

* * *

When they landed, an annoyingly cheerful driver was waiting for them at the airport. He was holding a little sign that read THE ROSS FAMILY, and he led them outside into the hot, humid air. He was bald, and his shiny head reflected the sun as Caitlin followed. She already felt sweat beading under her arms. She was at least glad to see that her mom had arranged for a decent car to take them to Danbroke—a black Cadillac Escalade.

"You two ride in back," her mom said, as the driver hustled to put their bags inside, no doubt hoping for a large tip. "I'm sitting up front." Caitlin had no idea why her mom wanted to sit in the front, but guessed it was so she could zone out in peace.

Caitlin followed her mom's instructions without bothering to reply and climbed inside the spacious interior. It was cool inside, which was a welcome relief, and the seats were far more comfortable than the ones in the airplane. The car smelled subtly of expensive perfume.

"Tight ride," Luke commented, as he piled into the back of the Escalade after her. "Two TV screens. DVD player. Nice."

"As if you need to watch any more movies," Caitlin muttered, as she applied some cherry-flavored lip balm.

"This is the kind of car I'm going to buy when I make my first billion dollars," Luke decreed.

"A billion dollars from what? Pimping? Luke, you're a joke."

"Naw, I'll do my pimping on the side. I'm going to design video games, produce movies, and have my own clothing line, like Diddy."

Caitlin had heard this inane fantasy before. "Just because you like playing video games doesn't mean you're smart enough to design them. You failed math last year. In fact, you failed most of your classes, am I wrong? You need better grades and a college degree before anyone will let you design video games." As she spoke, in her head she was thinking, *Why am I even bothering?* She knew it was pointless to use logic in an argument with her brother.

"Bill Gates didn't go to college. Neither did Diddy or Jay-Z." He sounded like his pride had been wounded, but maybe he was just putting on an act.

"Bill Gates went to college—he just didn't graduate. I think. Listen, why are we even talking about this?" She crossed her arms over her chest. "Besides, all those people are exceptions. Most people don't get that rich."

"Dad's rich."

"Not *that* rich."

"Did I mention I'm going to be a rapper, too?" Luke asked. "Like Eminem."

"Vanilla Ice, maybe."

He looked mortally insulted. "You've never heard me rap, Caitlin."

"And I thank God for that every single day."

He opened his mouth, as if he were about to burst into a rhyme, but then, like the spaz that he was, he suddenly changed gears and began digging in his grungy backpack. The driver started the engine and the car came to life. All around them swirled taxis and other cars picking people up from the terminal.

Caitlin's mom turned around, looking dazed, and said, "Mr. Gordimer's going to tell us about the trip to Danbroke. You have to listen now."

Caitlin realized that Mr. Gordimer must be their driver. She wondered how much he and the Escalade were costing her mom per hour. "Great," she said sarcastically, kicking her legs out in front of her. "Can't wait."

Mr. Gordimer either didn't catch her tone or chose to ignore it. "So y'all are from California, is that right?"

Luke burped as a means of response, and Caitlin said nothing, but that didn't dissuade Mr. Gordimer from continuing to speak as he pulled the car away from the terminal and toward a long stretch of highway.

"La Jolla's a nice place, or so I've heard. I bet the beaches out there are real pretty. Not as pretty as some of the beaches we got here, though, I'll wager." He chuckled throatily and Caitlin wished that he'd just stop talking. "Anyways," he continued, "it's about an hour and twenty minutes from here to the ferry that will take you to Danbroke Island. The ferry runs three times a day, as long as the weather's good. We'll probably hit it just in time for the six-thirty one."

He turned back to glance at them; Caitlin would have preferred him to keep his eyes on the road. The traffic had thinned out, and the long, winding highway was like a strip of gray ribbon unfurling across the desolate landscape in front of them. Unlike the open vistas of California, except for the road ahead, the horizon was hemmed in by thick green trees.

"It freaks me out that we have to take a ferry," Caitlin muttered. There was something oddly claustrophobic about living on an island in general—no way to get on or off it except by boat or air. "I don't like islands."

"Manhattan's an island," Luke piped up. "Does it freak you out when we fly to New York City to visit Dad?"

"Luke, shut up."

Mr. Gordimer heard their interaction and laughed, which irritated Caitlin. *Shouldn't the driver just be quiet and drive?* Sadly, he seemed to be one of those overly talkative types. "That's right, Luke. You make a good point. Besides, the ferry ride will be fun. You and your sister will enjoy it."

Caitlin noticed her mom was silent, and wondered if she were nodding out from the pills, or just general fatigue. Mr. Gordimer kept up his banter, trying to engage her and Luke in conversation, but neither of them had much interest in talking to him. Caitlin did pick up a couple useful bits of knowledge, neither of which made her feel any better about how life would be on Danbroke.

The total population of the island was only a thousand people, not including the small number of tourists that came every summer. Because it was so far down the Outer Banks, it wasn't a hot spot for vacationers, like Wilmington or Cape Hatteras. Caitlin got the sense the island was nearly deserted.

"Danbroke has beautiful white sand beaches," Mr. Gordimer said rapturously. "Unspoiled. Some folks like it for the fishing. Some for the peace and quiet. The Pirate's Lodge, where you folks are headed, is the only hotel on the whole island that's got any size to it. The other two are bed-and-breakfast joints." He glanced at Caitlin in the rearview mirror. "Your mom knows the owner, is that right?"

This was news to Caitlin. She sat upright in the seat and looked over at Luke, but he hadn't heard. He'd taken out his own iPod and had his earbuds in.

"What?" Caitlin asked, confused.

"Your mom knows the owner of the Pirate's Lodge," Mr. Gordimer reiterated. "She's friends with him." He looked over at Caitlin's mom sitting next to him and then said, "Looks like she's taking a little catnap. Guess we better be quiet."

"No, wait, tell me more," Caitlin said, leaning forward. Now the driver had her interest.

"When your mother arranged this trip, I think she told me that she'd be staying at the Pirate's Lodge because the owner is an old friend of hers. Someone she's known since high school."

Now Caitlin was doubly shocked, because as far as she knew, her mom hadn't kept in touch with any "old friends" from

Texas. She'd always thought her mom had wanted to put her past far behind her.

"What's the owner's name?"

Mr. Gordimer seemed surprised that Caitlin didn't know about any of this. "Bill something," he said, sounding quizzical. "Bill Collins, maybe?"

Bill Collins, Caitlin thought, repeating the name several times in her mind. It was a generic-sounding name, and it didn't ring any bells. But not surprisingly, it was a guy's name. *Could this whole trip be some sick attempt on my mom's part to hook up with an old flame?* If so, her dad didn't know about *that* part, Caitlin was sure.

"And Bill is an old friend of my mom?" Caitlin asked earnestly, wanting to extract as much information as possible from the driver. "Is that why we're here?"

Mr. Gordimer suddenly turned a little nervous. "I think so," he said vaguely. "You should probably talk to your mother about it when she wakes up." He gave a forced laugh. "I don't want to interfere with family business, you know."

"You're not interfering, you're enlightening me. My mom didn't mention anything about an old friend named Bill Collins." Out the window, more green trees rushed past on either side.

"Huh," Mr. Gordimer muttered uneasily. It seemed his stream of chattiness had suddenly dried up. Caitlin wondered if he knew more than he was letting on. Either way, she couldn't wait to quiz her mom about it. She wanted to wake her up right away, but thought it would prove better to spring the newfound knowledge on her later, when it was just the two of them alone.

Or better yet, say nothing to her mom, but call her dad and let him know about it. Her mom was certainly the kind of woman who chased after guys, but usually ones richer and younger than her. It would be fairly insane to go all the way across the country after some random high-school crush. *And surely no one rich lived on Danbroke.*

They rode in near silence for a while, Caitlin listening to the faint sounds of her brother's iPod and the deep breathing of her mom emanating from up front. The hue of the sky was different here than in California, Caitlin noticed. It looked murkier and slightly faded, grayish brown, for whatever reason. She hoped the beaches were as nice as Mr. Gordimer had said. At least then she'd have the solace of the ocean to console her, even if she didn't have any friends to share it with.

From what she knew of Danbroke, it didn't sound like there'd be too many people her own age out there. There was—according to what she'd read online—a small high school on the island for locals, but most of the kids fled during the summer to work jobs on the mainland.

By the time they reached the ocean, Caitlin was beyond sick of traveling. They'd turned off the highway a few miles back and the road they were on eventually dead-ended into the ferry station. The ferry wasn't a very encouraging indication of what the island would be like. It was small and flat, old and rusty, and it made Caitlin a little nervous. A man in a tan uniform waved the Escalade onto the ferry, behind a beaten-up white van. There were only three other cars on the ferry, and all of them were dilapidated. Ahead stretched the choppy water of the Atlantic Ocean, dappled by the sunlight. Mr. Gordimer parked and turned off the engine.

"Let me know if you need the windows rolled down back there," he said. "It can get stuffy."

"Whatever," Caitlin replied. It was the first thing he'd said since the Bill Collins discussion. Her mom was still asleep. Caitlin looked out of the window at the water lapping at the giant wooden pylons to the left of the dock. The water looked cold, dark, and less inviting than the Pacific.

Luke was looking out the window, too, his earpieces now around his neck. "Has a ferry ever sunk out here?" he asked Mr. Gordimer. He didn't sound nervous or worried, just excited, like he was hoping it would happen.

"Not that I know of," Mr. Gordimer replied.

"Really," Luke said, sounding skeptical.

"Don't get any ideas, Luke," Caitlin told him, fearing that her brother was hatching some sort of terrorist plan, but he just laughed in response.

"One day I bet it sinks, and I bet all the passengers drown."

"Thanks for sharing." Caitlin heard her mom stirring in the passenger seat.

"Are we on Danbroke yet?" her mom mumbled, sounding dazed, and Luke laughed again. Her mom sounded like a little kid.

"No, ma'am," Caitlin heard Mr. Gordimer say. "But we're onboard the ferry. Danbroke's only another hour and a half from here, due south."

"Good." Her mom fell silent again. *Had she gone back to sleep already?* Caitlin wondered what it must feel like to be on pills all the time. It was probably like being drunk, she guessed, but even weirder because the sensation lasted twenty-four hours a day. It couldn't be a good feeling.

Caitlin opened her door and stepped out onto the metal surface of the ferry, shutting the door behind her. She was afraid Luke was going to burst out after her, but fortunately he didn't. The air was sticky, but at least there was a breeze as the ferry cut through the water. Caitlin took a deep breath, glad to be out in the fresh air. She walked over to the low wall at the edge of the ferry and looked down at the foaming water below.

I have to find out more about this Bill Collins guy, she thought. *And above all else, I have to make sure we get back to La Jolla as soon as possible.* Caitlin knew she couldn't stand living someplace so isolated, where it felt like the real world was a million miles away. *I'm going to get myself back home,* she vowed, still staring at the swirling ocean left in the wake of the ferry. *No matter what.*

4
island in the sun

By the time the ferry docked in Danbroke, Caitlin was back in the Escalade with Luke and her mom. Mr. Gordimer drove it off the ferry onto a narrow road, the tarmac pitted with potholes and asphalt scars. The island looked bleak and barren. On one side of the road were white sand dunes, blocking Caitlin's view. On the other side was a thick marsh that gave way to the ocean beyond. Sand drifted off the dunes in the breeze and blew across the road, making strange patterns on it like snow. Caitlin remembered the maps of Danbroke she'd seen online and realized they were traveling down the main artery of the island.

Shit, if the main road looks this bad, I can't imagine what the other roads look like, she thought. The island was extremely narrow, and she knew on the other side of the dunes lay more water.

There was literally nothing visible on the thin, flat island. No buildings, no people. Only the white van and the cars in front of them. Caitlin could tell even Luke was surprised at how deserted it seemed, because he was silent.

"This here is all national park," Mr. Gordimer explained helpfully. "Just sand and swamps. The town is closer to the other end of this road, which is why you can't see it from here."

Caitlin's mom was finally awake, jostled too frequently by the poor condition of the road to stay sleeping. "The Pirate's Lodge . . . it shouldn't be too far?" she murmured hopefully.

"That's right. It's just eight miles ahead, on the other side of the town."

There's something extremely creepy about Danbroke, Caitlin thought, as she looked out the windows. It was the perfect setting for a horror movie. She felt a nervous knot in her stomach about seeing the hotel, and the town, that would be her surrogate home for the summer.

Even Mr. Gordimer seemed odd, albeit in a banal kind of way. Caitlin couldn't quite put a finger on what was making her feel so uneasy. Maybe it was just being in such an isolated environment, so far away from home. It didn't help that she was trapped in close quarters with her mom and her brother, either: two people she generally tried to avoid. But there was still something fundamentally uncanny about Danbroke. The sand dunes and ocean reminded her a little of La Jolla, yet they were different enough to be completely alien. *Danbroke is like some nightmare version of home,* Caitlin thought. *Some twisted tangent universe.*

Luke shifted restlessly in his seat, oblivious to the unsettling ambience of the island. "They have a movie theater here, right? And a place to buy vids?"

Caitlin saw Mr. Gordimer glance at him in the rearview mirror. "You mean video games? I don't think so, young man."

"What exactly *is* on Danbroke?" Caitlin asked, sick of hearing and thinking about all the things it didn't have.

"There are several restaurants. Only one of them's open all year 'round. Lita's Pub. But in the summer, you've got your choice of at least three or four. Then there's a surf shop near the marina, a bait and tackle place, and some other stores. It's a nice little town. It's quaint."

Quaint. Caitlin hated quaint. It made her think of retired people in Florida.

"Danbroke's lame if it doesn't have a place to buy video games and DVDs," Luke opined. "What the hell am I going to do all summer? Mom, I didn't know this place would be such a dump."

With effort, their mom turned around in the seat and eyed Luke blearily. "I told you I'd buy you a four-wheeler. Just focus on that, okay? You can go riding on the sand dunes. You won't need to hide in your video games and movies anymore."

"Yeah, right." Luke didn't sound convinced. Caitlin wanted to point out that he should have taken her side and fought harder against going to Danbroke in the first place, but it was too late now. "You better get me that four-wheeler soon," Luke said. "Or else I'm going to get my paintball gun and go people hunting."

Caitlin smiled despite herself, because she had a sudden, almost post-apocalyptic, image of Luke riding around shirtless on his four-wheeler, shooting unwitting pedestrians—a demented child of the island. Her smile faded and she shuddered. The vision was all too real.

"They do have a bookstore on Danbroke—" Mr. Gordimer began, but Luke cut him off immediately.

"Books suck," he said. "I'm not going to waste my summer reading."

Mr. Gordimer chuckled dryly. "The bookstore's small, but well-stocked. It's part of a coffee shop called the Danbroke Coffee Company." Then, apropos of nothing, he added, "Books will help expand your mind, Luke."

Caitlin knew there was no way Luke would ever get into reading—a book to Luke was like a crucifix to a vampire.

"I hate books, and I hate coffee too," Luke mumbled.

"You hate pretty much everything," she said, turning toward him.

"So do you!" he retorted.

"But I'm not bitching about it constantly, am I? It doesn't count if I don't say it. Give us all a break." Caitlin looked out the window again. It was still just marsh and ocean. She hoped they'd get to the town soon, no matter how crappy and bleak it was. Anything had to be better than this desolate landscape.

"Why is everything so empty?" she asked Mr. Gordimer as they drove. "It's like there's nothing out here at all. Are we still in the national seashore part?"

"No, now we're just outside the township. There used to be some homes here, but they got destroyed by Hurricane Faye five years ago. Most of the people who still live here rebuilt closer to town, or moved off the island."

Luke's eyes sparkled with excitement. "Hurricanes. Cool."

"Don't say that. They're scary," Caitlin said. Now she had a whole new worry to think about. "Does Danbroke get a lot of them?"

"They pass through occasionally," Mr. Gordimer admitted, "but usually later in the year, around September."

Another good reason to be out of here soon, Caitlin thought. Her mission was becoming crystal clear: *Make Mom hate the island so we don't end up here for good.*

Luke leaned across Caitlin and looked intently out at the ocean through her tinted window. "I bet it'd be cool to be here when a hurricane hit. I bet the waves get huge. I could go body surf them."

"Yeah, Luke. That sounds great," Caitlin said, with deliberate overemphasis. "Remember what happened to New Orleans? Was that cool? Do you want all your stuff to get ruined and washed away?"

"No arguing," her mom intervened weakly, sensing that Caitlin and Luke were about to get into a fight. "Save it until you're out of the car."

Luke ignored her. "Caitlin, we don't have any stuff here yet. Most of your stupid, trashy outfits are in your closet back home. They'll be fine when a hurricane hits Danbroke. Relax."

Caitlin took a deep breath. She wished it were possible to go selectively deaf.

"Look, we're coming up to the outskirts of town now."

When she heard Mr. Gordimer's words, Caitlin strained to look out the front windows, but the few ramshackle buildings they were quickly approaching didn't resemble anything like a real town. *More like a ghost town,* Caitlin thought.

There were just a few broken-down buildings on either side of the road, wilting under the bright sun. She saw the obligatory crummy gas station, complete with a broken sign and a heap of old tires next to it. Everywhere she looked, weeds had grown through the cracked pavement.

"The town's been struggling since the hurricane," Mr.

Gordimer said by means of explanation. To Caitlin, it didn't look like the kind of place that had ever been doing well.

She saw a few people walking around here and there, but everything was in a state of decay. The closer they got, the more buildings she saw emerge. Some were fairly solid structures, but others were clearly trailers, mounted up on cinder blocks. Trees hung down over them, giving shade, and she saw people sitting out on their stoops. It was all pretty disheartening.

They passed a stand by the side of the road with a hand-painted sign on plywood that read FRESH SHRIMP AND BAIT. A guy with a scruffy beard was sitting there next to a couple of Styrofoam ice chests. He waved lazily at the car as it passed.

"You're lucky you're staying at the Pirate's Lodge," Mr. Gordimer continued. "It's the best hotel on the island by far, and the oldest. The hurricane scared a lot of visitors off, so some places just shut down. Still, I bet you'll be very happy here for the summer."

I seriously doubt it, Caitlin thought, annoyed at Mr. Gordimer's persistent optimism. Caitlin guessed it had never crossed her mom's mind to rent a car and do the driving herself.

"I'm bored," Luke volunteered. "When are we going to get there?"

"See that big building?" Mr. Gordimer pointed at something dark up ahead through the windshield, but Caitlin's view was blocked by Luke, who leaned right in front of her. "That's it, right there. The Pirate's Lodge. Built in nineteen-twenty-one . . . or so I believe."

Caitlin peered around Luke's head, trying to scout out the place. The building was massive, rising up from the land like the hotel from *The Shining*. It was built out of red brick, but had wooden walkways and terraces jutting out of it at various levels. Even at a distance, Caitlin could see it was run-down and derelict in appearance. What might have looked glamorous in the 1920s just looked ancient now.

"Mom, this place looks like shit," Luke blurted out, stating the obvious. He sat back in the seat, and for the first time on the trip, Caitlin could tell he was genuinely disturbed. Mr. Gordimer was being silent again. Caitlin's mom turned around to stare at her and Luke.

"Just because it's not La Jolla doesn't mean you have to immediately dislike it. You're acting like five-year-olds."

"I didn't say anything," Caitlin pointed out.

"You didn't need to. Give this place a chance." Her mother's eyes darted over to Luke. "That goes double for you, mister."

"I'm just being honest. You don't want me to lie, do you? All of us can see this hotel is a shit hole, even Mr. Gordimer, I bet."

Mr. Gordimer wisely stayed quiet.

"No backtalk," Caitlin's mom said tiredly.

The Escalade continued its slow approach. The hotel's lawn was poorly maintained, and patches of it had turned yellow and died under the heat of the sun. Other areas were verdant and overgrown, as if the sprinkler system were dysfunctional. It was a far cry from the lush, manicured lawns back home. *I never thought I'd be nostalgic for our lawn.* Caitlin thought dully. Mr. Gordimer drove them down the road until they reached the winding entrance to the hotel, a cobblestone drive that curved up to the main building and the large, beveled glass front doors of the entryway.

Mr. Gordimer parked the car and Caitlin got out, stepping into the thick air that felt almost tropical to her. She peered back down the road and saw that its surface was shimmering a little in the heat. Then she looked back up at the sweeping walls of the hotel. There was no one around to meet them; no sign of the mysterious Bill Collins. Just silence, and the hum of insects in the heat.

Caitlin heard Luke get out from the other side of the car. "So is hunting allowed on the island?" he was asking Mr. Gordimer, a note of challenge in his voice. "Are there any firing ranges?"

"I don't think so," he replied.

Caitlin's mom finally got out and walked around the front of the car, smoothing down her light blue Hermès blouse. There were sweat stains under her armpits. Caitlin followed.

"Are you serious about moving us here?" she asked her mom softly. She didn't say it bitchily; she was being sincere.

Her mom looked up at her, squinting because the sun was in her eyes. "I'm very serious, Caitlin. This place is going to do us good."

"I'm not so sure about that."

Just as Luke and Mr. Gordimer came around from the other side of the car, the front doors of the hotel swung open. A very tall, slightly stooped man about her mom's age emerged and lumbered down the flight of short stairs.

"Kathryn!" he called out. "You're here!"

Caitlin had never seen the man before in her life, but to her surprise, her mom yelped, "Bill!" and rushed to meet him. The two of them embraced, hugging long and hard. While still in his arms, Caitlin's mom turned around and said to her and Luke, "This is my friend Bill."

No shit, Caitlin thought. She knew in that instant that this guy was the whole reason they'd been dragged to the island for the summer—not because her mom wanted her and Luke to experience a new environment. Bill could only be a prospective boyfriend of her mom's, or an ex-boyfriend. Caitlin didn't know how or when the two of them had reconnected, but she could tell there was something between them. They were clearly more than just friends.

"Hey there, kids," Bill said in an awkward, and not particularly friendly, way. He had a strong Texan accent. Caitlin gave him a halfhearted wave, while Luke just stared at him blankly.

"Mom, how do you know Bill?" he asked, trying to put the pieces together. Caitlin realized he had to be even more discomforted than her by this turn of events.

Caitlin's mom and Bill looked at each other. At least they weren't hugging anymore, but they were still standing very close together—so close they looked like a couple. The thought made Caitlin feel queasy. Bill wasn't good-looking by anyone's standards. He had a patchy beard, sagging jowls, and his skin looked doughy in the sunlight. His receding brown hair was lank and unkempt, too long for a man his age.

He looked scary, like the kind of guy you see in the news wanted for armed robbery, or child molestation. *Something's not right here,* Caitlin thought. It was just a gut feeling she had, that there was some kind of mystery about Bill yet to be explained. Her mom always had terrible taste in men—her dad excepted— but she was really scraping the bottom of the barrel with Bill.

"Yes, Bill. How did we meet?" her mom asked rhetorically, giggling nervously. She looked at Caitlin, even though it was Luke who'd asked the question. "We've known each other since we were teenagers and Bill was the star basketball player at Belmont High. I've known him since before your dad." She paused, preparing to unveil her obvious secret. "We used to see each other in high school."

"We recently got back in touch," Bill added, "over the Internet. And we've talked on the phone a lot in the last six months."

Caitlin let this gruesome nugget sink in, as her stomach dropped ever further. *How could I not have known about this?* she wondered. "You're not married, are you, Bill?" she asked, already guessing what the answer would be.

He shook his head. "I'm single."

Mr. Gordimer cleared his throat. He'd unloaded their bags from the Escalade and was standing there in the sun. Caitlin could only guess at what he made of the strange, tense situation. "I'd better be going, ma'am," he said. "Unless I can be of further service?"

"No," Caitlin's mom said, barely glancing in his direction. If he was hoping for a tip, he was out of luck. Her mom's eyes were back on Bill's face. *Doesn't she notice how deformed this guy looks?* Caitlin wondered.

"Well, follow me and come inside," Bill said, wearing a phony-looking grin. "I'll get Michael to take your bags—he's the bellhop here." With Caitlin's mom at his side, he turned around and started heading into the hotel.

"This is some really fucked-up shit," Luke said loudly, to no one in particular. He looked around, appearing disoriented. Caitlin heard the engine of the Escalade start up and felt a pang of fear at being stranded at the hotel. Luke heard it, too, and stared longingly after the gleaming car as it pulled away. "Mr. Gordimer's leaving," Luke said.

"I know," Caitlin replied. "I think Mom's gone completely

crazy this time. What the hell is she doing, and why did she need to bring us with her?"

"Don't ask me," Luke said, after a pause. And then he added, almost wistfully, "She's acting like a ho. Most women are ho's."

Caitlin wondered where he'd picked that line up from. *Probably another stupid gangster movie.* "Thanks for the insight, Luke," she said. "I'm glad to see you're still an immature, sexist pig. If your mom's a ho, what does that make you?"

She didn't wait for his answer. Brushing sweat away from her eyes, Caitlin followed Bill and her mom into the cavernous foyer of the Pirate's Lodge.

5
the lodge

Despite its tacky name, the Pirate's Lodge looked like it had once been kind of grand inside. The foyer was large, with a huge oak check-in counter on the left and an array of chairs, tables, and couches positioned under massive crystal chandeliers. Caitlin noticed only about half the bulbs were still working, which meant the foyer was dark and shadowy. A far larger problem was that there weren't any guests in the lobby, and no one was manning the desk. A fat guy in a tan uniform, who Caitlin assumed was Michael, hustled past them to get their bags. Other than that, the place was silent and still.

"Bill owns this hotel," Caitlin's mom said. She was standing with him in the middle of the foyer, looking around. "Bill and I are probably the only two people from Belmont, Texas to ever make something of themselves."

Caitlin just nodded. She didn't know if her mom had suddenly gone blind, but she was acting like Bill and his hotel were amazing, when they were both total disasters.

"Bill made a fortune in the stock market in New York, and then he bought this place fifteen years ago. Isn't that right, Bill?"

He nodded, seeming eager to agree.

"Why aren't we staying somewhere nicer?" Luke asked. Caitlin's mom and Bill pretended they hadn't heard. Caitlin guessed there was nowhere nicer, like Mr. Gordimer had said.

"Bill, can you get me something to drink?" Caitlin's mom suddenly asked. "I need to take my medicine." Caitlin knew her mom's "medicine" was just a tranquilizer that she didn't need.

"Of course," Bill said. "Just a moment." He hustled off down a narrow hallway located to the side of the front desk.

"So what do you think?" Caitlin's mom asked her, beaming in a deranged way.

"You don't want me to answer that question."

"Why not?"

"Did you drag us here because of Bill Collins? Because that's what it looks like." Caitlin noticed one of the chandeliers was flickering. "What's the deal with you two, and why all these weird secrets? You know Dad's going to flip out when I tell him . . ."

Caitlin's mom frowned. "We're divorced, Caitlin. I'm free to see other people just like he is. That's what a divorce means."

"So you want to start dating Bill?" Caitlin lowered her voice. "One little question. *Why?*"

"Bill was my first real boyfriend—" her mom began.

There was a sudden crashing sound as a lamp fell down onto the marble floor. The lamp didn't break, but the bulb sparked and flared out. As Luke was only standing a foot away, it was easy to deduce who the culprit was.

"Luke!" Caitlin's mom yelled. "Why'd you do that?"

Luke turned around to look at them, an oddly serene look gracing his face. "To get your attention. Now that I have it, I want to ask you how soon we're leaving this island, because I hate it here, and I don't even care about getting a four-wheeler anymore."

"I don't want to discuss this right now."

"There's never a good time to discuss things with you, Mom," Caitlin said, hoping that maybe both she and Luke together could make her mom see what a terrible mistake she'd made in bringing them here. "You're never sober—"

"Caitlin!" her mom hissed. "Be quiet! I won't have you ruining my reputation here, especially when we've only just arrived."

"What reputation?" Caitlin snapped back.

In the moment of silence that followed, Bill reemerged bearing a crate of bottled water. Caitlin got the feeling he might have been standing there listening, waiting for the right moment to appear. He didn't mention the downed lamp.

"I thought you all might be thirsty," he said. "We've got a whole lot more than water to drink, but it's in the storeroom downstairs."

"Does this place have a restaurant?" Luke asked, as Bill passed out water. "I'm hungry."

"It used to, but I closed it two years ago. It wasn't economically feasible to keep it running anymore. There are places to eat nearby." Bill spoke in an odd, stilted cadence. *Maybe he's just not used to speaking to kids,* Caitlin thought, *or to people in general.* He was large and ungainly, not at all her mom's type physically. He had the height of a basketball player, but that was about it. It looked like it had been years since he'd done any physical activity.

"As you can tell, the hotel's almost empty," he added. "Only two of our forty-five rooms are currently booked. You kids and your mom are going to be staying in a special section of suites in the back."

"I'll get my own room, right?" Luke asked Bill urgently. "I don't want to share with her." He pointed at Caitlin.

"Of course," Bill said. "You and your sister will get private suites of your own, as will Kathryn."

Caitlin glanced over at her mom and saw that she was busy swallowing two little yellow pills. She wished her mom would just lay off the stuff altogether, but she guessed it would take some serious rehab to make that happen—and Danbroke clearly didn't have any rehab centers.

"Why don't you show us our rooms, Bill," her mom said, gulping down water. "I want to see what they look like and get the kids settled."

You mean get us out of the way, Caitlin thought.

Bill said, "Sure."

Caitlin, Luke, and their mom trundled after Bill as he headed up a wide, shabbily carpeted staircase to the left of the foyer. Luke kicked at some of the banisters as they walked. *He's going to go nuts from boredom out here,* Caitlin thought. *And honestly, so am I.* It seemed surreal that they were actually on Danbroke, in this hotel. If she'd known the trip was just so her mom could chase down an old boyfriend, she would have thrown a total fit and refused to go anywhere. Now it was way too late to do that, and she was trapped thousands of miles from home with no way to get back. She hoped when she told her dad about her mom and Bill, he'd intervene and rescue her, but her faith in her dad had been shaken recently.

When they reached their suites, it was more bad news for Caitlin. Just as she thought, the rooms were large, but musty and dark. Caitlin's suite, number 302, consisted of three rooms: a bedroom, a kitchen area with a fridge, and a living room with an old television set in it. Caitlin wondered if the place even had cable, because the TV had an old-school rabbit-ear antenna stuck to the back of it. It was the sort of place her mom usually would never consider staying at in a million years. Caitlin hoped it didn't have roaches.

"You probably won't be spending much time in here," Bill said to her as she looked around glumly, while Luke and her mom stood in the hall. "There's so much to do on the island, you'll be outside most of the time. Of course, there aren't many kids your age here, but I'm sure you'll find people to make friends with. Everyone here is friendly." He paused. "How old are you? Fifteen?"

"I turned sixteen four months ago," she corrected him.

He smiled. "It's unbelievable to think Kathryn has a daughter that age. You know, that's the same age your mom was when we started dating in tenth grade."

All this talk of dating was grossing Caitlin out. She never liked to think of her mom being into any guy who wasn't her dad. And prior to today, she'd never even heard of Bill Collins. She wondered why that was, and also what had happened to break them up. Until now, her mom had kept Bill a well-hidden secret.

After checking out her room, Caitlin went along with her

mom and Luke to look at their similar suites on the floor below. There was no sign of any sort of maid service, although Caitlin guessed there had to be maids around somewhere. Every now and then Luke made monkey noises for attention, but it was a perfunctory effort on his part and everyone ignored it.

"Listen," Caitlin's mom said to her when the brief tour was over and they'd been given keys to their suites. "I need to have some alone time to catch up with Bill, so you and Luke go off and amuse yourselves for a while, okay?"

"Sure," Caitlin replied, standing outside her mother's suite with Luke, wondering if her mom still thought she was ten.

"Those keys also open the front door to the hotel," Bill added. "So you can go in and out whenever you want. The island's safe, so feel free to go anywhere. Just be sure not to lose the keys."

Caitlin nodded, thinking it would only be a matter of hours until Luke's keys were long gone.

"I'm going to scope out the terrain," Luke said. He turned to Caitlin. "I'll let you know what I find."

"You do that, loser," she said, leaning against the wall because her back ached and her legs were cramped from the journey. She felt tired enough to take a nap, but she also felt a weird sort of manic energy, an electric undercurrent that wouldn't let her rest. She had to keep reminding herself this wasn't a movie, this was real life. It was strange to think that back in La Jolla, the world went on as usual without her. She knew Alison was missing the hell out of her, but probably the rest of her friends would quickly get over her absence and continue with their normal lives. *But maybe I'm just being pessimistic . . .*

Caitlin decided to stop thinking about home because it was

too depressing. Instead, she decided to focus on her goal of getting the hell off of Danbroke. Luke had already headed down the hall to explore the hotel, so she followed, gripping her keys in her hand. Caitlin glanced down at the thick green-and-orange–checkered carpet as she walked, thinking, *How tacky.* The Pirate's Lodge had an unintentionally retro feel to it, like it hadn't been remodeled since the 1970s. The wallpaper was flowery and peeling off in places, and the white paint on the railing of the stairway was chipped. The grime was just too authentic to be chic.

Caitlin saw Luke disappearing down the stairs toward the lobby and wondered how long it would take for him to find trouble. If Danbroke was anything like home, not very long. His paintball gun was probably being shipped with the rest of their stuff and would arrive at the hotel soon. When that happened, it was only a matter of time before he did irrevocable damage to something, or someone.

Caitlin went back up to her suite and shut the door, locking it so Luke or Mom couldn't barge in uninvited. She went over to the windows and pulled back the heavy yellow curtains, hoping for a decent view. There wasn't one, of course. She found herself staring out the back of the hotel, into a wall of thick trees behind an empty parking lot. There was a rusted Dumpster there, with a pile of moldering cardboard boxes next to it. *Nice.* She decided to shut the curtains again.

She sat down on the dusty, itchy couch and pulled out her cellphone to call her dad, Alison, and Ian—in that order. But she didn't get any reception. She figured she might fare better outside, so she put away the phone. Then she walked over to the fridge and opened it. She'd been hoping for a fully stocked mini-bar, like most good hotels had, but not surprisingly, the fridge was completely empty. It didn't even have any bottled water or juice in it, let alone alcohol, and Caitlin was craving a drink. Her little metal flask was in her suitcase, but unfortunately it was empty, so it wouldn't help her much. She took out a cigarette and lit it, figuring it was okay to smoke, because the room already smelled terrible.

Caitlin went back to the couch and flicked on the TV. Just as she figured, it didn't even have basic cable or satellite. She turned it off again. There was no ashtray in the room, so she flicked ash onto the carpet. She stood up, thinking she should go back outside. They'd passed a few buildings near the hotel that looked like they housed stores, so maybe she could find a fruit smoothie place and make her telephone calls.

Right then, as she was gathering her things to leave, she heard a knock at the door. She looked through the peephole and, to her complete surprise, it was Bill Collins himself. Reluctantly, she opened the door.

He stood there awkwardly, smiling down at her. Caitlin saw that he wore his slacks too high, like an old person. *Christ, what a weirdo,* she thought. *Why would Mom be into this guy?*

"Can I help you?" Caitlin asked.

"Just came to check in on you," Bill said, stepping into the room as Caitlin moved back to make space for him. He was so tall, he had to stoop to pass through the doorway. "I wanted to see how you're doing. You can treat this place like home, Caitlin. You're going to be here for a while, and with the hotel so empty, you pretty much have the run of the place."

"I'm doing fine," she said. Caitlin hadn't invited him inside her room, but as it was his hotel, she figured he could go wherever he wanted. "Danbroke's pretty different from La Jolla."

"Good, good," he said, nodding, like he didn't understand what she meant.

There's nothing good about it, buddy, she thought. The door to the room was still open, but Caitlin felt a little blocked in by Bill because of his size. "I was just heading out . . ."

Bill continued nodding. The way he was looking at her made her feel weird. It was a strange look, like he was having all kinds of thoughts he didn't want to share. *This guy is such a creep,* Caitlin thought. She was looking forward to telling her dad all about Bill Collins.

"Want to know something?" he asked, a faint smile playing at the corners of his mouth.

She didn't, but she asked, "What?" anyway.

"You look *exactly* like Kathryn. I mean, how she used to look when she was your age." His gaze grew more intense. "It's remarkable. You could be the same person, practically."

"We're not the same person, Bill. In fact, I'm nothing like my mom."

Bill chuckled to himself. "Of course you're not. I understand. No teenage girl wants to be compared to their mother in that way, am I right? You're your own person."

"Maybe." She didn't want to agree with him. About anything.

He continued smiling, in his strange knowing way. "Parents can be embarrassing."

"Do you have any kids, Bill?" Caitlin suddenly asked, thinking it would make him seem less creepy to know he had daughters of his own.

He shook his head. "No, Caitlin, I sure don't."

She didn't like hearing him say her name. She was hit with a pang of longing for her dad, wishing the divorce hadn't happened. No one was around to protect her anymore. Here was yet another slimy guy that her mom had unearthed, but this time it was worse than back home, because they were stuck in his domain.

"I'm going to get some fresh air," Caitlin said, not caring if she was being curt.

"That's a good idea," Bill replied, sounding agreeable enough, but Caitlin could tell he hadn't wanted the conversation to end so abruptly. His eyes found her chest and lingered a moment too long.

With her purse slung over her shoulder, feigning a self-confidence she didn't feel, Caitlin said, "Tell Mom I went out."

"Sure, sure," he said, as she walked past him and through the open door of the room. "Say 'hey' to your little brother if you see him out there. He's a handful, eh?"

Caitlin didn't respond, but just kept walking down the hall, and then the stairs, and then out the front doors of the Pirate's Lodge into the warm, swampy air that came as a welcome embrace.

6

Luckily, Bill didn't follow Caitlin outside the hotel. She even looked back over her shoulder to make certain, but didn't see any sign of him. She wondered if he were still back in her room, maybe going through her things. *Ugh.* The less she saw of Bill, the happier she'd be.

She looked around, but didn't see Luke anywhere. What she did see were omnipresent signs of decay. A shingle from the roof lay on the brown grass, and there were some beer cans in the ditch along the road. When she looked down the road leading to the hotel, she saw a short, shabby strip mall. She began walking toward it. She noticed a tacky red neon sign for a place called Buckley's Pizza, so she figured she could get something to drink there, maybe a beer if they didn't card her. She tied her hair back in a knot as she walked, because she knew it made her look older.

She was surprised she couldn't see the beach from the road, but the land here sloped upward on either side and blocked her view. She knew that there was water close by, and she could feel a slight cooling breeze blowing over her, carrying with it the faint scent of brine.

As she walked, she tried to figure out a plan of action, but her thoughts were suddenly interrupted by loud war whoops coming from her left. She knew instantly who it was.

"Luke!" she yelled out. "Where are you?"

She didn't get a response, but heard more gleeful yelling. She paused and then began climbing up the hill in the direction of the sound. When she got near the top, she realized she was even closer to the ocean than she'd previously thought. She was standing on the crest of a massive sand dune, looking directly down on a long beach beyond which sprawled a vast expanse of water. The ocean was curiously quiet and calm, gently lapping at the slight slope of the beach.

What wasn't quiet and calm was her brother, who was leaping up and down on the beach, stabbing at a dark lump on the sand with a stick. Other than Luke, the entire beach was deserted as far as Caitlin could see. It stretched out to the horizon in either direction, beautiful but stark.

"What are you doing?" she yelled.

Luke turned toward her, raising his stick in the air like a weapon. "I found a dead turtle!" he called out. "Check it out. Its head came off."

Caitlin sighed, putting her hands on her hips. "You probably killed it, didn't you?"

"No, it's all dried up. It's been dead for a long time." He brought the stick down and whacked at it, as if to show her. Caitlin looked away.

"Listen, I'm going to get something to drink from the pizza place," she said. "Want to come with me?" Usually she never would have made an offer like that to Luke, but she figured for once it was better to be with him than all by herself.

"No way. I'm staying down here. I want to go swimming . . ." He paused. "Naked!"

Caitlin realized she was an idiot to think he could chill and act normal. As she turned away from him in silent resignation and headed back to the road, she took out her cellphone and managed to get a signal. As she walked, she called her dad and then Alison, but neither picked up, so she left them messages.

Finally she reached the run-down row of stores. There were two old pickup trucks in the parking lot and no one on the streets. The sun was baking her skin, making her feel like she was going to burn, despite the fact that she already had a decent tan from California. The island was so deserted it felt like the inhabitants had suddenly fled a natural disaster or plague. *I'm starting to feel like a character in one of Luke's zombie movies,* Caitlin thought. *One where there's only a few humans left alive.*

She knew she was being overly dramatic, but figured she'd feel better when she actually saw some other human faces. She'd never thought of La Jolla as particularly crowded, but she now realized there was always a steady flow of traffic and pedestrians.

She got to Buckley's Pizza, which had airbrushed artwork of a giant pepperoni pizza across its grimy windows, and pushed open one of the glass doors. The restaurant was tiny, with an ancient Mortal Kombat video game in one corner, unplugged. It looked like the kind of place that primarily did takeout. It was really hot and smelled like freshly baked bread. There was only one customer inside, a girl about Caitlin's age, with dark hair, olive skin, and Gothic black eyeshadow. She was reading an

Anne Rice paperback. She didn't bother looking up when Caitlin came in.

No one was behind the counter so Caitlin stood there for a moment, until a short guy with his hair in a ponytail, wearing a grease-splattered white T-shirt, emerged from the back and asked, "Can I help you?"

Caitlin hadn't even looked at the menu yet, but doubted they had anything good. *Probably just cheap beer.* Trying to look and sound older than she was, she said, "I'll take a Bud Light."

He shook his head. At first she thought it was because he knew she was underage, but then he explained. "We lost our liquor license two months ago. Didn't you see the sign on the door?"

"No." She scanned the menu hanging on the wall behind him. "You got any bottled water then? San Pellegrino? Voss?"

"Nope. We got Coke, Diet Coke, root beer, and Sprite. That's it. There's a water fountain outside the bathroom if you want water."

"I'll take a Diet Coke. Make it a large," Caitlin said. She hoped some caffeine and a cigarette or two would reenergize her and clear her thoughts.

The guy paused. "Anything to eat?"

Caitlin was hungry, but she'd once read that a single slice of pizza, depending on the toppings, could contain as many as nine hundred calories, most of them from fat. Since then, she hadn't been a big pizza eater, as much as she loved it. "Naw, I'm fine," she said, figuring she could eat someplace later.

The guy took out a cup and got her Coke from the soda machine. But Caitlin ran into problems when it came time to pay.

She had her Visa card out and in her hand, but when the guy saw it, he said, "We don't take credit cards."

Caitlin was momentarily puzzled. "Are you serious?"

He nodded. "Yep, this is a cash-only joint. No credit cards, no debit cards, and no personal checks, neither."

Caitlin dug around in her wallet, already knowing that there wasn't any cash inside, because she used her credit cards to pay for *everything*. She couldn't even remember the last place she'd been to that didn't take credit cards. "Fuck," she muttered as she searched. She found a nickel, but she needed a dollar and fifty cents, which meant she was out of luck.

"Cash only," the guy reiterated, even though Caitlin hadn't said anything to encourage him. Then again, "Didn't you see the sign on the door?"

"No, I didn't see the sign," Caitlin said, getting annoyed.

"There is no sign," spoke a voice from behind her. Caitlin glanced back and saw the dark-haired girl staring at her intensely, her brown eyes boring holes into her. "Joe's just fucking with you."

The guy behind the counter laughed, a scratchy nasal sound. Caitlin looked back at him and then at the girl again.

"There's no sign," she continued. "But it's true they don't take credit cards. I should know, I used to work here."

"And you were a terrible employee," Joe said to her. "The pits. If you hadn't quit, I would have ended up firing you." He was still laughing a little.

The girl was still staring at Caitlin. "Let me guess. You're not from around here."

"I'm from California," Caitlin said.

"Where in California?"

"La Jolla. North of San Diego, south of L.A."

"I know where it is. I've got relatives in Carlsbad." The girl dug in a backpack next to her. It reminded Caitlin of Luke's bag, except the girl's had patches and stickers all over it, mostly for bands. Caitlin recognized some of the names—Joy Division, Bauhaus, and Sisters of Mercy. From what she knew, they were all Goth acts. Definitely not the kind of music Caitlin listened to herself, but better than the mainstream crap a lot of people her age liked.

The girl took out a couple dollar bills and waved them at Caitlin. "I got you covered," she said. "Don't worry."

"For real?"

"Yeah. You can pay me back later. If not, two bucks isn't going to break the bank."

"Thanks," Caitlin said, as she walked over and took the money. "And I *will* pay you back. What's your name?"

"Danielle. Yours?"

"Caitlin."

Joe leaned over the counter. "So now you got some money, you can afford your Coke, huh," he called out. "Come get it before the ice melts."

Caitlin walked up to the counter, gave him the money, and took her drink. "By the way, thanks for fucking with me," she said to him. "I really appreciate it."

She heard Danielle snicker behind her.

Joe grinned widely. He was missing one of his upper front teeth. "Comes free with the pizza."

"I'm sure it really encourages customers to tip you." Caitlin took a sip of Coke.

"Listen, honey, no one tips well on Danbroke. No one has

any money. Now bartenders, they do a little better. If I were smarter, I would have opened a bar instead of a pizza joint. Ah well, too late now."

"Let him keep the change," Danielle called out to Caitlin. And then she added, "When I worked here, I used to steal from the register all the time. It's payback . . ."

Joe just laughed. Caitlin put her Coke down on one of the small, round tables and took out her pack of cigarettes.

Danielle was watching her closely again, as she zipped up her backpack. "Hey, mind if I bum a cancer stick off you?"

"'Course not." Caitlin tossed the pack over to her, and the girl took one and lit it. "It's the least I can do after you bought me a Coke, right?"

"Perfect synergy," Danielle pointed out, tossing the cigarettes back. She hoisted her backpack over her shoulder. "Want to come sit outside with me while you drink that? Joe's cool, but he can annoy the hell out of me."

Caitlin nodded.

"I heard that!" Joe called out, but he didn't sound offended. It was clearly just friendly banter between the two of them.

"You were meant to," Danielle told him, as she and Caitlin headed out the front door.

Danielle was slightly shorter than Caitlin, and pretty, with a pale face and forehead accentuated by the way her short, dark hair was parted in the center. She had a slim body too, Caitlin could tell, but it was masked by her loose black top and long black skirt. Danielle also had on a pair of well-worn thick-soled black boots, possibly Doc Martens, dented and scarred at the front.

Caitlin and Danielle walked over to a short wall near the edge of the parking lot and leaned back against it. Danielle tossed her backpack onto the ground where it made a heavy thump. From the wall, they could see the road and the hotel, but not the ocean.

"So, California, huh? Why'd you come all the way out here to the middle of nowhere?"

"Good question." Caitlin fiddled with her lighter, trying to figure out how much she could tell this girl. Even though they'd just met, she had a weird feeling, like she knew Danielle from somewhere. It was kind of like déjà vu in an odd way—the sense that there was some kind of preexisting connection between the two of them. And Danielle had bought her a Coke, an atypically generous gesture for a stranger.

"My mom's crazy," Caitlin finally said. "She moved me and my brother here for the summer." She pointed at the Pirate's Lodge, presiding over the landscape. "We're staying there."

Danielle's eyes widened a little. "That place? I've never been inside. Bill Collins is the manager, right?"

"Right."

"He's an infamous island weirdo. He even stands out from all the other losers who live on Danbroke." She paused. "You ever seen *Psycho*? The original, not the shitty remake."

Caitlin shook her head.

"Oh well. Anyway, Bill reminds me of the crazy killer in that movie."

"Good to know," Caitlin said, thinking, *I wish you hadn't just told me that.*

"I'm sure he's harmless, though," Danielle hastened to add. "I mean, he's been here for years, since before I got here."

"Where are you from?"

"Toronto."

Caitlin was surprised. "Canada?"

"Yeah. Not too many half-Filipina Goth chicks come from that far north, right? But that's where I was born. My parents still live there, but my grandmother lives on Danbroke. I stay with her down near the beach, a couple miles from here."

Caitlin wanted to ask why she wasn't living with her parents, but figured it might be a sensitive subject.

"Grandma's kinda old and needs help," Danielle added. "My parents can't do it 'cause of their jobs, so it's up to me."

"How long have you been here?"

"Too long." She frowned. "It'll be two years in August. Two very long fucking years."

Caitlin took a drag on her cigarette. She couldn't imagine what it would be like to spend two years in a place as desolate as Danbroke. "So you go to school here and everything?"

"Yep. I'll be a junior next year, which means I only got two more years left until I can get the hell out of Dodge. I don't know if you've met too many locals yet, but you can live here for twenty years and still be considered a newbie. They think of me as a 'tourist,' if you can believe it. After two years."

"Crazy." Then Caitlin added, "I'll be a junior next year, too." *Just hopefully not here.*

"There aren't that many people our age on the island. Locals, I mean. The kids that do live here are pretty lame. All the girls have big eighties hair and are dumb as a bag of rocks. Most of them aren't planning on going to college, if they even graduate high school. The guys are even worse. There are only eighteen kids in my whole class."

"Sounds awful."

"It is. I can't wait until I get off the island. I want to move to New York and study design at NYU, maybe painting."

"Cool," Caitlin said. "I love New York City."

"Me too."

There was an awkward silence, as both girls contemplated how very far away they were from New York at that moment. Caitlin thoughtfully took another drag on her cigarette.

"So why'd your mom bring you here again?" Danielle finally asked.

"She said she wanted to take us someplace different, where we'd get a change of pace from life in California, or some parental bullshit like that." Caitlin wondered if it would freak Danielle out to know how rich her family was. It didn't matter with her friends back home, because their families all had money, too, but she could tell that Danielle's probably didn't. *But maybe I'm just jumping to conclusions.*

"Yep, that's some bullshit."

"My mom grew up with Bill Collins and went to high school with him in Texas," Caitlin said. "They're friends, I guess." She was too embarrassed to tell the girl everything about her mom.

"Look," Danielle suddenly said, distracted. "Over there." She pointed to where a shadowy figure was leaping up and down on top of the sand dune running between the road and the beach. "Is that kid crazy or what?"

Caitlin sighed, exhaling a plume of smoke. "That's my little brother." She stared at the figure moving toward them, wishing he would disappear into the hazy air of the island.

Danielle said, "I guess I should be glad I don't have any siblings."

As Luke grew closer, Caitlin heard that he was yelling her name. *Why can't he just leave me alone?* she thought. She took another sip of Coke as she watched his approach with narrowed eyes.

7

the danbroke blues

"Who the hell are you?" Luke asked Danielle when he got there, completely ignoring Caitlin. He was still clutching the stick, with bits of dead turtle hanging off the end of it.

"I'm Danielle. Who the hell are you?"

In a phony Cuban accent he growled, "You can call me Tony Montana!"

Danielle laughed. "Right. Like from *Scarface.* Gotcha."

"Luke, why are you such a weirdo?" Caitlin asked.

"No reason," he replied, swinging the stick in her direction.

"If you touch me with that thing, I'll kill you." The stick got closer to her bare leg, so Caitlin snapped, "I mean it!" The stick retreated. She looked over at Danielle and said, "His name's not Tony, it's Luke. I call him Lukus Pukus." It was a name she hadn't used in years, since they were little kids, but it made Danielle laugh.

"Hey there, Luke," Danielle said, but Luke didn't respond.

Instead, he turned to Caitlin and asked bluntly, "What do you think is up between Mom and Bill?"

Surprised to hear a relatively rational question come out of his mouth, she didn't know how to respond. "What do you mean?"

"Mom's into him, right? He's one of her ex-boyfriends. Is that why she made us come here?"

"I think so," Caitlin admitted haltingly, wishing they could have the conversation in private. She didn't want Danielle to know how screwed up her family was. Maybe Danielle sensed it, because she put a hand on her backpack and picked it up by one of the straps.

"I'd better get going," she said. "I told Grandma I'd be back in time to help with dinner. But I come to Buckley's almost every day to read and just chill with Joe, so you know where to find me if you want to hang out. All the places in town are filled with assholes. Besides, Joe gives me free slices of pizza, so it's cool."

"And you know where to find me," Caitlin said. "Come by the hotel sometime. I'm in suite three-oh-two." She was touched that the girl had been so friendly. "I can pay you those two dollars back."

"Don't stress about it," Danielle said with a smile that looked genuine. "See you around, Caitlin." With a wave, she headed down the road toward town, her backpack hanging off a shoulder.

Caitlin noticed that Luke was staring after her. *Maybe the little freak has a crush on her,* she thought. As Luke usually wore all black, too, maybe Danielle was a fantasy come true. But Caitlin was pretty sure Luke wasn't mature enough to be into girls yet. Thinking about her brother's potential sex life grossed her out, so she blotted it out of her mind.

"What do *you* think the deal with Mom and Bill is?" she asked him.

He shrugged and dropped the stick. "Mom wants to bang him." He made a circle with one hand and stuck a finger through the hole with his other, moving it back and forth.

"Do you always have to be so disgusting?"

He grinned. "Yeah, I do."

"Luke, what the fuck are we going to do? I know neither of us wants to spend our summer here, even though Mom tried to bribe you with that four-wheeler—"

"She better come through," he interrupted. "Or I'm going to be really pissed."

"Luke, forget about the four-wheeler for a moment," Caitlin pleaded. "Just think, you'll get bored with it in a day or two, like you get bored with everything. And then you'll be stuck here. There aren't even that many people around, so what are you going to use for target practice? This place has nothing on it for either of us."

Luke seriously considered her words for a second. "Have you tried calling Dad yet?" he asked.

"Yeah, I called, but he didn't pick up." In the distance, Caitlin could still see Danielle walking down the side of the sandy road. Caitlin wondered why the ocean was so quiet on Danbroke. It wasn't like that in La Jolla because even from her bedroom she could hear the sound of the surf if she kept the windows open. Here she was even closer to the water, but she never would have known it. *It's like everything's dead on this island,* Caitlin thought. *Even the waves.*

"We have to make sure Mom doesn't move us here for good," she said. "Agreed?"

"Yeah, this place sucks worse than home . . . I didn't think that was possible." He burped. "I'm going back to the hotel. I want to hook my Xbox up to the TV."

Caitlin was surprised. "You brought your Xbox?"

"And half my games. That's what was in my suitcases. I figured I'd just get my clothes and everything else sent later." He turned boastful: "I didn't even bring my toothbrush."

"I'm glad you've got your priorities straight. I think you're addicted to video games."

He shrugged. "You're addicted to cigarettes."

"At least they'll only rot my lungs and not my brain. Listen, I'm coming back to the hotel with you. I want to talk to Mom about the island. If we both gang up on her, maybe she'll change her mind."

Grudgingly, like he was doing her a huge favor, Luke nodded.

Together, the two of them headed back up the road to the Pirate's Lodge. When they got inside and walked up to their mom's suite, they discovered that the door was locked. Caitlin didn't know if her mom was inside or not, so she went back to the lobby. Fortunately, there was no sign of Bill anywhere. Luke sneaked off to his suite, and she knew he was just going to disappear into his Xbox. There was still no call back from Dad or Alison, either. As Caitlin slumped down on one of the couches, under a chandelier, Michael appeared from the back and stood behind the front desk, sweaty and disheveled.

"Hey," Caitlin said.

He nodded in response. "Hey yourself." He wiped his brow.

It looked like he'd been working hard at something. "Good to see you again."

"Are you the only person who works here?"

He nodded. "Yup. Bill let everyone else go in March when the hotel got underbooked. He couldn't afford to keep the staff. There were only four of us by that point, anyway. There used to be twelve." In a softer voice, he added, "This place is falling apart, in case you haven't noticed."

Startled by his candor, Caitlin got up and walked over to the front desk. "So there aren't even any maids?"

He pointed a finger at his own chest. "You're looking at them. I do everything around here—clean the rooms, fix the toilets, change the lightbulbs. Bill helps out, too, sometimes. The sheets get changed once every three days, at best."

There was obviously no way two people could keep a place this size running. If Caitlin's mom weren't hooked on drugs and Bill, she certainly would have recognized what a weird situation she'd put them in.

"So what happened exactly?" Caitlin asked, playing with one of her rings. "I mean, why is the hotel so abandoned?"

He shrugged. "Danbroke's changing. The few people who still come to the island want to rent houses, because it's cheaper and easier. They're building nice places at the far end of the island, away from the ferry. This hotel is a relic." He pointed at the wall behind him, at a faded photograph in a tacky gold frame. Caitlin squinted and realized the person in the photo was Sean Penn, standing in the lobby, looking very young. "This place has seen better days since the likes of him stayed here. That was back in the eighties, before I worked here." He sighed.

Caitlin remained surprised he was being so honest. "Is the hotel going to close down?" she pressed, thinking optimistically that if it did, she'd get to go back home.

He grinned crookedly. "Hope not, because then I'd be out of a job." He leaned across the desk. "And don't tell Bill any of what I just said. He has a temper and I don't want him bitching at me. He can bitch worse than an old lady with hemorrhoids."

"I won't tell."

He seemed convinced and leaned back. "You guys would have been better off renting a house."

Caitlin nodded. "Sounds like it." She knew her mom could have rented a mansion if she'd wanted, not that Caitlin had seen any so far on Danbroke. Clearly the only reason they were staying at the Pirate's Lodge was for Mom to be close to Bill. She hadn't even known her mom had been communicating with some random guy over the Internet. It was more than a little disturbing. She knew deep down her mom loved her, but she also knew her mom's bad habits and poor choices were destroying what little of their relationship was left.

Right then her phone rang, so she took it out and saw it was her dad. *About time,* she thought. *Jesus.* She walked toward the stairs, in the direction of her suite, and away from the front desk and Michael as she put the phone to her ear.

"Dad?" she asked.

"It's me," she heard her father say, his comforting voice loud in her ear. "How are you doing, kiddo? Enjoying the island?"

Was he serious? "Uh, Dad, there are a few things about this trip I bet Mom didn't tell you."

"Like what?" She could hear typing sounds in the background, so she said, "Dad, quit using the computer and give me your full attention. I'm begging you."

She heard him laugh. "Sure."

"Listen, did Mom tell you that she knows the guy who owns the hotel we're staying at? That the two of them went to high school together? And dated?"

There was a pause, and she noticed the typing had stopped. "What?!"

So he didn't know. "The guy's name is Bill Collins. Mom grew up with him in Belmont, way back when. Have you ever heard of him?"

"No, Caitlin, I haven't," her dad replied slowly. She could tell she had his full attention now, and that he was worried for her and Luke. "What in the world is going on down there—"

"Hang on a sec." Caitlin reached her suite and opened the door, went inside, and locked it behind her. "Bill is extremely weird and Mom's doped up on pills, so it's a pretty crappy place to be. Oh yeah, and the Pirate's Lodge isn't a resort—it's a wreck. Even the guy who works the front desk told me it's going to close down soon. It's an appalling situation."

Her dad sighed heavily. She could picture him at his desk in his Rockefeller Plaza office, head in his hands. "This is news to me, Caitlin. I don't know what to say. Are you and Luke okay?"

"Technically, yes, but not really. We need to get off the island." She paused, biting her lip, thinking about the way Bill had checked out her breasts earlier. "I'm worried, Dad. Honestly, I don't feel safe here."

"Has anything happened to you?" her dad asked, concern filling his voice.

"Not yet."

"I should have known Kathryn would do something like this. She's obviously as unstable as she's always been. One of the reasons I supported the trip to Danbroke is because I thought it might help her, too." He paused and collected his thoughts. "I'm going to call her right now and get to the bottom of this."

"She might be passed out." Dismayed silence answered her, so she added, "Luke hates it here, too." She figured she might as well guilt-trip her dad into actually doing something to help them. *He practically threw us to the wolves by letting Mom drag us to Danbroke.* He probably hadn't been thinking straight, what with having to keep The Model happy and all.

"I'll try your mother and call you right back," he said finally. She could hear the strain in his voice.

"Thanks, Dad. I love you."

"I love you, too, Caitlin. Very much."

"'Bye." She hung up and put the phone back in her pocket. She hoped her dad would procure tickets back to California for her and Luke right away. After that, she wasn't sure what would happen. She and Luke definitely wouldn't be allowed to stay in the house by themselves, and she guessed her dad wouldn't take them in for the summer. She tried to stay calm and hope that somehow a miracle would happen, and her dad would talk—or maybe yell—some sense into her mom.

She opened the curtains again and stared out at the dingy trash heap outside, waiting for her dad to call back. He did, about a minute later.

"Couldn't get her," he said, sounding businesslike. He often did when he was upset. "She didn't answer her cellphone, so I called the front desk and got transferred to her suite. No one picked up. I'll try again later—" He broke off for a second and then came back, sounding distracted. "It's Julie." Julie was his tough-as-nails secretary. "I forgot I have a meeting right now. I can't afford to miss it."

"Dad, come on. I really need your help. Can't you just send me and Luke plane tickets?"

"I'll have to talk to your mother first. There are custody laws, and I can't break them, especially because of Luke's age. You know that, Caitlin. But I promise I'll do everything I can. I left a strong message for your mom, so I think I'll be hearing from her soon. Just keep your head up and keep plugging away, okay? I'll call as soon as I can."

"Thanks, Dad," Caitlin said, but she didn't feel very grateful. She felt bummed out.

"Have to run," he said. "Chin up, and we'll talk soon."

"Ditto," she replied, and then the line went dead. She tossed her phone onto the bed, frustrated. She felt alone and isolated in her strange, dark suite of rooms. The only bright spot in the whole day had been meeting Danielle.

Caitlin walked into the bathroom, contemplating a shower because she felt grimy and sticky. Then she noticed all the mold between the tiles and decided to postpone showering until absolutely necessary. Michael wasn't kidding when he'd said the place was falling apart. She wondered how her mom was coping with the lack of luxury, assuming she'd noticed it.

Caitlin was hungry, so she decided to go back and ask Michael about what places were in town and how to get there. Without a car, she didn't know how she'd get around, but maybe the hotel had a vehicle she could borrow. She didn't feel like walking the long stretch of road in the hot sun and getting even more sweaty than she already was.

She headed out of her room, thinking, *Am I a total sucker to believe that Dad will help me?* Yet there was no one else for her to put her faith in. After she figured out a way into town, she thought she'd try to call Alison again. She could use some support. And then maybe after that she'd finally try Ian.

She walked down the stairs to the lobby and right up to the front desk, where Michael was sitting with his feet up, reading an old issue of *Maxim.*

"Hey Michael," she said. "Is there a car I could use? I want to go into town and see what's down there. Explore, you know? Get some food."

"A car?" he repeated, putting the magazine facedown on the counter. "Naw, there's no car. But come with me, 'cause I got something a whole lot better."

8
the last place on earth

The "something better" turned out to be an old red bicycle that Michael wheeled out from a dusty storage room in the back. It looked like a guy's bike, and the wheels were thick, like it was meant for rough terrain.

"We used to rent them back in the day," he said, "but people kept stealing them, or wrecking them, so we quit. This is one of the only ones left."

"Thanks," Caitlin said, as he rolled it in her direction. When she touched the handlebars, dust came off on her hands. She wiped them clean on her shorts. It was a pretty big comedown from a Mercedes to a bike.

"Probably needs a little oil, but it might be okay. It's yours for the summer, or however long you end up staying. I'm sure it'll be cool with Bill. I don't even think he remembers we have these bikes."

Caitlin was grateful for the bike, but also embarrassed. *I suppose this is teaching me a lesson about appreciating the things I had back home, or something like that,* she thought. But she didn't want a lesson—she just wanted to be back in La Jolla. She took the bike from Michael and rolled it across the lobby to the front doors. It was big and clunky, but she thought she could probably handle it. There was a chain with a key lock wrapped around the frame.

"Have fun," he called out, as he retreated back to his desk and his magazine. "Just don't leave the bike outside if you can help it." As it was already covered in rust, Caitlin didn't think some time outside would hurt it. But she didn't want to offend Michael, who'd been nice to her so far. She wished that he was the one who owned the hotel, and not Bill.

Caitlin wondered if Bill were off with her mom somewhere. *God, what if they're sleeping with each other already?* Caitlin thought, the idea popping unbidden into her mind. It was a difficult and disturbing mental image to shake.

When she got outside, she adjusted the bicycle seat to its lowest position, got on awkwardly, and began riding down the long dusty road toward town. It had been a few years since she'd even ridden a bike; the last time had probably been with her dad. She struggled to keep the sticky pedals moving. The wind started pushing her hair back as she finally got moving at a decent speed.

In the fifteen minutes it took her to cycle into town, she barely saw anyone else on the road. There was just long grass and sand on either side of her. She thought maybe she'd run into Danielle on the way, but she didn't. When she got to the center of town, which was just a clump of dingy stores and restaurants, she found a bike rack at the side of the gas station and locked up the bike.

She wiped her hands on her shorts again as she looked at her surroundings. The town was a little less desolate than the road. There was a family nearby eating sandwiches at a picnic table, and a group of fisherman slowly walking past to her left. She also saw people going in and out of a general store. Next to it was a tiny shop called the Sweet Tooth, which advertised homemade ice cream in the window. Caitlin thought ice cream sounded good, because of the heat, though it was probably worse for her than pizza.

When she got in the store, she realized that maybe she'd made a mistake. It was dirty, cramped, and not particularly cold for a place that served ice cream. There was an old lady with two little girls sitting in one of the few seats inside, pressed up against the back wall. Behind the counter was a chubby woman with a frizzy hairdo, her clothes a size too small.

"You know what you want?" she asked, as Caitlin perused the meager selection of flavors.

"Still deciding," Caitlin said.

"Well, hurry up. I need a pee break."

"Thanks for sharing," Caitlin muttered, horrified that the woman would say something like that. Her desire for home-made ice cream was fading fast, but she decided to order some anyway because she was hot and craving the sugar rush. "Got any mint chocolate chip?"

The woman shook her head dolefully. "Just chocolate, vanilla, and strawberry." She fixed Caitlin with a frown that wrinkled her sun-leathered brow. "You're not from here, are you?"

And thank God for that, Caitlin thought, although she wished it weren't so obvious. She hated being marked as an outsider everywhere she went.

"Because if you were from here, then you'd know that's all we ever have," the woman continued. "Nothing fancy. We're not that kind of place. If you're looking for fancy, you won't find it on Danbroke."

"Got it," Caitlin said. She wanted the ice cream badly enough not to walk out of the store. "I'll keep it simple and go for chocolate."

The woman scowled even harder, as Caitlin wondered what was up with her. Danielle hadn't been kidding when she'd said the people here really sucked. "One scoop or two?" the woman asked, her voice as rough as a bark. "Cone or a cup?"

"One scoop, in a cone," Caitlin said slowly, as the old lady and the little girls stared at her from the corner.

Caitlin watched as the woman bent down and dug out a scoop of ice cream that looked half-melted. She plopped it into a cone and said, "Two dollars."

Caitlin had a moment of internal panic as she realized that once again she didn't have any cash on her. *If I can't pay for the cone, will this woman just throw it at me?* she wondered. But fortunately, at that moment Caitlin saw a Visa sticker on the side of the cash register and breathed a sigh of relief. She took out her card, paid for her ice cream, and then headed back outside into the heat and sunshine.

She found a ramshackle picnic table under the shade of a large oak tree, so she sat down. As she ate, two guys caught her eye walking across the town's courtyard. They were headed toward the bait and tackle shop across from the general store. She could tell right away they weren't locals, because they were actually decent looking and well-groomed. They looked about seventeen or eighteen. One of them had short, dark hair and sunglasses on, along with a bit of a smirk. He looked a lot like Adam Brody. His friend was half a head shorter and a little blonder, but still attractive.

She watched them secretly as they walked past. They didn't seem to notice her because she was far enough away, and hidden by the shade of the tree. They walked into the bait store and the door swung shut behind them. As long as there was any indication there might be a few cool people roughly her own age on Danbroke, Caitlin felt a little better about being there—but not a lot.

Out of nowhere, her phone rang and startled her. She took it out right away, without even looking at who was calling, and said, "Hello?"

"Caity!" exclaimed Alison's voice on the other end. "Omigod, I'm so sorry I didn't call you right away. My mom got a flat tire on Route Four and we got stuck out there, and I didn't have my phone on me for once. God, are you okay?"

"Don't even worry about it," Caitlin said, relief surging through her body at hearing her friend's voice.

For the next fifteen minutes, Caitlin told Alison all about Danbroke, and everything that had happened so far on the island. As usual, Alison listened, said all the right things, and made her feel better. After another ten minutes of chitchat and gossip about their friends back home in La Jolla, Caitlin was feeling a lot more like herself.

"If you see Ian, tell him I love him and I'll call him tonight," she added. By the time Caitlin hung up, her mood was so much better than it had been earlier, she felt almost happy. She couldn't wait for her dad to call back, and hoped that Danbroke would soon be a distant, unhappy memory.

She decided to bike back to the hotel because the locals kept staring at her. As she unlocked her bike and prepared for the return journey, she thought about the two guys she'd seen heading into the bait store. She wondered if they came from the other end of the island, the place where Michael mentioned that people rented houses. She wondered if the other end might be any different, and therefore better, than this end. She figured she'd go exploring tomorrow and see what she could find out.

As she brought her bike onto the road, something caught her eye. There was a mysterious little trail heading off through a grove of trees toward the side of the island that faced the exposed ocean. Wondering where it went, she decided to take it, and quickly found herself on a narrow asphalt path running parallel to the main road she'd come down. It appeared to be some kind of biking or jogging trail. The main difference between it and the road was that the trail had a spectacular view of the ocean. It ran up high above some sand dunes, so by looking down, Caitlin could see the beach and the water stretching below her. She decided to stay on the trail, hoping it would connect back up with the road.

The trail was a little winding in places, so it took her about twenty minutes to reach a narrow dirt path that served as a cut-through to the road. She biked along it until she reached the road and saw that she was close to the Pirate's Lodge. The sun was starting to set, coming in at such an abrupt angle that it reflected off the hotel's windows into Caitlin's eyes. She blinked and looked away. Seeing the hotel again depressed her, and made her nervous, because it reminded her of Bill.

I'm going to have to be really careful around that guy, she thought. There was something undeniably disturbing about him. She wondered if Bill had been a different person back in high school than the hunched-over husk who presided over his dying hotel. Bill and her mom had been stuck in a hick town, of course, but from photos, she knew her mom had been pretty hot back when she was young. She hoped Bill didn't have some kind of drug or alcohol problem of his own that might explain why he looked and acted so weird. *Just what Mom needs.*

When Caitlin reached the Pirate's Lodge, she took the bike inside and leaned it against one of the walls by the front doors. Because Michael was no longer at the desk, and there was no sign of anyone else, Caitlin decided to investigate the hotel a little. She walked back around the front desk and discovered a rabbit warren of offices along with the staff kitchen. Everything was pretty messy, and there were crates of bottled water and tins of food everywhere for some reason. She looked for alcohol, but didn't find any. Piles of paper were stacked up against the walls, and an old, funky-looking Apple computer sat on one of the desks. Caitlin grabbed a bottle of water from a crate and headed back up to her room.

You're going to get out of this place soon, she told herself. *No worries, no stress.* She took a deep yoga breath, holding it and then letting it out slowly, as she reached the door to her suite, opened it, and went inside.

9
bill

Unfortunately, things didn't work out like Caitlin had planned, and as the next few days passed, she realized there'd be no easy way off the island. She talked to her dad four more times, but he was either unable, or unwilling, to help her and Luke. He'd talked to her mom, but of course her mom minimized things—aka *lied*—and made it sound like Caitlin was complaining about everything because she was spoiled. Her mom did admit to her dad that Bill had been an old high school boyfriend, but maintained they were now just friends.

Caitlin could tell her mom was full of crap, and realized her dad was just turning a blind eye to the obvious. *It's only a matter of time before Mom and Bill hook up, if they haven't already,* she thought to herself, and she told her dad the same thing. But he didn't care, so it looked like she'd be stuck on Danbroke for the summer.

My parents suck, she thought, brooding in her room at night. *Some people get two cool parents, but I got stuck with two selfish ones.* To make it worse, there was nothing she could do about it.

In the first few days on Danbroke, she spent most of her time alone, or trying to fend off various attacks from Luke. Just as she'd predicted, he was running around crazily on the island. Partway through the week their belongings arrived, including his paintball guns, so soon the sides of the hotel had grown vivid splotches of red and green paint. No one seemed to notice except Michael, who was constantly chasing him and trying to confiscate the gun.

Caitlin spent a lot of time on the phone talking to Alison. She also called a few other friends and they helped share her misery. She'd talked to Ian twice, but he'd seemed distant and unsure of what to say.

More than anything else, Caitlin felt bored—at least until she started hanging out with Danielle. She ran into her at Buckley's Pizza four days after meeting her, and they sat outside and talked about music and movies. Caitlin could tell that Danielle was a little wary of talking about anything too personal, and she understood. Still, it was nice to have a friend of any sort on the island.

Caitlin realized Danielle was probably lonely, too. Living with her grandmother couldn't be much fun. Caitlin knew Danielle loved her grandmother, but probably felt burdened by the obligation of having to take care of her. To make it worse, Danielle and her grandmother lived in a small, ramshackle trailer down the road. In California, gross white-trash types often lived in trailer parks, but here on the island everyone was so poor, trailers were pretty common. Danielle hadn't ever invited her over, maybe because she was embarrassed.

The slow pace of island life was infectious, and Caitlin felt herself being dragged into somnambulance by its lazy rhythms. She still wasn't sure how to arrange a return to California, but she now thought she could at least get by and survive until the end of August.

That was, until something terrifying and unbelievably awful happened at the end of her first week on the island.

It was a slow Sunday afternoon, and she was watching television in her room alone because it was too hot outside. She'd just got back from sunbathing on the beach; Danielle had had to take her grandmother to church on the mainland, a ferry ride away. As Caitlin didn't have cable, she was satisfying her TV addiction by watching some cheesy soap rerun on CBS. Sometimes the image would get fuzzy, and she'd have to get up and bang on the top of the TV. She'd had a DVD player shipped to them, but the TV was so old that she couldn't figure out how to connect it.

She'd spent the morning in town with Luke, having breakfast and then heading to the beach. There'd been no sign of Caitlin's mom the whole day, so she figured she was off with Bill somewhere. This turned out to be a misguided assumption.

As Caitlin slumped on the couch in her room, she heard a knock on the door. *Shit, I forgot to lock it,* she thought, an instant too late, afraid it was Luke coming to shoot at her. Instead, the door swung open, and she looked up to see Bill standing there, a weird grin on his face.

"Hello there, Caitlin," he said stiffly, like he was nervous. "What are you up to?"

She was a little aggravated that he'd just barged in. "What does it look like I'm doing? I'm watching TV."

He forced a laugh. "Of course you are." He continued to

stand in the doorway, eyeing her. Although he wasn't doing or saying anything, there was something aggressive about his posture. It made her uncomfortable to be scrutinized so closely. "Anything good on?"

If you had cable, there might be. "Naw."

Caitlin immediately regretted her answer, because he took a shambling step farther into the room. "Then you don't mind if I interrupt?" At least the door remained open, which made her feel a little better. "Are you liking Danbroke so far?"

Caitlin nodded, her eyes flitting back toward the TV screen. She hoped he'd get the hint and leave, but he didn't.

"You like the beach?" he prompted. The silence grew. He was staring at her so intensely she felt like she had to respond.

"Sure. It's okay."

He chuckled oddly. "Danbroke gets better with time. It'll grow on you."

Yeah, like a virus, Caitlin thought. She still kept her eyes on the TV. A skinny blonde was about to kiss her Ken-doll boyfriend.

"Yes, ma'am. You'll learn to love Danbroke. I think we'll make a convert out of you yet." He took another step forward. "Kathryn and I have really grown closer these past few days. It's like all those years between now and Belmont just up and vanished." He paused. "She's thinking about moving here for good, you know."

Caitlin felt sick. "I know all too well."

"And what do you think about it?"

There was no reason to lie. "I don't want to leave La Jolla," she said, turning her head to look sideways at him. "All my friends are there. I don't think I'd fit in very well on Danbroke."

Bill didn't appear to appreciate that response. "You might be surprised, Caitlin. People are very . . . adaptable." He shuffled a bit closer, like he thought Caitlin might not notice. She thought she detected a whiff of alcohol coming from him. It smelled sweet, like some kind of hard liquor was seeping out of his pores, maybe whiskey. *He smells like a hobo,* she suddenly thought.

She realized if she stayed on the couch there was a possibility he'd come over and sit down next to her, which was something she definitely wasn't going to allow. So slowly she stood up and walked away from him, around the back of the couch and into the small kitchen area.

Unfortunately, he followed. She opened the fridge and took out a bottle of sparkling water. She'd taken a couple of them from the hotel kitchen and stockpiled them. She took a sip from the bottle as Bill looked on.

"So you're worried about fitting in, huh?" Under the fluorescent lights of the kitchen, he looked sallow and vampiric, with sunken eyes.

"I guess so." She was thinking, *What the hell is up with this guy?*

He was nodding. "That's natural. Made any friends yet?"

"I'm working on it." She supposed everything he was saying sounded normal enough, but his weird diction and body language were subverting his words. She leaned against the counter.

"I thought I saw you with that local girl . . ."

So he's been watching me. "You mean Danielle?"

"Yes, her. But it's only been a week. I bet you'll make more friends here quickly." His pale eyes moved up and down her body. "A pretty young girl like you will fit in just fine, here or anywhere else." She noticed his Texan accent was becoming more pronounced for whatever reason. *Just like Mom.*

"If you say so, Bill." She took another sip of water, feeling the bubbles tingle on her tongue. She didn't like him praising her looks because it was creepy, but it turned out he wasn't done yet.

He stepped closer, about to invade her zone of personal space. The smell of alcohol was stronger now, and she put down her bottle of water. "All you need to do is dress up in one of your sexy little bikinis and go into town," Bill said softly. "I've seen what you've been wearing on the beach. The local boys will be on you like flies on shit, isn't that right?"

Disgusting. She felt her skin start to crawl. "I already have a boyfriend."

"Do you now." A faint smile played at his lips again. Caitlin was starting to realize that Bill was screwing with her, but it was all happening in grisly slow motion, like a car accident. "Your boyfriend's not here, is he? He's back in California. Kathryn told me about him, name of Ian. Do you think he'll be faithful? Teenage boys aren't known for their fidelity, especially ones with bad reputations . . ."

Something had shifted in the air, and Caitlin now felt a palpable tension. An inner alarm had started going off, and she got the sense that Bill might be dangerous somehow. "It's not your business who I'm dating. Really." She kept her voice calm and firm. "You're not my dad."

"Damn straight, I'm not Daddy." He stooped down, leaning in closer next to her, his hot breath on her face. "And I wouldn't want to be. I like things the way they are. God, you look so much like Kathryn. So beautiful and so young . . ."

At that moment, Caitlin got the horrible knowledge that Bill was about to try to kiss her. She wanted to throw up, but instead she just ducked away from him, passing under his gangly arm and moving to the other side of the kitchen, as he pursed his lips. In that instant, she went from being concerned to being absolutely terrified. Bill was a big guy; she wouldn't be able to defend herself against someone like that if he cornered her. She stood with her back to the wall, her heart racing.

Bill looked annoyed as he turned around and took a pace in her direction. "Where are you going, Caitlin?" He reached out a large hand toward her, groping at her breasts.

"Don't touch me!" she snapped. She felt light-headed. "What the hell's wrong with you?" He backed away a little, but only slightly. She was still close enough to smell him. She tried to stay calm. "I'm going to start yelling for help if you put your hands on me. Stay away."

"It doesn't matter what you say," he murmured, not listening. "Kathryn took some pills, your brother's on the beach, and I gave Michael the afternoon off. No one's going to hear you, even if you scream."

Her blood ran cold at his words. "Stop it!" she snapped in terror, holding her arms across her chest. Despite herself, she was starting to completely freak out. She still couldn't believe this was actually happening to her—it was the sort of thing you heard about, or read in a magazine. The kind of thing that happened to girls who let down their guard, or got drunk at a party, or who were just plain dumb enough to put themselves in harm's way. Or at least that's how Caitlin had thought of it, until it happened to her—and she knew she wasn't stupid, or an easy victim.

"I'm going to tell my mom what a pervert you are," she hissed at Bill, not sure it was good to show him anger, but unable to stop herself. "I can't believe you. Are you nuts?"

His eyes were glazed over, like he couldn't hear. "Just you and me," he breathed woozily. "It'll be like old times, like it was in Belmont. Remember the time underneath the bleachers, after the spirit week parade? If I shut my eyes I can go right back there, like it was yesterday . . ." He did shut his eyes, and a sick grin played crookedly across his face.

"I'm not Kathryn," Caitlin said, trying to steady her voice again because she was so scared, she could feel it wanting to crack. She knew all too well there was no way out of the room other than the front door, and Bill was in the way. "I'm Caitlin. You're thinking about my mom."

He opened his eyes, his reverie broken, the look on his face curdling into a frown. "Don't tell me what I'm thinking. I know who you are." He stood there staring. Caitlin kept a hand over her chest to protect herself. "Let me tell you a little something about me," Bill continued. "I get what I want, Caitlin. I always have and I always will. I built myself up from nothing, understand? That's what your mother and I come from. *Nothing*. A blink-and-you'll-miss-it Texas crapper town." He gestured for emphasis. "Look what we've done with ourselves. I know this hotel has turned to shit, but I've got other investments, other opportunities. I can make money again. We've all got demons, Caitlin, but I'm not a bad person. You and your mom aren't any better than me."

He paused for breath, licking his lips and then exhaling raggedly. "Your mom is old and fucked-out. But you're not. You're like a doll. A little porcelain doll. I want you. I need you . . ." His words trailed away into a whisper, as though he realized he'd said way too much.

Each word hit Caitlin like a physical blow. She felt goose bumps rising up like an army on the back of her neck. His words spoke to some deep, dark fear inside of her, and it made her want to cry. *How could someone say these things to me?* Bill had stepped so far outside the bounds of normal human conduct, she didn't know how to deal with it.

"I'm going to tell Mom what you're saying, and Dad too, and Luke and Michael," she babbled, feeling like she was choking. "You're not going to get away with acting this way, with me or anyone else."

He didn't seem to care about what she said—which was the scariest thing of all in some ways. "No one will believe you. I'll tell Kathryn that I came here to talk to you in a fatherly way, and you started screaming about how much you hate Danbroke, and she'll believe me. You're just a poor little rich girl from Southern California. I bet you got diamonds in your pussy."

All she could think of in response to such a revolting line was, "My dad's going to fucking kill you."

Bill spread his hands wide. "He's not here. Just like your boyfriend." He smiled and then suddenly relented, like a cat with a mouse. He took a step backward, and then another, so that soon he was halfway out of the room. He wasn't done talking, though. *"I'm* here, Caitlin. Me and you. That's all who's here."

"Get out of my room," she spat, still barely believing what had just happened between the two of them.

"I'll be seeing much more of you, Caitlin," Bill said, the

threat apparent in the way he said the words. "And I don't care what you say about me. Try telling everyone. It won't work. Luke's the only one who might believe you . . . but what can a little kid do?" Bill winked. "And keep wearing those little bikinis—I like the view." Then he abruptly turned around and strode out through the door.

The door had been open the whole time, Caitlin realized, and no one had heard her yelling at Bill. No one had come to investigate. Bill could have kissed her if he wanted, maybe raped her, and she wouldn't have been able to stop him. *Holy shit.* She stood there shaking as she heard Bill's heavy footsteps moving down the hall until they faded into silence.

She instantly ran to the door, locked it, and slammed the deadbolt, acting on pure instinct. Then she sat down in the far corner of the room, facing the door, watching it and waiting to see if he'd come back.

She realized there was no way she was going to stay at the Pirate's Lodge for another night, but she didn't want to leave the room right away because she was safe for the moment. For all she knew, Bill could be lurking in the hallway. *He's been watching me on the beach,* was all she kept thinking. If her room had been on the first or even the second floor, she would have climbed out the window and run, but there was no way down, so she was temporarily stuck.

She tried to plan, her thoughts churning. *At least now I have a reason why we need to leave Danbroke ASAP,* she thought. The first thing she'd do was call her dad, then tell Luke and her mom, and then they could all get the hell out of this nightmare.

Tears kept trying to come into her eyes, but she managed to

blink them away. She told herself to stay focused and controlled. Bill had scared her badly, but for now she was okay. When she was strong enough to stand up again, she got her cellphone and dialed her dad's number, praying that this time, of all times, he'd be there to help her.

10

escape and rescue

When Caitlin didn't hear anything from her phone, she looked down and saw the battery was dead. She'd stupidly left the charger plugged into the wall in Luke's room when she'd been in there the night before. There was, of course, no phone in her suite, because the Pirate's Lodge was falling apart . . . *or maybe because Bill wanted it that way.*

I have to get out and find Luke, and then get to a phone, Caitlin thought. *There's no way to talk to Mom yet because she's probably doped up, and Bill will come back and find me if I stay in the hotel.*

She knew she'd escaped a dangerous situation and she vowed never to put herself in one like it again. She also knew Bill must be a flat-out psychopath to have acted like that.

She got her purse, crept to the door, and put her ear to it. When several minutes had passed and she was satisfied no one was there, she opened the door slowly and silently, looking both ways up and down the hall. *No sign of Bill.* She sneaked out of the room, shutting the door quietly behind her, and began walking swiftly down the hall. She held her breath as she approached the lobby, but fortunately it was empty. When she reached it, she started to run across the marble floor, straight out the glass front doors and into the sunlight. She didn't stop running until the hotel was several hundred yards behind her and she was safely on the road. Her chest heaving, she took a few deep gasps of air. She wondered why Bill had let her go.

Caitlin climbed up the dune at the side of the road to where she could see the beach and the ocean, looking for her brother. She was worried for a second that she wouldn't find him, but then she saw him out in the ocean, trying to bodysurf on the small waves and failing because he was too fat. Yet at the same time he looked tiny, a lonely, microscopic figure compressed by the vast space around him. Glad that she'd located him so easily, she began to climb down the dune, feeling sand get inside her shoes.

"Luke!" she called out as she walked, but either he didn't hear her or pretended not to. She got closer, stumbling onto the flat part of the beach that led toward the ocean. She passed Luke's clothes, a black bundle on the sand, resting next to his paintball gun and a canister of ammunition.

"Luke, it's me!" she yelled again, and this time he turned his head and saw her. He was still waist deep in the water and didn't show any inclination of coming out. *I'm going to get him out if I have to walk in there and grab him,* Caitlin thought. She reached the water's edge and stopped. "Luke!"

"What do you want?" he finally called back.

"Get over here! Something really bad just happened . . ."

He could tell she wasn't messing around because he began wading through the water to the shore. When he reached Caitlin, he stood there, dripping wet. "This better be good."

"It's not good. It's bad." She shielded her eyes from the sun's reflection on the water as Luke slicked back his hair. "Listen, this is sick, but true. Bill Collins just came into my room and tried to kiss me."

Luke looked surprised and blurted out, "What? No way!"

"He almost attacked me. He told me I looked like Mom when she was my age, and that he wanted to fuck me, basically. He's a psycho, Luke. And I'm not joking, or exaggerating, or anything. I'm telling it to you for real. I yelled at him and then I ran out. I'm never going back there and I don't think it's safe for you, either. Or for Mom." She paused for breath.

Luke was silent. Caitlin could tell he was thinking, and that he knew instantly she was telling the truth. It was one of the few times she'd seen him look so serious in years. "What are we going to do?" he finally asked.

"We need to call Dad, but my phone is dead. We can do it from Danielle's place. Dad will know what to do."

Luke frowned. "Dad is thousands of miles away."

"But he can make things happen. We'll call Mom, too, or maybe go back to the hotel to talk to her if we know Bill's not around. She'll believe us—if we get her when she's sober."

"She's never sober."

True. "We have to try." She blinked against the sun. "And from now on we have to stick together. Bill is seriously messed-up."

"I hate this stupid place," Luke said. He looked out at the ocean. "I want to go home."

"Me too, and maybe we can get there sooner than we thought."

Luke didn't respond right away, like he was lost in thought again. "Mom never got me that four-wheeler," he murmured finally.

"Don't worry about that now. It's not important anymore. Get your clothes and get dressed, and then let's go to Danielle's." For once, the no-nonsense tone seemed to work with him. They walked up the beach and he put on his black T-shirt and flip-flops, and picked up his paintball gun.

"How are we getting to her place?" he asked.

"How do you think? We're walking."

She knew he wanted to complain, but he was smart enough to keep his mouth shut. The two of them hurried across the dune until they got back down to the road. Caitlin scanned it for Bill, afraid he was going to pop out of nowhere like the monster in a horror movie, but the place was deserted.

It took a long time to reach the town. They passed one pay-phone on the way and Caitlin tried it, but it was broken. If she'd known where the police station was, she would have gone straight there, but she didn't want to waste time looking for one. On an island this small, she wasn't even sure they had one. She also wasn't sure what kind of crime she could even report. *Attempted assault? Extreme asshole-ness?*

After passing through town, they got to the trailer park where Danielle lived. Although she'd never been there, Caitlin knew where it was and remembered the address Danielle had once told her. Luke started bitching about how his feet hurt, but Caitlin ignored him. They walked across the lawn and up the three metal stairs to the front door of Danielle's trailer. Caitlin knocked and felt an overwhelming sense of relief when Danielle appeared at the front door, behind the screen.

"Caitlin," she said, surprised. She quickly ushered the two of them inside. "Grandma's asleep, so we need to be quiet. We just got back. It's good to see you, although I could have used some advance warning."

"Listen, we need to talk," Caitlin said urgently. "Something unbelievable just happened to me at the hotel."

"I told you that place had bad vibes. You want to go out somewhere? Or you want to come into my room?"

"Your room. I need to use your phone."

Caitlin noticed Luke's eyes scanning the interior of the trailer. She guessed he didn't even know people really lived in places this small, that not everyone could afford a mansion.

"Luke, why don't you go outside," Caitlin prompted, because she wanted to be alone when she talked with Danielle. "Don't go far, just stay on the lawn, okay?"

"Why?" Luke complained. "It's too hot. I'm going to get heat stroke."

"No, you won't." She noticed he was still toting his paintball gun so she said, "You can go shoot something if you want."

He seemed to brighten up a bit. "Good idea."

Then maybe the police will come, and I can tell them about Bill, Caitlin thought. "Just don't wander too far because we'll be right out." Feeling paranoid, she added, "If you see Bill anywhere, come inside right away."

"Sure." He was out the door fast.

Danielle took Caitlin down an impossibly narrow hallway and into her tiny room. There were posters for bands all over the walls, including a giant one for the Cure, and a blue cloth was draped over a lamp, making it feel like the room was underwater. The only pieces of furniture in it were a twin bed with a black comforter on it and a huge drafting desk that took up most of the room. Taped onto it were some black-and-white sketches in the style of Japanese anime.

"So what the hell happened?" Danielle asked. "You look really shook up." She sat down on the bed, and Caitlin sat across from her in the desk chair.

She suddenly felt nervous about telling the story, even though she knew it wasn't her fault at all. In some ways it had been easier telling Luke, because she'd still been caught up in the horror of the moment. Now she worried a little that Danielle would think she'd done something to lead Bill on, when in fact the opposite was true. Taking a deep breath, she mustered the courage to begin recounting the events.

She ended up telling Danielle everything, and when she was finished, the first thing Danielle did was give her a big hug.

"Jesus, he could have really hurt you," she said, shaking her head. "You're lucky you got out of there. That's awful."

"I know," Caitlin said, hugging Danielle back tightly.

"I always had a bad feeling about that guy. Always. He must have just gone off the deep end for good. It happens on the island sometimes." She took out a pack of cigarettes and gave one to Caitlin.

"I'm worried about my mom," Caitlin said, lighting up. "And me, and Luke."

"Shit, I don't blame you. There's something wrong with half the people on Danbroke, but most of them aren't quite that fucked-up."

"Can I use your phone to call my dad, and the police? I don't want Bill to get away with this."

"You won't have much luck with the police on Danbroke,"

Danielle said. "There aren't any on the island, believe it or not. The nearest police station's across the water. And Bill's a local. The police will probably take his side, no matter what. I know about these situations from personal experience . . ." Her face darkened, but she didn't elaborate. "Try your dad." She leaned over and handed Caitlin her phone.

Caitlin dialed the number. *Voicemail. Of course.* Right before she was about to leave a message, she hesitated. *What the fuck am I going to say?* She was filled with a strange kind of dread. Without fully knowing why she did it, she tentatively hung up the phone. "He's not there," she said to Danielle. "I guess I'll call back later?" Danielle didn't ask why Caitlin hadn't left a message, and Caitlin was relieved.

"You can't go back to the Pirate's Lodge," was all Danielle said, after a moment's pause. "Why don't you just stay here with us? I mean, until you get hold of your dad. Both of you can stay, you and Luke."

Caitlin was surprised by the sudden generosity. She found an ashtray on the nightstand and tapped her cigarette on it. "Are you serious?"

"Sure. You can even spend the night, as long as you don't care about sleeping on the floor in a sleeping bag. You and Luke can both stay in my room, or in the living room. Either way's cool with me."

"Won't your grandmother mind?"

"Naw. She's a little senile anyway. She'll barely notice. If she does, she'll just be excited I actually have some friends my own age."

Caitlin thought it over and realized it made sense. There was really no place else for her to go. "Just until I call my dad," she said. "Then he'll come and get us, or arrange for us to get off of Danbroke. It won't take long."

"I hope so, for your sake. Honestly, though, you can stay as long as you want."

"I can call Mom from here, too, and get her to come over. I want to tell her in person. She needs to know what kind of guy Bill Collins really is."

Danielle nodded her agreement. "A total fuckhead."

Caitlin stubbed out her cigarette. "I better go get Luke. Just in case Bill is nuts enough to have followed me here."

Caitlin and Danielle went outside the trailer, Caitlin worrying that Luke would be gone. Fortunately, he was across the street, trying to shoot out a streetlight with his gun.

"You don't want to do that, Luke," Danielle warned. "I live here. Remember? Besides, that light doesn't work anyway."

Luke lowered the gun. "So did you two geniuses think up a plan?" He sounded accusatory and spoiled. "What did Dad say?"

Caitlin shook her head. "He wasn't there."

"What about Mom?"

"We're about to call her. We thought we'd come get you first."

"Whatever." He feigned nonchalance as he followed them into the trailer, but Caitlin knew her brother well enough to know that he was worried about the situation, too. The three of them crowded back into Danielle's room and shut the door.

"Did you draw those?" Luke asked when he saw the sketches on Danielle's desk.

"Yeah, I did."

In his typical fashion, Luke didn't bother praising them

or anything, even though Caitlin guessed he was impressed. He just pretended to get distracted by a pile of CDs in the corner.

Caitlin picked up the phone again. She knew it wasn't worth calling her mom's cellphone because her mom rarely turned it on. She dialed the number for the hotel, hoping there'd be an automated way to connect directly to her mom's room. The phone rang once, then twice, then three times before someone picked up on the other end.

"Hello?" the voice asked pleasantly. Instantly, Caitlin slammed the phone down, startling both Luke and Danielle.

"It was Bill," Caitlin said, looking around in revulsion. Just hearing his voice made her feel scared, like she was back in the confines of the kitchen with him. Caitlin suddenly felt like she couldn't breathe again.

"No more calls for right now," Danielle advised. "We'll call your mother later tonight, after you've had a chance to relax. I can even call and ask to talk to her. Bill won't recognize my voice, so maybe he'll put my call through. Okay?"

Caitlin nodded, still trying to regulate her breathing. "Sure. It'll be fine."

But what she was thinking was, *This island is a nightmare, and I can't wait to wake up.*

11

Later that night, after a dinner of Kraft macaroni and cheese, Danielle placed the call for Caitlin and got through to Caitlin's mom. Danielle handed the phone to Caitlin, who could tell right away from her mom's voice that she was all doped-up. Caitlin didn't tell her what had happened yet because she knew things would work better face-to-face.

She was also afraid Bill might be there in the room with her mom, listening. So all she said was that she was spending the night at Danielle's, and had taken Luke with her. Strangely, her mom didn't seem to care too much, although she'd never even met Danielle. Caitlin knew her mom wouldn't have been this lax back in La Jolla, and she hoped Danbroke wasn't making her mom lose even more of her grip on sanity.

"I have to see you tomorrow to talk," Caitlin told her on the phone, nervously gripping the white plastic receiver. "Alone, and away from the hotel."

"What in the world is this all about?" her mom asked.

Caitlin ignored the question. She was aware that Danielle

and Luke were watching her face closely. "We can meet at Buckley's Pizza," she continued to her mom, "down the road from the hotel, at noon." She was pretty sure her mom had never been to Buckley's, but the vivid neon sign made it easy to find. Unfortunately, her mom didn't sound interested in seeing her.

"I don't think so, Caitlin," her mom said, her voice getting fainter as though she'd put the phone down and was moving around the room. "I'm going sailing with Bill on his yacht at one, and I need time to get ready."

Caitlin flinched at the mention of Bill's name. She remembered seeing his crappy old yacht, docked in an inlet near the beach by the hotel. She wondered if her mom would be safe on it. "Fine. What about eleven?"

"That won't work either. Just come and find me in my room if you want to talk, Caitlin. I'll be busy tomorrow." Caitlin wondered if "busy" were a code word for "loaded"—*or maybe for "fucking."*

Caitlin realized she'd have to lie to get her mom's attention, and she knew exactly what button to push. "Well, I talked to Dad a few minutes ago, and he told me something really important . . . about him and Sofie."

Her mom got agitated instantly, her voice getting louder and more strident. Needless to say, she hated The Model. "What did he say about that slut?!"

"I can only tell you in person," Caitlin replied ominously.

"Is he marrying her?" her mom yelled. Caitlin heard coughing sounds on the other end of the line. "I knew it! I knew they'd get engaged. He popped the question, didn't he?"

"Meet me at eleven at Buckley's if you want to find out."

Then Caitlin did something she knew would drive her mom crazy—she hung up.

She looked at Luke and Danielle and said, "Well, that went shittily, like I knew it would."

"Why isn't Mom more normal?" Luke asked.

Caitlin didn't answer. She was glad Luke was on her side, but she knew his allegiance was fleeting. If their mom had come through with the four-wheeler, then he'd probably still be at the Pirate's Lodge, talking crap about Caitlin. "She better turn up tomorrow," was all she said.

* * *

After spending a long night in Danielle's room—during which she was plagued with nightmares of Bill and woke up twice in a cold sweat—she met her mom at Buckley's, accompanied by both Luke and Danielle. She knew that the two of them were probably nervous, too. *Danielle must be some kind of saint to get dragged into my family's mess,* Caitlin thought. She clung to the hope that if things went well, she'd be off the island soon.

Caitlin's mother was sitting outside Buckley's at one of the flimsy metal tables, her mouth contorted into a scowl. She had her huge dark Chanel sunglasses on, and a wide-brimmed black felt hat to cover her face. It looked like she was nursing a major hangover. "I tried calling your father, but he didn't answer," she said, her voice a little slurred.

Caitlin took a seat across from her. The smell of the ocean was heavy in the air, and there wasn't much of a breeze, so she felt sweaty. Danielle followed Caitlin's lead and took a seat, too.

Luke hung back, leaning against the brick wall next to them, kicking it with the heels of his shoes.

Danielle introduced herself to Caitlin's mom, who just responded with a tight nod. *How rude,* Caitlin thought. *Mom would go crazy if I acted that way to one of her SoCal friends.* She noticed her mom was sipping coffee out of a cup and prayed there wasn't any Frangelico or Kahlua in there.

"I need to know every word your father said," Caitlin's mother began, speaking through clenched teeth. "I knew the two of them were up to something recently. They don't want me to know about it, do they? Both of them are—"

"This isn't about Dad," Caitlin interrupted. "It's about Bill."

Her mom looked puzzled. "Bill?"

Caitlin began telling the hideous story. She realized that each time she told it, it got harder and harder and made her feel worse about herself. Bill had put her in a terrible position. But this time, she only got partway through—to the point where Bill leaned in for the kiss—before her mom held up a hand and stopped her, shaking her head. Caitlin's words slowly trailed away into confused silence.

She heard her mom take a slow, thick intake of breath, as if preparing to scream. But instead, she simply said, "You're lying to me, aren't you? You must be, because I don't believe a single word you're saying."

Caitlin was stupefied. She knew her mom might have a violent reaction to the news about Bill, but she hadn't truly thought her mom would outright accuse her of being a liar. "No— It's true—" she stammered. "What I'm telling you is exactly what happened! Wait until you hear the rest."

Her mom's face was rigid and expressionless. *She looks angry,* Caitlin thought. *But why should she be angry at me? Shouldn't she be mad at Bill?*

"I've already heard enough," her mom said. "I won't let you talk that way about Bill, especially in front of Luke, and"—her eyes flicked dismissively behind her sunglasses to Danielle—"strangers." Her mom's head turned back toward her. "You don't need to hide behind strangers, Caitlin. I'm your mother. You shouldn't have brought anyone here to listen to your lies."

Caitlin was frankly terrified, because if her mom didn't believe her, then she was in big trouble. "I'm not hiding behind anyone," she protested. "If you don't believe me, then you're the one who's hiding—hiding from the truth. At least let me finish telling you what happened."

"Bill would never do the things you said. You're jealous of my happiness with him," her mom said, the words coming out angrily. "I brought you here to help you, to show you a different part of the country, but you don't care, do you? You want to spoil my relationship with Bill before it even gets started. You don't care about anyone except yourself."

How can she not believe me? Caitlin screamed inside her mind. *She's my own mother!* She fervently hoped it was the pills and alcohol talking, and not her real mom. Luke had been right when he said their mom was never sober. She glanced back at him, and his face was pale and tight, but he wasn't saying anything. Danielle looked vaguely stunned, like an unwitting witness to an abrupt and gruesome car accident.

"Mom, think about it logically. Why would I lie?" Caitlin pleaded. "I'm telling you the truth, swear to God. Bill tried to attack me, and none of us are safe at the hotel. We can't stay here any longer. Bill kept talking to me like I was you—I think he has mental problems. I'm scared, Mom. You have to listen—"

"Don't tell me what to do!" Caitlin's mother retorted angrily, pushing her sunglasses up the bridge of her nose. The situation was spiraling downward, out of control, and Caitlin didn't know how to stop it. "I don't believe a word you're saying. I've known Bill Collins since I was twelve, and he's a good, hardworking man. He was my first boyfriend, Caitlin. We went to junior prom together!" This was news to Caitlin, who felt a mounting sense of doom. "How dare you make these ludicrous accusations against him?!" Her mom's voice continued to rise in volume and pitch, like the mother on some bad soap opera. Caitlin wondered if Joe could hear from inside the restaurant. "How dare you!"

Some cold, hard part of Caitlin's mind remained detached from her emotions, and she thought, *So this was clearly one big fucking mistake, huh?* She'd realized, too late, that to criticize Bill was to implicitly criticize her mom—both her mom's choice in men, and the fact that her mom had brought her own children to such a dangerous place without being more careful. Her mother wasn't prepared to face that reality or assume any guilt. In fact, Caitlin knew her mom had difficulty facing everyday life, which was why she took pills.

Caitlin kept her face blank as her mom continued to scream at her. She wasn't even listening to the words anymore. It really didn't matter what her mom was saying, or how she rationalized what had happened. All that mattered was that her mom had chosen not to believe her. Her mom had chosen Bill.

Partway through her mom's diatribe, Luke got up and walked away. Clearly he couldn't take it anymore, and Caitlin didn't blame him. *But I won't run,* she thought. *I'll sit here and let my mom yell at me and take Bill's side, and I won't forget she did this—ever.* It would be a good, if harsh, lesson never to trust her mom again. She knew that later she'd cry over it, probably long and hard, but not in front of her mom.

When her mom ran out of invectives and began to calm down, dabbing at her eyes showily with a Kleenex under her sunglasses, Caitlin felt Danielle lightly touch her arm.

"I think we should go," Danielle whispered.

The words were meant just for Caitlin, but her mom heard and wearily said to Danielle, "Who in God's name are you, anyway? Just some Mexican. No one cares what you think."

"She's my friend," Caitlin said, startled by her mom's casual racism. "I care what she thinks."

"I'm Filipina," Danielle added softly. "Not Mexican."

Caitlin stood up slowly, realizing that her legs were feeling shaky. She addressed her mom stiffly, or at least what she could see of her mom behind the glasses and the hat. "I shouldn't have told you."

"You're right. I'm tired of lies. You lie all the time back home, about boys and about partying, and you're lying all the time here. I was hoping Danbroke would change things."

Oh, but it has, Caitlin thought. *Just not for the better.* Yet she said nothing, as Danielle stood up, too, right next to her. She was glad for the girl's support because she wasn't sure she could have made it through the trauma on her own. She wondered what Danielle would think of her, now that she'd met her mom and seen what a mess she was.

"You must be very disturbed to make up such terrible accusations," Caitlin's mom opined. "More troubled than I thought." From Caitlin's angle standing up, her eyes were now completely hidden by the emotionless black glasses. "How did I go so wrong in raising you? You don't even know the difference between the truth and a lie anymore. Are you doing drugs? You must be."

The irony wasn't lost on Caitlin. She merely said, "I want to let you know that Luke and I won't be returning to the Pirate's Lodge. It's not safe for us there. I can't stay in the suite because I know Bill has a master key and can come in anytime. For all I know, he's crazy enough to hurt me. From now on, we'll be staying with Danielle and her grandmother in town."

She wanted her mom to argue with her, to fight for her and Luke to stay at the hotel, which would at least show that she cared. Instead, her mom said, "Good. Don't come back unless you're ready to apologize to me, and Bill as well. And you shouldn't let your own anger ruin Luke's time here or his relationship with Bill."

"He has no relationship with Bill and neither do I. Bill isn't our dad, if you haven't noticed. He's a monster."

"If your father's so great, and loves us so much, then why did he leave?" her mom replied sharply. "Don't forget, he didn't just leave me. He left all of us."

Caitlin flinched. "Thanks for rubbing that in, Mom."

Her mom stood up, holding onto the table. Drugs were no excuse. Caitlin knew her mom's reaction was flat-out wrong, no matter what the reasons. Yet it planted a seed of doubt in Caitlin's mind about telling her dad. She'd been certain she was going to tell him about Bill, figuring there was no way he'd disbelieve her, but then she'd thought the same thing about her mom.

If there were even a half-a-percent possibility that he'd think she was lying, then it wasn't worth telling him. She couldn't risk losing both parents, because that's what it felt like with her mom: a loss. *A loss of confidence, a loss of trust, and a loss of love.*

"I'm going back to the lodge," her mom said quietly. "I'm not going to tell Bill about our conversation. I know you want to leave Danbroke, but making up fantasies about Bill isn't going to work. I'm not going to let you ruin my day—or my summer. I'm going sailing on Bill's yacht this afternoon, like I planned. I'm through with you until you change your bad attitude."

Caitlin was smart enough to know the real reason her mom wasn't going to mention their conversation to Bill was that, deep down, she was afraid it might be true. Caitlin stood there watching as her mom began tottering unsteadily away from the table. She looked like she needed a cane to keep her balance. She stumbled awkwardly back down the path toward the main road in the direction of the hotel.

After a moment, Caitlin felt the weight of Danielle's arm around her shoulders. "Don't worry," Danielle whispered. "I believe you, and so does Luke, and so will everyone else." Then she added, "My mom's crazy, too. She's an alcoholic. She's been in and out of rehab a hundred times. That's why I live with my grandma. I know what it's like."

Caitlin fought the urge to cry, feeling a hard lump in her throat and trying to swallow it away. Danielle's empathy almost made the floodgates open and the tears come out. *Almost.* She wondered where Luke had run off to, and what they were going to do now. They were basically stranded. Orphaned.

"It's going to be okay," Danielle said calmly. "I'm going to help you, like I promised."

Caitlin brushed back a wayward strand of hair. "My own mom hates me."

"She's just messed-up. I've seen my mom act worse, if that's any consolation." It wasn't.

Why couldn't Dad, or someone, have stepped in earlier and done something for Mom? Caitlin wondered. She continued to watch her mother's receding figure as it picked its way across the barren landscape. She was torn between hatred and pity—and hatred was winning. She stood there watching silently for a long time, with Danielle at her side.

"Let's go find Luke," Caitlin finally said.

12
life with danielle

By the time two entire weeks had passed—a span of time that seemed much longer than merely fourteen days—things had completely changed for Caitlin. She hadn't returned to the Pirate's Lodge at any point, and she'd basically abandoned all her possessions and clothes there. *I'd rather look like crap than go back there and see Bill, even for a second,* she thought. She just borrowed stuff from Danielle. It wasn't the designer outfits she was used to, but the clothes fit, and that was enough.

Caitlin daydreamed about going back to the hotel, hoping she might avoid Bill and run into Michael instead, but she didn't have the courage to do it. She also hadn't found the courage to tell her dad, deciding instead to remain quiet about what Bill had done. It wasn't the smartest decision, but it was the one she had made.

It was mainly because she was afraid of her dad's reaction, but also because things were looking up for her at the moment. She and Luke, due to the kindness of Danielle, had moved into the trailer for the time being. She was sort of amazed at how quickly her admittedly high standards for living had plummeted in the face of Danbroke. Caitlin could barely believe that just a few weeks earlier she'd been living in luxury and splendor back in Southern California. Still, she'd learned it was far better to have a humble bed—or rather, a sleeping bag—in a trailer where she was safe, than a whole suite of rooms in a hotel owned by a dangerous creep.

Luke had recovered from the shock of the events and was back to his normal, obnoxious self. He was enjoying the most freedom he'd ever had in his life. It almost didn't matter what he did on the island—Mom wasn't there to yell at him, and there were no police to bring him home in their patrol car if he vandalized something. Yet in a strange way, having no restrictions gave him nothing to rebel against. He spent most of his time swimming in the ocean or shooting his paintball gun at trees, which were far more numerous than cars.

Caitlin saw her mom only twice from a distance during those two weeks. Both times her mom was being escorted by Bill in his Lincoln Town Car. It seemed insane to Caitlin that her mom wasn't making more of an effort to get her and Luke back. She imagined by now her mom might be completely lost, especially if Bill were enabling her bad habits.

I don't care if I ever see her again, Caitlin thought wildly. She'd told her dad that Mom was acting crazy and had basically abandoned them, but he'd thought she was exaggerating. The conversation had been frustrating, and brief, and it made her glad she hadn't risked telling him about Bill.

She didn't have to worry about money, because she still had her credit cards and access to her bank account. Her mom hadn't stopped either of them, probably out of laziness. *Or maybe Mom doesn't even remember.* She thought about fleeing the island on her own, but then there was Luke to worry about, and she didn't know where the two of them could go. Caitlin wondered if her mother was happy things had turned out this way, because now she was free to be alone with Bill.

Living at Danielle's place was okay for the short term, but a bit awkward. Her grandmother, Rina, nominally took care of Luke and helped make the food, but she was old and sometimes disoriented. She was a tiny, shrunken Filipina woman in her seventies, with thinning gray hair in a bun and a perpetual smile. Danielle called her Rinita, and at her urging, Caitlin soon adopted the habit. At first, Caitlin had thought that maybe Rinita couldn't speak English because she was pretty quiet, but Caitlin soon learned Rinita spoke English just fine. Rinita just wasn't too interested in speaking, preferring to spend most of her time watching game shows on the small TV in her bedroom.

Caitlin realized she'd found a good friend in Danielle, and marveled at how insanely generous she was. *Who the hell would take in some strange girl and her crazy brother?* Caitlin wondered. She knew she probably wouldn't have done the same thing had their situations been reversed.

Caitlin still talked to Alison, of course, but it was frequently hard for them to get hold of each other. She'd bought another cellphone charger, but service was sporadic on Danbroke, and often it was impossible to get a signal. Even regular phone service got interrupted sometimes because the phone lines were so old. For one of the first times ever in their friendship, Caitlin was keeping a secret from Alison and hadn't told her what Bill had done. She didn't doubt that Alison would believe her; she just couldn't face saying the words out loud anymore. It felt like reliving the moment each time she was forced to repeat it.

Caitlin and Danielle spent a lot of time together, although Caitlin slept in later than Danielle on most days. Sometimes she'd wake up on the floor in her borrowed sleeping bag, the bright rays of the morning sun streaming through the small window, and see Danielle sitting at her desk, drawing. Caitlin didn't ask too much about Danielle's art, not because she wasn't interested, but because she could tell it was something private. Danielle almost never hung her drawings on the walls of her room, but filed them away in a series of large black portfolios she kept under the bed. After she'd been there a week, Caitlin asked Danielle if she ever thought about hanging the art up or showing it to anyone. Danielle had shook her head.

"I never even take it out of my room," she'd told Caitlin. "Pretty lame of me, I know." She tried to turn it into a joke: "I must have low self-esteem, right?"

"They're really good," Caitlin insisted. "Seriously, I know I couldn't draw anything like that."

Danielle grinned, but Caitlin could tell she was slightly embarrassed and not used to praise. "You're staying at my house, Caitlin. It's not like you'd tell me they're shit, even if they are."

"I wouldn't say they were shit—I just wouldn't say anything about them. I'm totally serious when I say they're awesome."

Danielle made a face. "Rinita doesn't think much of them. She just tells me to study hard at school and not let boys touch my breasts. Oh, and to never drink or do drugs. That's pretty much all the advice she has. It didn't work too well with my mom, so I don't know why she thinks it'll work with me."

"At least she cares about you. Look at my mom—what a joke."

Danielle sighed. "Things are backwards with both our parents. We're the teenagers, not them. Shouldn't we be the ones doing drugs?"

Caitlin agreed, but she realized that somehow the conversation had been skillfully steered away from Danielle's art. After that, Caitlin hadn't pressed too much about Danielle's sketches. She had other things to think about.

Ian, for example, was a whole other disaster area. He'd become a virtual nonentity in her mind, which made her wonder if she'd even liked him much to begin with. He wasn't good about returning her phone calls, and their conversations were clumsy and short, both of them struggling for things to say. He didn't seem too interested in her, and Caitlin counted that as a major turn-off. She had a sense that their relationship probably wasn't going to work out in the long run. *Fuck it,* she thought, with manufactured nonchalance. *Someone better will come along . . .*

By the end of the two weeks at Danielle's place, Caitlin almost thought of the girl as a sister. She enjoyed living with her friend and she felt like she'd already grown closer to her than she would have guessed. Danielle was even responsible for helping her get her first job.

Danielle was just starting a new part-time job at the tiny grocery store in town, bagging groceries. It was uninventively called the Food Stop, but everyone referred to it as "the Stop." It didn't sell alcohol, so it wasn't a popular location with the locals, who lived on cheap beer and box wine. There wasn't much to do on Danbroke but drink. Caitlin just wished the island was like

La Jolla, where even the most microscopic minimarts stocked Veuve Clicquot, and sometimes Cristal. She had shared quite a few mystery-brand bottles of red wine with Danielle so far, and they'd tasted like cough syrup. *Still, they'd got the job done.* When she was drunk, she was free.

Caitlin had offered to pay Danielle rent and help her out while she was staying at the trailer, but Danielle refused. "We're doing fine. Grandma gets a pension and my dad sends money sometimes." Still, Caitlin made sure to pick up the tab anytime they went out for food just to show her gratitude. She'd never forget how Danielle had given her two dollars that first day they'd met at Buckley's.

Danielle and her grandmother certainly weren't rich, but Danielle claimed she was taking a job just for something to do—not for the money. "I've had a bunch of summer jobs here," she told Caitlin, "but I usually end up quitting after a few weeks because they're so lame. Or I get fired. But I get really bored just sitting around doing nothing, and I figure that working is good inspiration for my art." She scrunched her nose. "There are enough freaks on Danbroke to fill an entire portfolio . . ."

Caitlin went along with Danielle on her first day of work at the Food Stop and, out of sheer boredom, as well as a desire to hang out with the one cool person on the island, she applied for a position there, too. Luckily Danielle had a couple bikes they used to get around. Rinita owned an old station wagon, but didn't let anyone drive it, except to go to the ferry on Sundays for church.

"This feels really fucking weird," Caitlin admitted to Danielle as she filled in the one-page application at the Stop.

She couldn't even remember her Social Security number at first. "I've never had a job before."

"Just lie and say you did," Danielle told her. "They don't give a shit here. They just want some sucker who doesn't mind working for minimum wage."

"How much is minimum wage, anyway?"

"You don't want to know."

"Should I say I worked in a grocery store before?"

"Why not? Say you were assistant manager and maybe they'll pay you an extra ten cents an hour."

It turned out that Danielle was right about lying, because Caitlin got the job, bagging groceries for the occasional customers who wandered in each afternoon. She worked side by side with Danielle for a few hours every day. It wasn't a difficult job, and usually there were more people working there than shopping. The manager, whose name was Curtis, spent most of his time in the office on the phone, so Caitlin and Danielle just hung out and talked, and did as little work as possible. The only other employee was an old woman named Sally, who glared at them as she mopped the floor and popped her dentures in and out.

If any of my friends in La Jolla could see me now, they'd think I'd totally lost my mind, Caitlin thought. *I wouldn't even set foot in a store like this back home, but here I am now, working in one.* She'd mentioned to Alison that she'd got a job, but she'd made it sound better by saying she was working at a bistro.

Only one thing bothered Caitlin at the Stop. She continued to nurse a fear that Bill would barge into the store one day. She knew on an island as small as Danbroke, he probably knew exactly where she was. But for whatever reason, he seemed to be keeping his distance. *He's probably got his hands full with my mom.* Still, the lurking fear of Bill made her uneasy, and it dogged her like a shadow. She was glad Danielle knew about the situation because if Bill ever did show up they could fight him off together.

There was only one weird event that was maybe connected to Bill, although Caitlin wasn't sure. It happened when she was using the tiny bathroom at the back of the Stop. When she sat down in the stall and shut the flimsy metal door, to her surprise she saw that a photograph had been taped onto the back of it. Surprised, she squinted at it, trying to figure it out. The photo was blurry, but it looked like two girls on their bikes, riding near the beach. Caitlin tore the photo off the door and looked closer.

Shit, is that me and Danielle? she wondered. The image was too indistinct for her to be sure, but it looked like someone had snapped a photo of the two of them from a distance. Caitlin wondered if it was Danielle playing a joke, but it didn't seem like something she'd do. *Could it be Curtis?* But their boss was completely humorless, so that was doubtful.

Caitlin tried not to think about Bill Collins and how it seemed like he'd been following her around. It gave her the creeps to imagine that he might be secretly watching them and snapping photos. *And why would the photo be taped up in here? Does it mean that Bill's been inside the store? Without me knowing?* Each question that she asked herself made her feel more uncomfortable. She knew she should do something about it, but she couldn't bring herself to face it. If Bill were trying to scare her, then it was working. Without thinking it through, on gut instinct, she tore the photo up and flushed it down the toilet. And, knowing it was probably the wrong decision, she didn't mention anything about it to Danielle.

Hopefully, it's nothing, she told herself, trying to forget about it. *Just some random photo that's not even of us.* Yet she couldn't shake the ominous feeling that something very bad was going to happen to her unless she was careful and watched her back on Danbroke.

Then, on a sleepy Tuesday afternoon, just as Caitlin and Danielle were heading to work, a different kind of event occurred that shattered their newly established routine. It happened in an unexpected way, as both girls were standing on the corner in town, smoking. They were trying to finish their cigarettes quickly, because Curtis didn't allow smoking in the Stop. Of course, when he wasn't around they sneaked as many cigarettes as they could.

As Caitlin stood there, talking and smoking in the heat, she saw something that really surprised her coming down the road. It was a red Mercedes sports car, new and shiny, like the kind of car she saw every day on the roads around La Jolla, but never on the island. It was even newer than her Mercedes back home, and its rims sparkled in the sun. Caitlin had grown used to the fact that nearly every car on Danbroke was a complete rust bucket. The only nice vehicle she'd seen on the island was the Escalade that had brought them there on the very first day.

Danielle noticed the Mercedes, too. She turned to Caitlin and derisively said, "Check that thing out. Probably some Wall Street yuppie on vacation who got lost heading to Miami."

Caitlin laughed, but as the car got closer, she recognized both the driver and the guy sitting in the passenger seat. It took her a second to place them, but then she realized she'd seen them a few weeks earlier in town. It was the Adam Brody look-alike at the wheel; his blond-haired friend was sitting next to him. Three other boys she didn't recognize were crammed into the backseat, one of them with his shirt off and another wearing a backward baseball cap.

The car was driving slowly, but somewhat erratically, and Caitlin and Danielle stepped back onto the side of the road as it approached. The guys barely noticed them. The ones in the back were laughing and joking, and the blond-haired passenger was drinking a beer, not even trying to hide it. Caitlin could hear unidentifiable hip-hop blasting out of the car as it passed them and continued unevenly down the road.

"Look at those morons," Danielle said, staring after them. "Spoiled rich kids."

Caitlin didn't want to point out that Danielle's description could have once perfectly fit her, and maybe still did. She just said, "They're not locals, right?"

"No way. Their car is too nice." Danielle frowned. "And they have all their teeth . . ."

"I saw two of them in town, before the whole Bill thing happened."

"Really?" Danielle tossed her cigarette butt on the ground and snuffed it out with the heel of her boot. Caitlin had noticed she always wore those boots, even though she knew Danielle owned other pairs of shoes.

"Yeah, the two of them caught my eye because they looked so out of place on Danbroke. I remember thinking I felt a little better about things to see guys our age here. Besides, I guess they're kind of cute. At least the driver . . ." She broke off, not sure if she should have confessed that. Unlike Alison and her friends back home, Danielle was a little more guarded when it came to talking about boys.

"I didn't get a good enough look to tell if they're cute," Danielle said. "Besides, they're not my type."

Caitlin took a final puff on her cigarette and tossed it onto the gravel. She wondered what, exactly, Danielle's type was, but her friend didn't elaborate. She imagined it was probably arty, Gothic-type guys. *Not too many of those on Danbroke.*

"Why do you think they're even here?" Caitlin asked.

"I dunno. Probably to get drunk on the beach like everyone else. Maybe they're slumming by coming this far south. They better be careful with that car, though. The local good ol' boys won't take kindly to a bunch of rich kids in a Mercedes."

"Do the locals take kindly to anything?"

Danielle laughed. "Other than inbreeding and alcoholism? No."

Caitlin checked her watch. It was already 2:15 and they were supposed to be at work at 2:00. It was probably no mystery why Danielle got fired because she was always running behind. *Just like me,* Caitlin thought. "Shit, we're late."

"Does it matter?"

They both started laughing again for no reason in particular. Caitlin realized that it really didn't matter, that—in a good way—nothing mattered at that moment. It was strangely liberating.

Caitlin and Danielle began trudging their way down the road to the Food Stop. Caitlin was hungry, and was looking forward to getting there and eating some Macadamia nut cookies. Both she and Danielle pilfered the snack counter at will, although they weren't supposed to even eat on the job, let alone steal the food. *My diet's gone to shit,* Caitlin thought.

They chatted as they walked and were almost there before they heard the sound of a car approaching, now blaring classic Beastie Boys.

"Look who's back," Caitlin heard Danielle mutter, but she knew it was the red Mercedes before she even turned around.

13

T he car pulled up right behind them, and a voice yelled out, "Hey! Girls! Stop—we want to talk to you!"

The guy doing the yelling was the blond-haired passenger, who was leaning partway out the window, the bottle of Budweiser still in his hand. He was dressed in typical preppy-chic attire, wearing a light blue vintage T-shirt that probably cost at least a hundred bucks. *Definitely not from Danbroke,* Caitlin decided.

"Yeah, you!" he said, as both Caitlin and Danielle looked at him. He'd put a pair of sunglasses on, and his tousled hair hung over them. To Caitlin, he looked like one of the generic surfer boys she saw nearly every day hanging out in La Jolla. He was wearing a silver stud earring. The guys in the back of the car continued to talk and snicker, obviously about her and Danielle. Only the dark-haired driver seemed uninterested in them, nodding his head in time to the music, staring straight ahead at the road.

"Where are you guys headed?" the blond-haired boy asked.

"Guys?" Danielle retorted, somewhat haughtily. "Do we look like 'guys' to you?"

The blond-haired passenger looked a little taken aback, but he forged ahead. "No, you don't. I just meant 'guys' as a general term for 'people,' understand? Don't be so friggin' touchy. My name's Nathan."

The driver revved the engine for no particular reason. One of the guys in the back of the car reached down and pulled out a beer, taking a long swig. He was wearing a UCLA sweatshirt, which made Caitlin wonder if he was from California.

"I'm not going to tell you my name," Caitlin heard Danielle telling Nathan.

"Me neither," Caitlin added, because now Nathan was staring at her. *Or maybe "leering" was a better word.* He looked sloppy drunk.

"I didn't ask for your names, did I?"

"Drinking and driving is going to get you idiots arrested," Danielle said, over the music. "Just so you know."

"Arrested by who?" Nathan asked, and then he cackled as his buddies in the back egged him on. "There aren't any police around that I can see." One of the guys in the back leaned forward and whispered something in his ear.

"What do you want with us?" Caitlin asked, irritated.

"We just wanted to say hi," called out one of the guys from the backseat.

"Hi!" blurted out another of them.

"Okay. So now you've said hi, you can keep driving," Danielle replied.

"Don't be such a hard-ass," the guy complained. "Jeez. Where are you two from? I know it's not Danbroke."

"California," Caitlin said. She nodded at Danielle. "She's from Toronto."

"Don't tell them anything more," Danielle said.

"No, please, tell me more—" Nathan pleaded, leaning out the window even farther. He looked ridiculous, like he was going to fall out of the car.

Caitlin touched Danielle's arm and said, "Let's go." She found the guys and their car more annoying than threatening, because they looked and acted like the jerks back home. It wasn't uncommon for some sleazy guy in a sports car to roll the window down and yell at her while she was jogging down Girard Avenue on the way to the beach. *At least these guys are about my age,* she thought. Often in La Jolla, guys old enough to be her grandfather would hit on her without any shame whatsoever.

Danielle nodded and said, "Yeah, you're right. Let's go. These guys are nobodies."

"Ooooh," Nathan said, overhearing her comment like he was supposed to. The driver continued to ignore them, completely disengaged. "Is it your time of the month or something?"

Oh my God, he sounds just like Luke, Caitlin thought, rolling her eyes.

"You're exactly right," Danielle said to Nathan, her voice dripping with sarcasm. "I'm a total PMSing bitch. And you're a drunken asshole. So I think you should just leave me alone and then we'll both be happy."

"Hey, I might be drunk, but at least I can sober up," Nathan retorted. "It'll be harder to de-bitch you."

Caitlin interrupted because she could tell Danielle was about to get really mad. "Listen, stop fucking with us," she said. "If you're trying to pick us up, in some sick, twisted way, then don't bother. We have boyfriends, okay?" It was a lie, because Danielle didn't, and Ian was in flux, but it felt like the right thing to say.

"Who said anything about trying to pick you up?" Nathan asked, encouraged by his friends in the back again. "Don't flatter yourselves."

Danielle stepped toward the car like she wanted to punch Nathan in the face.

"Listen, we have to get going," Caitlin told the guys as she reached out her arm again and grabbed Danielle's shoulder, trying to reel her in. "Unlike you, we actually have things to do."

"Like what? There's nothing to do on this island. We've only been here a few weeks and we're already sick of it."

True enough. But she didn't want to give him the satisfaction of agreeing with anything he said. "We have jobs."

"Where?" Nathan asked.

"Wouldn't you like to know?" Danielle replied.

The driver revved the engine again, like he was losing patience with his friends. Alone among the five guys, he was the only one who hadn't said anything to Caitlin and Danielle or whispered about them. *Probably the only sane one,* Caitlin thought. *Or the only sober one.*

Nathan turned to him, saying, "Evan, wait—I need one more minute." But his words didn't have any effect, and the Mercedes began moving forward, picking up speed. Caitlin saw one of the guys in the back spill beer on his preppy yellow shirt as the car lurched forward.

Nathan leaned out the window, the wind rippling through his hair. "See you around!" he yelled back at them. Then he tossed his empty beer bottle onto the road, not in their direction, but over the roof of the car and onto the other side. It failed to break, and just bounced once, before rolling away into the grass.

"Why do guys have to be like that?" Danielle asked when the car was gone, shaking her head. "I don't get it." She paused. "I mean, I *do* get it. I just don't like it."

"Where do you think they came from? Where do people like that stay on Danbroke?"

She shrugged. "They're probably renting a house somewhere. Maybe on the other end of the island? They're building new places there to entice rich tourists to come. It's never going to work." Caitlin hadn't been up there yet with Danielle. "If they are on the other end of the island, they can stay there," Danielle continued. "I hate that kind of attitude, like they own the whole place just because they have money."

"Don't worry about them," Caitlin told Danielle. "Like you said earlier, they're idiots. They'll probably drive their Mercedes into a tree and total it."

"I can only hope." Danielle sighed. "But even if that happens, their parents will just buy them a new one."

"Yeah, but their parents can't buy them brains or better social skills."

Danielle paused as they walked, seemingly lost in thought for a second. They were almost at the store, so Caitlin lit a final cigarette, just to get a last-minute hit of nicotine before work began.

"The kid who was driving," Danielle finally said. "He looks like that guy from TV . . . you know the show I mean? The high school one? I don't know if it's even still on. I never watched it that much . . ."

Caitlin could tell she was lying—trying to sound cool—and

she smiled inwardly. *So the driver had caught Danielle's eye, too.* "You mean *The O.C.?* Adam Brody."

Danielle nodded. "That'd be the one."

* * *

Caitlin wasn't expecting to see the driver so soon after the encounter with him and his drunk friends. But later that same day, as she was stocking the barren shelves with dented cans of Campbell's chicken and rice soup, the front door opened and he came in all by himself. Danielle was in the back, unloading some crates, so Caitlin was working alone.

She noticed him right away because he looked so different from most of the Stop's usual patrons. She kept her head down because she didn't want him to see her. She didn't think he knew that she and Danielle worked there, but it seemed like an awfully big coincidence that he'd just turn up out of the blue. From the corner of her eye, she saw him peering up and down a couple of the dimly lit aisles. She wondered if he were looking for something. She definitely wasn't going to get up and introduce herself after the way his friends had acted earlier in the day.

She looked away as she saw him glance in her direction. *Shit, what do I do?* she wondered. She was wearing her uniform over her clothes, a dumpy red smock with the Food Stop logo on the back, so maybe he wouldn't recognize her.

It turned out she had no such luck. Even though she was no longer watching him, she knew he was approaching because she could hear footsteps getting closer, and he was the only customer in the store. Slowly, she stood up, not sure what to say.

"Hey there," she heard a voice call out, deep and with a barely perceptible Southern drawl.

Caitlin turned around, coming face-to-face with him. Or rather, face-to-chest, because he was a good six inches taller than her. His sunglasses were off, hanging from his shirt, and she could see that his eyes were an unusual shade of washed-out silver blue.

"Hey," she said. If he was as much of a joke as his friends were then she didn't want to encourage him.

"I saw you earlier," he said. "On the street."

"Yeah, I remember." She brushed back her hair and then put the can of chicken and rice that had been in her hand on the shelf. "What are you doing here?"

He looked vaguely embarrassed, his eyes drifting away from hers for a second. "I wanted to come and . . . apologize," he finally managed. His eyes returned to hers. "At least that was the plan."

So he *had* come here to find her, after all. "How did you know where I work?"

"I asked around."

"I was that easy to find?"

"Kind of." He paused again. She hoped he wasn't like Ian, impossible to talk to. But then he loosened up a little. "I just wanted to say I'm sorry for how everyone acted earlier today. Nathan can get pretty unruly, and we were all kind of drunk. I know it was childish . . ."

"It's not too smart to drink and drive," she said, thinking, *What am I, an after-school special or something?* This guy was old enough to make his own decisions.

"You're right," he said. "I just happened to be the least

drunk, which somehow made me the designated driver." He grinned crookedly, in a way that was disarming. "My name's Evan."

"I already know. I'm Caitlin." She figured there was no reason to keep her name secret if he knew where she worked. "Caitlin Ross."

"Nice to meet you," he said in an overly chivalrous way that made both of them laugh a little bit. "Anyway, I'm sorry about what happened earlier. Nathan always turns into an asshole when he drinks. I guess I did, too, for letting them make me stop the car and harass you like that."

Caitlin had a sudden thought. "Are you and Nathan brothers?" She didn't know why she asked it; maybe because the two of them sounded a little similar.

He smiled and shook his head. "People ask us that sometimes. We're just good friends—we grew up together in Richmond."

"So that's where you're from?"

He nodded. The more they talked, the more comfortable Caitlin was starting to feel. "All of us are from Richmond," Evan explained. "We're down here for eight weeks this summer. Nathan's dad is a contractor, and he just got done working on this huge mansion down at Murray's Point." Caitlin recognized the name and knew it was on the opposite end of the island from the Pirate's Lodge. "We're helping clean up a little and staying there for free until it goes on the market. We spend most of our time just surfing, grilling food, and hanging out."

Sounds like home, Caitlin thought. *Where do I sign up?*

"We only got here a few weeks ago," he added.

"How many of you guys are there?" she asked.

"Twelve. We all go to Richmond Prep."

"Twelve guys in one house. Raising hell, huh?"

"There's not much hell to raise on Danbroke, but some of us have been trying." He grinned again. "You can imagine what Nathan's been up to . . ."

She could, but before she could formulate a response, she heard the door to the storage room open and saw Danielle come out dragging a cardboard box. "Hey, Caitlin, can you help me with this thing? It's heavier than a corpse," Danielle called out in the moment before she looked up and saw Evan standing there. She stopped moving.

"You," she said in an unfriendly tone of voice.

Evan looked sheepish. "I came here to find you and apologize for earlier. We didn't mean anything by it."

"You followed us here?" She let go of the box and stood up. "Are you some kind of stalker?"

"No, he's okay," Caitlin spoke up. "He's cool."

Danielle looked annoyed to be contradicted. She wasn't comfortable with guys, Caitlin realized. Or maybe just not this type of guy.

Evan didn't seem fazed. "I wanted to come and invite you down to our house for a barbeque tonight. I talked to Nathan and the others, and I told them not to bug you. Not all of us are crazy, you know."

"Why would we go anywhere with you?" Danielle asked frostily. "I'm a vegetarian. I don't want to go to a barbeque with a bunch of drunken wannabe frat boys. Jocks aren't my scene."

"God, I'm definitely not a jock," Evan said. "I suck at football and soccer. The only thing I'm decent at is basketball 'cause I'm tall."

Not wanting to betray Danielle, but also kind of wanting to go to the barbeque, Caitlin said, "Nathan's dad is renovating a mansion at Murray's Point. It might be kind of fun . . ."

"Oh, they live in a mansion, do they? Then I bet they're awesome."

"I didn't mean it that way," Caitlin said, bristling at the sarcasm. "I just meant it might be fun to go grab some food and have a night out." Caitlin hadn't realized how much she'd missed hanging out with a group of friends until Evan turned up and made his offer.

"There'll be a bunch of other girls there, too," Evan said, "so you don't have to feel awkward, or whatever. I just thought you might want to come."

"We'll think about it," Danielle said, in a tone of voice that meant, *No fucking way, buddy.*

"The address is twelve-oh-eight Glencove Road," Evan said. "You can't miss the house because it's big and there's still construction equipment everywhere outside. It's right on the beach. There aren't any other houses anywhere around it."

Caitlin made a mental note of the address. Despite Danielle's reluctance, she was hoping there'd be a way they could go. She wasn't worried about Nathan and the other guys—Luke had been good training for handling brats—but she was interested in spending some time with Evan. She couldn't help entertaining a fantasy that he'd been intrigued by her California looks.

"The barbeque starts at seven, but you can show up anytime. We'll probably make a fire pit when it gets dark." He lowered his voice, and added, "If you guys are into smoking up, we scored some quality weed, too. Not that we're stoners or anything."

"Like Danielle said, we'll think about," Caitlin told him.

"Yeah, and now we have to get back to work." Danielle picked up the cardboard box. Evan moved to help her, but she walked past him.

"So maybe I'll see you guys later," Evan said to Caitlin.

"Maybe."

Evan took that as his cue to say good-bye, which he did awkwardly.

"Well, that was an interesting experience," Caitlin said once he was gone, trying to gauge what Danielle thought. The girl didn't look too happy.

"I think if we go to the barbeque, we'll be making a mistake," she finally said. "What about you?"

"Probably," Caitlin admitted. Then, pushing back her hair, "I still want to go." But she didn't want to go alone.

Danielle stretched her arms above her head and feigned a yawn. "I don't know what I think," she said. "Could be trouble."

As it wasn't a definite "no," Caitlin thought she could talk Danielle into it. Evan's looks and demeanor clearly made the barbeque a more appealing proposition. If it had been Nathan who had come through the doors of the Stop, Caitlin knew there was no way either of them would have considered the offer.

"Here's why I think we should go . . ." Caitlin began, and by the time the work day was done, she'd managed to convince Danielle that it would be a laugh to turn up at the mansion. "If the barbeque sucks, we can always leave and go get pizza at Buckley's," she added as she hung up her smock. But something told her that the barbeque wasn't going to suck at all.

14

the barbeque

To get to the mansion, Caitlin and Danielle had to bike all the way down the island to the other end, past mostly desolate marshes and forests. It was spooky enough during the daytime, and Caitlin half expected a hillbilly to pop out of the forest with a chain saw and menace them. She hadn't forgotten about Bill, or that weird photo she'd found in the bathroom. She hoped Luke was safe with Rinita. She was also worried about the bike ride home in the pitch dark and hoped they could get Evan or someone else to drive them back to Danielle's place—assuming all the guys weren't too drunk. Evan had mentioned that Nathan's dad was working on the house, so Caitlin assumed that he lived there. Because of that, she doubted the barbeque would get too out of control. *Maybe Nathan's dad could even drive us back,* she thought.

Caitlin and Danielle reached the mansion a little after 7:45, figuring it would look stupid if they arrived precisely on time. Caitlin hoped she looked good—she'd made the best of Danielle's limited wardrobe. She was wearing jeans and a tight black top. Danielle was in black, as always, her eyes rimmed with dark eyeliner.

Just like Evan had said, the house was easy to find. In fact, Caitlin was kind of shocked to see it there, right on the beach, with multiple balconies sticking out over the water's edge. It was nearly the same size of her house back home in La Jolla, and it looked just as nice, if a little out of place. The sun was starting to set, and it was the magic hour, when everything was bathed in a golden glow. After weeks of being in an environment so different from California, it was almost a relief to see something familiar.

"Look at this tacky monstrosity," Danielle said, as they slowed on their bikes. "It's pretty much what I figured it would be."

Caitlin didn't want to tell Danielle how much it reminded her of home, so she just said, "I can't believe anyone with enough money to buy this place would actually want to live on Danbroke."

"No kidding." Danielle brought her bike to a stop and so did Caitlin. "I can't even tell where the front door is. Evan and Nathan are lucky bastards to spend the summer in a place like this."

No one on Danbroke is lucky, Caitlin thought. "I guess we should go around back and see if we can find the barbeque."

Danielle didn't look too happy.

Maybe it'll be good for her to loosen up and hang out with a group of people, Caitlin thought. *It'll definitely do me some good.* She wondered if Evan had a girlfriend or not and figured that he probably did. She knew boys that good-looking were rarely single, unless they were screwed-up in the head, or permanent playboy types. But as Caitlin had a boyfriend back home, or at least assumed she still did, it shouldn't even have mattered to her. *Yet somehow it does . . .*

Caitlin followed Danielle down a winding path cut through the tall grass that ran alongside the house, hoping it would take them to the backyard. As she and Danielle approached, faint noises of people talking and laughing grew louder.

The grass turned to sand as they stumbled forward and found themselves at the edge of an elevated deck. About forty people or so, mostly their age, were hanging out on it, drinking beer out of blue plastic cups. Bob Marley was playing from inside, reggae blaring through the open windows looking out onto the beach and the water. A few couples were playing with a Frisbee in the shallows. To Caitlin, it looked like a typical keg party transplanted straight from La Jolla to the middle of nowhere.

A few girls saw them coming as they walked around the deck to a flight of wood stairs, and waved as if they knew them. Caitlin waved back to be friendly, but Danielle didn't bother.

"Local girls," she muttered under her breath, like they were a dangerous new species. "Beware." Caitlin's interactions with them had been almost nonexistent so far, but she supposed she trusted Danielle's judgment.

Caitlin and Danielle went up the stairs and onto the deck, with its spectacular view of the placid water below and the darkening blue sky above. Caitlin could smell burgers sizzling on the grill, which was sending up a plume of hazy gray smoke into the air.

"Hey there," a guy with dark curly hair, wearing a pink Lacoste shirt, said to them. He had a flat nose, but was good-looking in a bland kind of way. "What's up?"

Danielle brushed past him, and Caitlin followed in her wake. "Let's find the keg. I need some alcohol to make this thing tolerable."

"Sure," Caitlin said, looking back at the guy, hoping they hadn't offended him. But he'd already moved on and was talking to another girl. She hadn't expected the barbeque to be so crowded. This was actually the largest group of people she'd seen in one place since being on Danbroke. The crowd was maybe two-thirds local girls and one-third Richmond guys, with a few random people thrown in for good measure. *Including us,* Caitlin supposed. She and Danielle didn't really know anyone there except Evan, and there was no sign of him.

I miss my friends so much, Caitlin thought as she waded through the crowd to get to the keg, which was sitting just outside an open French door. She realized the barbeque was making her feel homesick. Instead of looking around and seeing Alison and everyone else she loved, she just saw a bunch of strangers.

There were some eyes staring back at her, too. She could tell some of the girls were sizing her up and that some of the guys were checking her out. Caitlin noted the prevalence of outdated fashions on the girls. She was surprised the guys would even be into girls like these, but then she guessed there wasn't much of an alternative on the island, and these girls were probably considered "easy." She supposed some of them were cute, in an innocent farm-girl kind of way, and guys in general were dogs. *So maybe it's a perfect match.*

When Caitlin and Danielle finally got to the keg, a smarmy-looking guy wearing glasses was standing next to it, leaning back on the edge of the deck. "Allow me, ladies," he began, and Danielle laughed right in his face.

"I know how to operate a keg, chump," she said. "Back off."

"Of course you do," he said, holding up his hands in a gesture of peace. He backed away and disappeared into the crowd. *Danielle definitely has a way with people,* Caitlin thought, bemused by her friend's attitude, and wondering why her guard was up so high.

They got their drinks and stood there, surveying the group of revelers. Caitlin sipped the warm, watery beer from the plastic cup. She was looking for Evan, but she still didn't see him anywhere. *I hope he shows up,* she thought. Then she worried that her interest in Evan—which was dangerously close to a crush—might be some sort of betrayal of Ian.

Just as she was thinking about it, she saw the back of Nathan's blond head in the crowd. As though sensing her gaze, he turned around and saw her and Danielle.

"Hey!" he waved, excited. "You came!" He made a beeline for the two of them. Nathan seemed to be as drunk as he was earlier, but he looked a little tired, and the gleam in his eyes had dimmed by a few degrees. Caitlin speculated that a full day of drinking had probably worn him out.

"I don't know your names," he blurted when he reached them. "Evan told me, but I already forgot."

"I don't want you to know my name," Danielle said, looking him right in the eye. "Remember?" He thought she was kidding so he laughed, but Caitlin knew Danielle was dead serious.

"Enjoying the barbeque?" he continued, oblivious of Danielle's contempt. "If you're in the South, you gotta dig the barbeque, right?"

"We only just got here," Caitlin said, before Danielle could say something else mean. She felt kind of sorry for Nathan—maybe because he reminded her of Luke.

"Sorry about how I acted earlier," he said, taking a swig of beer from his cup. "You guys probably think I'm a total jerkoff."

"Do you care what we think?" Danielle asked.

He seemed to consider the question for a moment, with drunken earnestness. "I guess I do."

"Good answer," Caitlin replied.

He touched her arm and said with unexpected sincerity, "Thanks."

Danielle turned to Caitlin and said, "I have to go to the bathroom." Caitlin could tell she was just trying to get them away from Nathan.

Because she didn't want to be stranded by herself, Caitlin said, "Me too."

Nathan pointed toward the house. "Right that way. Go inside, first door on your left. Bang on it when you get there, 'cause I saw Tom head in there with a girl, and I don't think it was to go pee pee together."

"Thanks, Nathan," Caitlin said, thinking, *This might be what Luke grows up to be.* Then she felt depressed because thinking about Luke reminded her of her mom and Bill, and the total collapse of her family. She was looking forward to getting some more alcohol into her so she could forget her troubles, if only for a moment.

As they walked into the house, Danielle whispered to Caitlin, "Remember that show *Dawson's Creek*? I feel like we're trapped in a bad episode."

"I know what you mean. I was hoping we'd see Evan."

"The cute one."

"Exactly." *Do Danielle and I have our eye on the same guy?* she wondered. She knew that could lead to trouble fast, but she shrugged it off, thinking, *I want to try to have fun for one night.*

Even though the house was huge, there was only one bathroom visible nearby. "I really do have to go," Danielle said. Fortunately, the bathroom was actually empty, so she went in first. As Caitlin was waiting outside, she finally saw Evan sitting on the edge of the deck. He was surrounded by a cluster of three blonde-haired girls. When he saw her wave, he broke away from the pack and headed in her direction. She met him halfway.

"Caitlin, you made it," he said, sounding pleased.

Ignoring the angry glares of the blonde girls, she smiled at him and said, "Of course I did."

He gave her a hug. He was slim but wiry, and she could feel the muscles under his shirt and his smooth skin. Then she drew back quickly, because she didn't want the hug to go on for too long.

"Where's your friend?" Evan asked. "Danielle."

Caitlin pointed inside at the bathroom. "We got trapped by Nathan so we sought refuge."

"Smart. As much as I love the guy, I can't blame you."

As they waited for Danielle outside, they chatted briefly, and Caitlin tried not to think about how attractive he was. She mentioned how the mansion reminded her of her mom's house.

"You ever read *The Great Gatsby*? You know, for school?" Evan asked.

Caitlin shook her head. It was a good sign that he actually read books—unusual for a guy. "Reading the SparkNotes online doesn't count, does it?" she asked.

He grinned. "Nope. Anyway, that's what I thought of when I

first saw this place. The big house in *Gatsby* on the water. That whole vibe. If you ever decide to read it, it's a pretty cool book."

Caitlin wondered for an instant if he was trying to pose as more intellectual than he actually was, to impress her, but then she dismissed the thought. "Maybe I'll try it sometime," she said. She didn't want to mention that she'd tried it and hadn't been able to get past the first two chapters due to extreme boredom, hence the SparkNotes. "Have you ever read *The Beach*?" She was trying to think of a book she'd read that wasn't chick lit, or too young-sounding.

"The one they made into a Leonardo DiCaprio movie?"

"That's the one."

It was his turn to shake his head. "No. My sister has the DVD, though."

"You have a sister?"

"Yeah, she just finished her first year at Vassar. Her name's Amy." He didn't seem to want to talk about her because he quickly said, "So, *The Beach*. Any good?"

"It's my favorite book. Well, second favorite to *Harry Potter*, but I grew up with those, so they're different. And they aren't really literary, or whatever. Maybe we can do a book swap or something. *The Beach* for *Gatsby*."

"That'd be great."

It was a refreshing change for Caitlin to be talking to a guy about books, instead of sports, music, or video games, which was what the guys back home talked about to the exclusion of everything else. She almost felt bad for Ian; he wasn't stacking up too well against Evan so far.

Evan ran a hand over his short-cropped hair. "Listen, I better get back and keep an eye on everyone. Especially Nathan."

"Sure."

Caitlin worried for a second that he was blowing her off, but then he said, "We should talk more about books and stuff sometime." He paused. "You're not like the other girls around here." She assumed it could only be meant as a compliment. He tilted his head to one side, eyeing her. "Maybe we could get coffee tomorrow and hang out?"

"Sounds cool," Caitlin said, trying to sound nonchalant, but instantly feeling her face start to redden. She didn't want Evan to notice, but of course he did.

"Hey, are you blushing?" he asked, sounding amused.

"Naw. It just happens when I drink. It's the beer," she said, trying to play it off. *It's not like it's a date or anything,* she told herself. *Get a grip. Coffee means nothing.*

"What about noon at the Danbroke Coffee Company?"

Caitlin nodded.

Fortunately, Danielle turned up at that moment.

"Hey," Evan said to her, raising his drink in her direction. "Having fun?"

"Technically, no. Your friend Nathan banged on the bathroom door until I came out, and then he laughed and ran away. He's disturbed."

"Tell me something I don't know. His girlfriend just broke up with him before we came out here, and I think it's messed with his head. He's totally regressing. We've started calling him Frodo because he's so short and childlike."

"Got it." Danielle turned to Caitlin. "Listen, I think I'm ready to go if you are."

"You only just got here," Evan pointed out. "You didn't get any food yet."

Caitlin wanted to stay longer, but she knew that she already owed Danielle more than could ever be repaid. She'd also promised Danielle they'd split if Danielle didn't like it. And now that she had plans to meet Evan tomorrow, she didn't mind leaving so abruptly. Then she remembered the problem of actually getting home.

"Hey, Evan, can you give us a ride?" she asked. "Or get someone to give us one?"

She thought he'd say yes to the ride, but to her surprise, he wasn't too amenable. "You're safer on your bikes," he said, frowning a little. "Everyone here's drunk."

"What about you? You're not drunk." He'd probably had a beer or two, but he seemed far from intoxicated. *Okay, he's losing a few points here,* Caitlin thought. *Why can't he just take us back in the Mercedes?*

He looked sheepish for a second. "I, uh, had some car trouble today . . ."

"What? You were driving around just fine earlier."

He looked away, out at the trees. "I feel stupid, okay, but we actually had a little accident, and I got the car stuck in the sand. I was trying to park it closer to the deck so we could unload the kegs right onto it. I wasn't thinking too straight and it took an hour to get the car out. Nathan's dad won't let me drive anymore 'cause he's pissed. It's his car."

"Can Nathan's dad take us home?" Danielle asked. "We can throw our bikes in the backseat." Caitlin wondered what Nathan's dad would think of that—their muddy bikes trashing the leather upholstery.

"Nathan's dad is busy upstairs," Evan finally said.

"Doing what?"

"We don't ask too many questions about what he does. He's a real . . . character." Caitlin wasn't sure what Evan meant by that. "I don't think he'd be up for driving anywhere tonight. He's kind of eccentric, and that's a nice way of putting it."

"We'll just bike back then," Danielle said, looking at Caitlin.

Evan seemed relieved. "That'd be best."

Caitlin and Danielle said a quick good-bye to him, and then, as they were starting to walk away, he called out after Caitlin.

"Don't forget tomorrow!" he yelled over the sound of the music. Someone had just switched Bob Marley for Bloc Party, so now there was a din of spiky guitars to contend with.

"I won't," Caitlin called back in response, and then she turned to follow Danielle down the trail.

"What was that about?" Danielle asked as they walked down the dark path, illuminated by sodium lights on the eaves of the house. The noise of the party faded into the background. It had been a mildly surreal experience.

"Evan asked me to go get coffee with him tomorrow. At the Danbroke Coffee Company at noon."

"I thought you hated all the places in town, like me."

"I don't hate Evan."

"That's what I thought." Even though Caitlin couldn't see her face, she could sense the disapproval in her tone. She understood, but it also irked her. *Why should Danielle begrudge the fact that Evan likes me?* Besides, it was just coffee; it wasn't like they were getting married. Caitlin and Danielle walked the rest of the way back to their bikes in silence as Caitlin tried to think of the right thing to say.

"It's no big deal," she finally said as they got to their bikes. An idea suddenly occurred to her, and she added, "You want to come with me tomorrow?"

"No, it's okay," Danielle said, but the offer apparently appeased her a little. "I've seen enough of those guys for a while. Sorry I wanted to bail so quickly, but I got overwhelmed. I don't like crowds—at least not that kind."

"It's cool."

Danielle got on her bike, straddling the seat, and suddenly smiled. "That geeky kid with glasses by the keg . . ."

Caitlin burst out laughing. "I know. He called us 'ladies.' "

"What a freak."

"Probably the runt of the litter."

Their equilibrium restored, they continued talking and laughing all the way back to the trailer. That night the island didn't seem spooky at all, despite the heavy moon that hung over the forest, and the ominous droning of the insects. Their laughter and friendship warded all the bad thoughts away, at least for the moment.

15
coffee and cigarettes

When Caitlin arrived fashionably late at the Danbroke Coffee Company, she discovered it was a dusty, old used bookstore with a coffee counter and some circular wooden tables up at the front. There was an old couple browsing the stacks and a guy with a mountain-man beard and thick glasses sitting behind the counter.

"Hi," Caitlin said as she came in the door, because the man was staring right at her. He just nodded in response, but didn't stop staring. For a moment she thought she'd gotten there before Evan, despite being late, but then she saw his head sticking out above one of the stacks near the back of the store.

She headed past the coffee counter, in his direction, and he turned around to face her before she got there. He was wearing board shorts and a gray-and-red Chicago Bulls T-shirt.

"Hey," she said, smiling. "Sorry I'm running late . . ."

They hugged and he said, "No problem. I just got here myself. Let's get some coffee?"

Caitlin felt a nervous tingle of anticipation in her stomach. "Sure."

They walked back up to the front of the store.

"You know," Evan said, as they almost reached the counter, "I don't really like coffee that much. I just thought I'd tell you that."

"Really? I love it."

"Coffee? Or the fact that I just admitted something so intensely personal to you," he joked.

"Both . . . you're deeper than I thought," Caitlin teased.

"I like the smell of it," he elaborated, "and I like coffee-flavored ice cream. Just not coffee itself."

Caitlin wondered if he felt nervous. She always assumed boys got that way, too, but worked to conceal it. *Just like I'm doing.* They got to the counter and she ordered a double mocha and he got a Coke. When their drinks were ready, he paid, and they took a seat at one of the tables.

"You look great," he told her. "I like your hair that way."

"Thanks." She hadn't done anything special with her hair other than wash it. She kept telling herself there was no need to become monosyllabic just because she liked Evan, but it was difficult. "You look great, too," she added.

"I try so hard," he said, taking a sip of Coke.

They started talking, and maybe it was the caffeine, but Caitlin began to feel more lucid and could start forming complete sentences again. Evan asked where she was from in California, and she told him all about La Jolla and her life there, omitting the fact that her mom was a drug addict. She did mention that she was staying with Danielle instead of her mother; luckily he didn't ask why.

"Yeah, your friend Danielle is interesting," he said. Caitlin figured he was referring to the whole Goth thing. Then he said, "You know, I think Nathan's into her."

Caitlin almost choked. "Are you serious?"

"Yeah, I think so." Evan shook his head ruefully. "I know. You're wondering why he acted like a dickhead to her, right? Nathan gets goofy around girls. Simple fact."

"Somehow I can't picture Danielle and Nathan together."

He nodded. "Yeah, they'd make a sick couple."

She didn't know if he meant "sick" in a good way or a bad one, so she didn't ask for an elaboration. She was thinking, *Danielle will freak out when I tell her about this!*

They also talked about Luke, and Evan told her a little more about his sister Amy, who was majoring in psychology. It sounded like they were close. In general, the more she learned about Evan, the more she liked him. His dad was a doctor, and his mom was an investment banker at a firm in Richmond.

"You sure you don't have a girlfriend?" she asked him at one point, unable to help herself. He'd already told her that he was single.

"Why, do I seem sketchy?"

She shook her head and said, "No reason. I just get paranoid sometimes . . ." She wanted to change the subject because of the whole Ian issue, so she asked what college he wanted to go to.

"I don't know," he answered thoughtfully. "My dad went to Dartmouth, so he wants me to go there. Maybe UVA? That's where my friend Shep wants to go—he was at the barbeque last night, but I don't know if you met him yet." Caitlin shook her head. "Nathan might apply there, too."

"Keeping the whole gang together, huh?"

He raised an eyebrow. "Something like that."

"That's cool. I wish I could go to college with my friend Alison. She's a better student than I am, though, so she'll probably go to Stanford or Berkeley. Maybe we'll find a way to stick together somehow."

"You're only going to be a junior next year. You've got time to figure it out."

"True. Honestly, it's kind of scary to think about going to college." *Although it wouldn't be scary to leave home—that part would be a relief.* But it was strange to think about moving from La Jolla to some other city where she might not know anyone. *Of course, I guess this summer has been a trial run,* she thought.

Evan took another sip of Coke. "Yeah, it's freaky. I've been at Richmond Prep since first grade, like most of the other kids in my class."

"Same." She fumbled in her purse, suddenly craving a cigarette. "You think we can smoke in here?"

"Only one way to find out."

Caitlin spotted what looked like an ashtray on the counter, so she assumed it was okay. "Want one?" she offered as she extracted a cigarette.

Evan shook his head. "I quit because of basketball, and if I start up again, it'll be hard to stop. I have an addictive personality."

"Yeah, me too, but I just don't have the willpower to fight it." Caitlin lit up, and about five seconds after she did so, she heard a clatter and someone loudly curse, "Son of a bitch!"

Evan looked behind her and warned, "Here comes trouble." Caitlin's first thought was that it was Bill, but it wasn't. She swiveled in her seat and saw the bearded man from behind the counter standing a few feet away.

"Didn't you see the sign?" he raved, waving his arms around in a frenzy.

"What sign?" *It's like a repeat of Buckley's Pizza, except this guy isn't kidding,* Caitlin thought. *He looks furious.*

"Gee, I wonder what sign?" the guy snapped. "The No Smoking sign! Smoking is bad for the books. And bad for me!"

"Sorry," Caitlin said, looking for a place to stub out her cigarette. "Jesus."

"That's right, you are sorry," the man continued. "Someone who can't read signs shouldn't set foot in a bookstore."

Caitlin was about to retort, but Evan stepped in and did it for her. "Hey, don't be so uptight, man," he said, fixing the bearded guy with a stare. "She didn't mean anything by it. Just relax before you have a heart attack."

"No smoking means no smoking," the guy huffed, but maybe because of Evan's size—which was apparent even though he was sitting down—the man relented and stopped yelling. He did add, "Rules aren't made to be broken," as he headed back to his little domain behind the counter.

"Let's get out of here," Evan said to Caitlin, and she agreed.

As they walked out into the thick, wet air, Evan said, "Sorry I picked that place for us to meet. I figured it would be cool after we talked about books and stuff, you know? I looked for *The Beach* in the stacks, but they didn't have it. I've never been in there before."

"It's not your fault they suck."

"The only thing wrong with Danbroke is the people who live on it. At least that's what I heard Nathan's dad say once."

"I completely agree," Caitlin said, thinking it sounded like a sentiment Danielle would appreciate. She stubbed out her cigarette and tossed it into an overflowing trash can.

As if to hammer Evan's point home, a fat guy who looked like a troll from *Lord of the Rings* wandered by, clutching three fishing poles in one pudgy, grease-stained hand. He appeared to be talking to himself.

I have got *to get out of this place,* Caitlin thought, as a kind of reflex action. Yet now that she'd met Evan, she wasn't sure if she wanted to leave the island so much. She didn't think there was any way of talking sense into her mom at this point anyway, so she might as well make the best of it as long as she was stuck. There was Danielle, too, which meant she had a good friend, and even a part-time job. *Hell, I've almost got my shit together here better than I do back home,* she thought.

"I noticed some of your friends are really into the local girls," she said, curious to know what Evan thought.

"I guess they have low standards." He paused, a bit uncomfortable with the line of discussion. Caitlin wondered if he'd hit on, or maybe even slept with, any of the girls from the island. *Maybe it's best not to know.*

"What should we do now?" he asked. "We can go back to the house or hang out in town some more. Or maybe go down to a nearby beach?"

Caitlin didn't want to go back to the house because she knew there'd probably be a bunch of other guys there. And she was sick of the town, so she said, "Beach."

They headed down one of the pathways that led away from town and toward the dunes. When they reached the top of them, walking across the narrow bike path Caitlin had used weeks earlier, they got an amazing view of the beach and the ocean, stretching out as far as the eye could see. Caitlin had to admit it was beautiful, if a little bleak. The beach was nearly deserted. About a quarter of a mile away on her right, she could see a yellow pickup truck parked on the beach, and a tattered tent next to it. To her left was a man knee-deep in the surf, wearing wading boots as he fished. There wasn't any shade, and Caitlin soaked up the sun, feeling it pour down on top of her head.

She and Evan sat down on the sand together, staring out at the ocean.

"We don't have anything like this back in Richmond, that's for sure," he said. "I like to come down here sometimes by myself and think, or play guitar."

"You play?"

"A little. I'm not any good."

"I always wanted to learn how to play guitar, but I never had the patience."

"It's not hard."

"It is for me." She held her hand out in front of him. "Small fingers." She wiggled them. "Maybe you could try teaching me sometime?" She tried to make the question sound impetuous, but she was thinking it would be a good way to get closer to him.

"Definitely," he nodded, seeming to like the idea. "I have a great guitar at home, a handmade Gibson, but I only brought my crappy one to Danbroke. It's got a hole in it 'cause I stepped on it when I was trashed once. Still, it's good enough."

"I'm looking forward to hearing you play."

"It'll have to be just for you. A solo performance. The guys give me too much crap when I bust it out in front of them. They call me Baby Dave Matthews, which definitely isn't a compliment."

Just then, as they were sitting there having a nice chat, something whizzed past Caitlin's head, barely missing her face.

"What the fuck?" she said out loud, startled. Evan looked surprised, too. "Did you see that?" she asked him.

He looked around as Caitlin did the same. "I think someone just threw something at us."

Caitlin couldn't help thinking about the angry guy at the bookstore, or worse, Bill Collins. Then she realized there was a much simpler explanation when another projectile came flying past them and exploded in a colorful red spray on the sand.

"It's Luke," she said. "My brother." Evan still looked confused, so Caitlin clarified things for him: "Luke is firing his paintball gun at us."

"Are you serious? Why would he do that?"

"Don't ask."

Evan squinted. "I think I see him." He pointed at a small sand dune to their left, a few hundred feet away. Caitlin followed his gaze and saw the top of her brother's head poke out from around the side of the dune. "Want me to go after him?" Evan asked.

Caitlin nodded. "That would be the most awesome thing ever." She was thinking, *My prayers have been answered.*

Evan stood up. Right then, Luke must have realized he'd been spotted because Caitlin saw him flee the sand dune and run away from them down the beach.

The idea of her bratty brother being chased down by Evan appealed to her so much that Caitlin exclaimed, "Go get him!"

Evan looked back and grinned. "No problem." He took off

running down the beach, head down, sprinting fast in Luke's direction. It took him less than a minute to catch up with Luke, who he wrestled down to the sand in a second. Caitlin knew he wouldn't really hurt her brother. Indeed, when Evan returned, dragging Luke along with an arm around his neck, Luke seemed filled with more energy than ever.

"Fuck you! Let me go!" he was yelling. Evan was clutching the paintball gun in his other hand.

"You should get more exercise," Evan pointed out to him. "If you're going to shoot at people with paintball guns, you better be in good shape so you can run away afterward. I know I would be."

"Pick on someone your own size, bitch!" Luke yelled, continuing to squirm in Evan's grasp. Evan looked far more amused than pissed off.

"I think you should kick his ass and teach him a lesson," Caitlin told Evan. She didn't mean it; she just wanted to scare Luke. She looked down at her brother and said, "You got busted. What do you think about that?"

"I think that sucks. But hey, it's life. All's fair in love and war."

"Luke, you could have shot me in the eye!" she snapped as Evan turned him loose. "Can't you even apologize?"

"I wasn't trying to hit you. If I'd wanted to hit you, I could have." Luke stood there panting, his T-shirt a little looser around the collar. "I have perfect aim, Caitlin. I just wanted to get your attention. Remember what I've told you time and time again—if your face gets fucked-up, then you won't be profitable as one of my ho's. You'll have to work as a secretary in the back office, counting my loot, and it doesn't pay as much."

Caitlin saw Evan's face turn from amusement to surprise and horror, and then back to amusement again, which was a typical reaction for people encountering her brother for the first time.

"Luke, you're the least-likely pimp in the history of the world," Caitlin said. "Drop your stupid fantasy. It's super creepy. Evan's going to think you're Special Ed if you keep talking like that."

Luke looked Evan up and down. "So gorilla boy is your new boyfriend? What happened to Ian?"

Caitlin wanted to scream. Instead, she reached over and took the paintball gun from Evan, letting it dangle from her fingers. "See the ocean, Luke? Do you realize the tide is going out? Do you know where your gun is headed?"

He just cackled. "I don't care if you throw it in the water. I can just call and order more and get them shipped to Danielle's place."

"I don't think Danielle or Rinita is going to help you out. Besides, you don't have a credit card, loser."

"Yeah, I do. I stole one of yours last week out of your purse and you didn't even notice."

"Luke!" Caitlin yelled, at her wit's end. "What's wrong with you?"

"Bad parenting? A mom on drugs? I'm just the victim here."

Great. All the things Caitlin didn't want Evan to know about yet were tumbling out. "Mom's crazy, but at least she's not firing guns at me," Caitlin said. She could tell Evan was standing there listening, trying to figure the situation out. "Luke, let's have this discussion later, okay? For now, we're confiscating your gun. Just go back to Danielle's and hang out with Rinita, alright? And if you say, 'Make me,' then I'll get Evan to kick your ass all the way there."

Luke looked up at Evan and said, "You've won this battle, but you haven't won the war!" Clearly deciding he'd caused enough trauma for the moment, he followed his proclamation by running off into the dunes, his laughter fading from Caitlin's ears.

"Whoa," Evan said, letting the vague reaction stand for itself.

You don't know the half of it, Caitlin thought. Tossing the gun onto the sand, she asked, "Can we pretend none of that happened?"

He laughed. "Sure. You hungry?"

Caitlin said that she was, and she was definitely ready to get off the beach now that the peaceful mood had been completely ruined.

"Then let's go get sandwiches or something."

With Evan's words, the two of them walked up the beach and back into town. Caitlin realized she already felt at home with Evan, even though she'd only known him for less than twenty-four hours. It was a little strange to feel that way so soon, she knew, but it was the truth. And she was looking forward to getting to know Evan even better—if and when she got the chance.

16
the mansion on
the dunes

Several more days passed, and Caitlin began spending most of her time with Evan. They'd kissed the evening of their third day together, lounging drunk on the balcony at the house, watching the bright stars hang in the black sky. She'd wanted to kiss him since that first day they'd hung out.

The night they kissed, they were both drinking red wine out of the ubiquitous plastic cups, because there didn't seem to be any glasses, dishes, or silverware at the mansion. Evan had his arm around her, protecting her from the cool breeze coming off the water. Behind them, she could hear the noise of the perpetual party that went on at the mansion, and the screams of girls running up and down the stairs, laughing. As the house was basically in the middle of nowhere, there was no reason to keep the noise level down. And Nathan's dad didn't seem to care.

Caitlin had a feeling she and Evan were going to kiss even before it happened. They'd been talking about typical random stuff, but in the back of her mind she'd been thinking, *I hope he stops talking at some point and kisses me!* She was almost surprised to realize that's what she wanted him to do. *Is it wrong for me to be into Evan because I'm dating Ian?* she wondered. Yet Ian hadn't returned her last three calls, and Alison had told her she thought she'd seen him with another girl at a Box of Flowers show. She told herself she'd better not overthink the whole thing or she'd screw it up.

She deliberately held his gaze, hoping to signal what she wanted without having to come out and say it, or make the first move herself. She knew from experience some guys were really shy, but was she hoping Evan wasn't one of them. It turned out that he wasn't. He leaned down and kissed her on the lips, slightly forcefully. His lips were soft and warm. The kiss was over too fast, so automatically she raised her head up to his, shut her eyes, and kissed him back. Finally they pulled away to look at each other, and they both grinned.

"You're so beautiful," he said, and she'd kissed him again.

From that night things had progressed, not all the way, but to fooling around. Caitlin knew that Evan would end up liking her more if she didn't sleep with him right away. She often heard the other guys talking among themselves about which local girl they were "banging," and frequently laughing about them. It made Caitlin feel sorry for the girls.

Fortunately, she and Evan had drifted off into their own little world, and the rest of the guys didn't affect them too much. The other eleven formed a blur of similar faces and names, with the exception of Nathan. If any one of them gave Evan shit about spending a lot of time with Caitlin, he shut them down right away.

The only troublesome thing about Caitlin's relationship with Evan was that it was making Danielle feel left out. Danielle didn't like any of the guys, or the local girls, so she didn't want to spend much time at the mansion. Caitlin was torn because she knew Danielle had rescued her from the situation with Bill and her mom. Yet she also didn't want to pass up a relationship with a guy like Evan just to appease her friend. In an admittedly selfish way, Caitlin wished Danielle would hook up with one of the other guys, so they could all do things together. Unfortunately, the only person who expressed interest in Danielle was Nathan, and she had less than zero interest in him.

"Doesn't anyone else like Danielle?" Caitlin asked Evan. "She's cute, right?" Caitlin knew that Danielle would be even better looking without all the heavy mascara and the dyed black hair, but that was part of Danielle's image, and who was she to tell her to change? It was hard for a girl to come up with a look, and if it worked for Danielle and made her feel good, then so be it.

"Yeah, she's cute," Evan told her, "but when Nathan said he liked her, that kind of blocked anyone else from trying. He told everyone in the house how he felt, so no one's going to touch her. Especially when we're only here because of him and his dad. Besides, you know the whole deal. Bro's before ho's."

They were lying on the couch together and Caitlin was startled enough to sit up. *What the fuck did he just say?!* "Bro's before ho's?" she repeated, outraged. "I can't believe I just heard those words come out of your mouth, Evan. That's the stupidest thing I've ever heard."

He laughed, and then turned serious when he saw that she was mad. "Sorry, sorry. I've never actually said those words myself, and I don't think that way, either. I'm just saying that some of the guys use that expression to justify themselves. I

figured you'd heard the phrase before. I was using it kind of iron-
ically . . . or trying to."

"I hope boys don't really think that way. I hope *you* don't say
it again."

"Okay, I won't. But anyway, just so you know, no one's going
to make a move on Danielle because of Nathan. She's pretty
much taken."

"Is Nathan really that insecure?"

Evan scratched one of his ears. "I'll let you in on a secret,
Caitlin. All guys are that insecure. No one wants to see one of his
friends hook up with a chick he has a crush on. Think of it the
other way around. If you liked some dude and then Danielle
hooked up with him, wouldn't you feel bad?"

"Probably, but wouldn't you feel insulted if you liked some
girl and she said, 'Sorry, dude, chicks before dicks'? Or something completely ridiculous like that?"

He couldn't hide his sudden smile. "I'd probably just start
laughing my ass off. Chicks before dicks, huh?"

She swatted him with the sleeve of her jacket. "You're a complete moron sometimes."

"True."

"I better keep you away from Luke so you guys don't influence each other . . ."

Strangely, though, Caitlin had to admit that Luke was doing
really well at the moment. He and Rinita had settled into a
weird kind of symbiosis. Somehow Rinita instinctively knew
the kind of attention he needed, and Luke seemed to revel in her
doting. Often the little trailer smelled of spices and pastries.
Caitlin had figured out that Rinita was basically a nonjudgmen-
tal parental figure to Luke, one whom he didn't have to rebel

against all the time. Luke spent his days outdoors and then crashed on the floor at night, and Rinita seemed to be cool with all of it. She didn't even care too much one afternoon when he shot up the neighbor's trailer with paintballs.

Maybe this is what Luke needed all along, Caitlin thought. Other than the day at the beach when he'd shot at them, he'd been much more mellow, and Caitlin worried about him less. Leaving the hotel and her mom had been the best thing the two of them had done on Danbroke. She was almost glad Bill had acted as a catalyst for the move, or they might have remained stuck in the sad, gloomy interior of the Pirate's Lodge.

There was still no interaction between Caitlin and her mom. Her mom hadn't even tried calling her, which seemed beyond bizarre. But Caitlin had stopped complaining about the island to her dad and her friends back home. Evan had changed all that; he'd made things exciting and alive. She made a list of all the things she liked about him: his silver-blue eyes, his thick dark hair, his height, the way he played guitar and sang to her when no one else was around, his intelligence and sense of humor, his lips and the way he kissed . . . She felt like the list could go on and on.

A few days after they kissed, Caitlin was hanging out with Evan at the mansion, without Danielle, and it got so late that she ended up staying over. She called Danielle to let her know. She'd been drinking and couldn't face the long bike ride home. She didn't sleep in Evan's room, even though he offered, but in one of the finished guest bedrooms, on the floor in a sleeping bag. She made sure to lock the door, nervous that drunken revelers would come in and mess with her. She'd learned a hard lesson from her experience with Bill at the Pirate's Lodge.

It was an unfortunate coincidence that Nathan's dad reminded her a little of Bill. Luckily, he was almost completely absent from everyone's lives. Rather than watching over the twelve guys and monitoring their behavior, he spent his time at the top of the house, often on the upper deck, drinking and talking on his cellphone. He never seemed to do any work. He was heavy and wore all his fat on his chest, with a belly that protruded from his silk shirts, and a gold chain around his neck. Dealing with her mom had given her a sixth sense when it came to telling if someone was a bad parent. Caitlin knew it wasn't coincidence that Nathan was the most screwed-up of all the kids at the mansion. The more she saw of him, the more she was convinced he was regularly doing drugs—and maybe stuff harder than pot. She'd tried to ask Evan about it, but he got defensive if she pushed too hard when it came to Nathan.

"Nathan's cool," he'd always say in a vague manner, meaning, *Let's change the subject.* She already knew him well enough to read his body language. His eyes would get hazy and distant if he felt uncomfortable about anything. She didn't quite understand his relationship with Nathan, but she knew good friends could sometimes let things slide or make excuses for each other, especially among boys.

But talking about Nathan and his dad was the last thing she wanted to do when she was with Evan. In fact, often she didn't want to do any talking at all. There weren't any beds in the house, but there were a ton of air mattresses. It was almost like camping indoors, especially because the windows were usually open and the smell of the ocean filled the vast spaces. The house was so large that even with the mob of boys, it was usually possible to find a deserted area to be alone with Evan. He'd originally shared a room downstairs with two other guys, Mark and Shep, but when Caitlin came on the scene, he moved upstairs to a smaller, more desolate one so they could have some privacy.

"You know something?" he asked, the night she spent at the house. It was before she went off to her own room. They were lying on the air mattress and a pile of pillows, staring through the windows at the night sky as they listened to the surf. "You could just move into this place. If you wanted to . . ."

"Yeah," she said, not quite understanding what he was saying because she was tired and still a little buzzed. Then she said, "You mean into this house?"

"Sure. This room. This house. Whatever. You could have your own room here permanently. I'm sure there's more space here than at Danielle's place."

"I can't," she told Evan. "It wouldn't be right."

"Why not?"

"Luke's at Danielle's. I can't just walk off and leave him." She turned her head to look at him. "It's a cute offer, though. It's sweet of you."

Evan wasn't prepared to give up. He stroked her hair as he said, "I think it might work. There's no reason for you to be over there if you're spending all your time here." He paused. "If you think this is a way for me to try to sleep with you faster, then you're wrong. I just thought it might be cool."

"Who said I was *ever* going to sleep with you? It's way too soon for me to be ready for that. And obviously I've never lived in the same house as a guy I'm—" She cut herself off. She'd almost said "dating," but that wasn't the right word to describe their relationship. "Anyway, what I'm saying is, it wouldn't work. Besides, if my dad ever found out, he'd flip." She figured her mom was in such a coma, she was past the point of flipping out about Caitlin anymore. *If Mom didn't care that Bill tried to molest me, or that I went to live in a trailer park, then I doubt she'll care if I share a house with Evan.*

"Well, at least think about it," Evan said.

"I will." She pulled herself closer to him. There was a thumping sound in the hallway as someone ran past, laughing. Footsteps followed in hot pursuit. Caitlin just didn't think there was any way she could stay at the mansion on a permanent basis.

She pulled herself on top of Evan and smiled down at him. "Just think, Evan. If I was here all the time, you'd get sick of me. This way, you can look forward to seeing me every single day when I bike over here."

"I'll always look forward to seeing you," he murmured.

She bent down and kissed the top of his forehead.

Later, as she climbed into her sleeping bag alone in the room in the mansion, she couldn't help but consider Evan's offer. She wasn't ready yet, but maybe she would be soon.

Have I gone crazy to even be thinking about it? she wondered. *No parents, no California, no Ian.* So many changes had happened so fast.

She curled up on her side, thinking of Evan's touch and hoping that she'd dream of him.

17

The next morning when Caitlin returned, Danielle looked really pissed off, but wouldn't say much about it. "So you stayed over at the pit, huh?" *The pit*—that was how she'd started referring to the mansion, as a sign of contempt for its inhabitants.

"Yeah, like I said on the phone, I was too tired and drunk to come back here," Caitlin explained. "Stupid of me, I know. I hope it's okay."

"Sure. You can do whatever you want." Her tone was brusque, and she didn't look Caitlin in the eye.

"You're not mad at me, are you?"

"I'm fine," she replied in a voice that said she was far from fine.

To change the subject, Caitlin asked, "Where's Luke?"

"He went out with Rinita to get some ice cream. They'll be back soon."

"Ice cream sounds good. Wanna get some before work?" She was trying to be friendly.

"Not really."

"Oh. Okay." Feeling bummed out by Danielle's cold attitude, Caitlin decided to go outside and smoke a cigarette. Danielle didn't follow. Caitlin stood outside the trailer on the cement patio and gazed around dejectedly, staring at some of the other trailers. Most were run-down.

Things didn't get better quickly. Later that day, riding their bikes to the Stop, Danielle said out of the blue, "You know, I saw your mom the other day."

Caitlin was so shocked she almost fell off. "What? Where?"

"In town. It was while we were at work. I went out the back to take some boxes out and looked down the alley through to State Avenue. Right then she and Bill just happened to be walking across the road."

"Danielle, I can't believe you didn't tell me. I've been really worried about her." To be honest, she'd been starting to think maybe Bill had killed her mom or something awful, and buried the body in the basement of the Pirate's Lodge. *Okay, not really—but given how insane Bill had acted, wasn't anything possible?* It seemed weird that on an island this small, she hadn't seen or heard anything of her mom or Bill recently.

Danielle glanced over at her. "I didn't know what to say. I only saw them for a second."

"How'd my mom look? Was she okay? You have to tell me."

"She looked fine, but like I said, I only saw them for an instant. Bill looked weird, like he always does."

Caitlin shuddered inwardly. "I bet he did." Caitlin couldn't bear to think about what would happen to her when the summer ended. *Would they even go back to La Jolla? Would Dad finally step in and help?* Thinking about anything more than the immediate present was too overwhelming, so Caitlin tried to focus on the issue in front of her: the sighting of her elusive and deranged mother.

As if reading Caitlin's mind, Danielle said, "Your mom's probably worried about you, too. She probably wants to see you."

"Well, she knows where to find me if she gets the urge."

Danielle slowed her bike down a little, and Caitlin took it as her cue to do the same. "Maybe you should make the effort and go talk to her first."

"Why? She'll just tell me how I'm a liar and how great Bill is. I don't want to hear that crap again. You were there—you saw what happened."

Danielle hesitated. "What if she's changed her mind?"

"Pretty doubtful, don't you think?" Caitlin started to wonder what Danielle was getting at.

"Well, I think you need to talk to her," Danielle said, sounding frustrated. "You can't hide forever."

Although Danielle was right, Caitlin realized all of a sudden where the conversation was going, and what was really motivating it. "You want me to move out of the trailer, don't you?" she said slowly. "Back to the hotel."

"No, I just think you should try to work things out with her because she's your family. Enough time has passed since the argument. I didn't say to move out."

"You're mad because of Evan. I knew it."

"I'm not mad." Danielle swerved to avoid a broken beer bottle. "I'm a little disappointed, maybe. I thought you and I would have the whole summer to hang out, and then the instant Evan and the guys came on the scene, you split. You can see how that makes me feel."

"I didn't split," Caitlin protested. "Where am I now? I'm right here with you. It was just one night I didn't come home. You're acting like I've been blowing you off or something, but I haven't." *At least not completely.* Caitlin felt guilty.

"You're here physically, but mentally you're with them. You belong with them, Caitlin. I'd bet a million bucks they're more like your friends back home than I am."

Caitlin didn't answer. Instead, she said, "So you think I should just go back to my mom and Bill and get abused? What happened to all the stuff you said earlier about standing up for myself? Did that fly out the window because I'm friends with Evan?"

"You're more than just friends with him."

"I used the word 'friends' because I don't know what else to call us. It's not like you really liked him that much or anything, so why are you acting this way? You said all those guys were posers, Evan included—it shouldn't matter to you."

"I still say they're posers. They're a bunch of spoiled rich kids."

"Some of them might be spoiled, but Evan's not, and that's who I hang out with. If someone has money, it doesn't automatically mean they're a piece of shit, Danielle."

They reached the Stop and went inside, still squabbling as they pushed their way through the glass doors. Caitlin knew there was some truth in what Danielle was saying, but thought she was overreacting.

"Well, I'm glad you and Evan are happy," Danielle said,

grabbing her apron. "You can be the perfect little couple, the jock and the princess. The teen king and queen of Danbroke. All you need is a prom to go to."

At that very moment, Curtis came out from the back and barked, "You two girls are late!"

"Sorry," they muttered, almost simultaneously. *Why is he in such a bad mood?* Caitlin wondered. Everything seemed to be going horribly today.

"Don't be sorry," Curtis said, "just be on time."

Danielle gave him a salute. "Will do, Sarge."

Curtis glared at her. "Just do your job and do it right, okay? You too, Caitlin." Slowly, grumbling, they got to work under his angry gaze. They didn't talk, and Caitlin couldn't wait for the afternoon to be over.

The work day seemed much longer than usual, and Caitlin just went through the motions. When the afternoon ended, she and Danielle didn't resume their previous argument. Danielle was being polite enough now, but distant, and instead of riding their bikes back to the trailer together, as they often did, Danielle said she was too busy.

"I'm going out to Buckley's Pizza to see Joe and do some reading," she told Caitlin, making it clear that Caitlin wasn't invited. "I need some time alone."

"Cool. I'm going to meet Evan at the house. We might go jet skiing today."

Danielle just nodded, as if to say, *Figures—that's such a rich kid sport.*

Trying to make amends, Caitlin said, "You want to have dinner at the so-called pit tonight? Because I think they're grilling again. It might even be edible this time."

Danielle shook her head. "Naw. I'll pick up a slice at Buckley's and take it home."

"Guess I'll see you later, then."

"Guess so."

They might have sounded cordial enough to any casual observer, but Caitlin knew they were both putting on an act. It was depressing that their friendship was already under so much strain. Caitlin wanted to add that she'd definitely come back to the trailer tonight to sleep, but was afraid Danielle would say something cold in response, like, *"Whatever you say, Caitlin."* So she bit her lip as Danielle got on her bike and rode away with a brisk wave.

* * *

Just four days later, despite knowing it was probably the wrong decision, but unable to help herself, Caitlin moved into a room at the mansion. She realized she was doing something that on one level was completely irresponsible—and perhaps dangerous—but she was starting to feel like maybe she was falling in love with Evan, so how could it be wrong? Ian had, via Alison, relayed the information that he thought the two of them should take some time off. Caitlin didn't even care because Evan was on a whole other level. She told Alison to tell Ian that he'd actually done her a favor.

She and Danielle never got in a true fight, but the tension between them just kept getting worse. Caitlin got the sense that the girl was sick of her and glad to see her leave. When Caitlin told her about the decision to move, Danielle had looked relieved instead of angry. However, she'd still acted affronted when Caitlin told her the reasons why she was moving.

"Evan's really been pushing for it," Caitlin said, "and there's so much more space over there than here—"

"Of course there's more space," Danielle interrupted. "This is just a shitty trailer and they live in a beachfront palace, right?"

Caitlin felt thwarted, like she couldn't help putting her foot in her mouth no matter what she said. "I didn't mean it like that," she apologized. "Honest. I just mean it'll be easy for me to stay there. I'll have my own room and you'll have your room back." The main reason she'd even mentioned the space issue was because she didn't want Danielle to think she was moving directly into Evan's bed.

Danielle nodded. "It's probably for the best."

Caitlin proposed taking Luke with her, because Evan said they could clear a room out for him, too. She knew it wouldn't be a great environment for her brother, and she really didn't want him around her all the time either, but it was the only solution she could think of. Danielle agreed that Luke should go, too.

But it turned out that Luke didn't want to—and Rinita didn't want him to leave, either.

"Luke will stay here!" she said firmly, the firmest Caitlin had ever heard her say anything. There was something no-nonsense in the way her usually smiling mouth grew tight and her lips turned downward. She'd obviously, and inexplicably, grown attached to Luke.

"Are you sure?" Caitlin asked. She was thinking it would seem pretty peculiar to have her mom, herself, and her brother all living in separate locations on the tiny island. She couldn't help thinking, *Jesus, are we dysfunctional or what?* She also guessed that Danielle would be justifiably annoyed if Caitlin left Luke behind for her to deal with.

But Rinita couldn't be swayed, and Luke ranted and raved about leaving, so in the end, it was decided that he'd continue to stay at the trailer for the short term.

"I realize this is a pretty crazy arrangement and I can't thank you enough," Caitlin said to Danielle and her grandmother. She didn't offer them money to help out with his expenses because she was worried they'd get offended, like she was saying they were poor. But she remembered that Luke still had the credit card he'd stolen from her, so she planned on telling him to use it to pay for everything.

Rinita smiled and said, "Luke is a good boy. No problem at all."

Danielle just nodded, and didn't reveal her true opinion on the subject, whatever it might have been.

Evan came over and helped transport Caitlin's stuff back to the mansion in the red Mercedes. She'd bought some clothes in the past two weeks, just T-shirts, tank tops, shorts, and bikinis mostly, because the island was so hot. The local clothes weren't great, but she'd managed to make it work. She figured it was a sign she must be adapting somewhat to the island.

Caitlin felt sad to be leaving Danielle. She knew she'd see her at the Stop every afternoon, but it wouldn't be the same. As she and Evan pulled away down the gravel driveway, she said to Evan without thinking, "Don't let me down, okay?"

She hadn't meant to say it out loud—it just slipped out—and the words hung awkwardly in the air for a second. She thought he might laugh at her or say, "What the hell do you mean?" but he didn't. Instead, he understood, and put one of his hands on her thigh as he drove.

"I definitely won't. You know that."

"I hope so."

"You made the right decision to move in. We're going to have a total blast, and you won't have to go back and forth on your bike anymore."

"I'll still be going to work at the Stop," she pointed out.

"Yeah, but that's different." He patted her leg. "I think it's going to be really cool having you in the house."

"Same."

"And a lot more convenient for other stuff," he said playfully, moving his hand upward.

"Evan," she cautioned, "it's not the right time for that. I'm in my sensitive, worried mode, not my sex kitten mode."

"Sorry," he said, putting his hand back down, still smiling.

She was thinking, *Shit, I hope I just didn't make a big mistake,* so she said, "You were kidding, I hope. I'm not one of the Danbroke bimbos. You know I think you're awesome, but this isn't going to turn me into your slut." She had to be firm because she knew most guys lost respect for a girl they could get too easily. It was just something hardwired into them, an awful but integral trait.

Evan stopped smiling and looked worried, rushing to reassure her. "Of course, Caitlin," he told her, squeezing her hand. "You know I think you're awesome, too. I was just fooling around. And believe me, I know you're nothing like those other girls."

"Much better." She squeezed his hand back. "Just don't forget it."

"I won't," he said. "Promise."

She decided to believe him.

18
pushing and pulling

It turned out moving into the mansion was the worst thing Caitlin ever could have done, and not because of Evan. She quickly learned there was no chance to get any peace, because of the nonstop party. The halls reeked of pot smoke, there were crushed beer cans overflowing from the few trash cans in the house, and the toilets were always backed up. Caitlin had noticed these things before, but somehow they'd seemed manageable when she wasn't living there. Now they just seemed like torture.

Danielle had been right when she called it a pit, she thought on more than one occasion. But it was too late to go back.

Nathan's dad turned out to be a very strange landlord. Even though he didn't seem to care what anyone did, he yelled at Nathan hysterically every time he saw him. Evan had told her that Nathan hated his dad, and Caitlin could understand why. The few times Caitlin had encountered the man since moving in, he had a bottle in his hand. *He's just as bad as my mom,* Caitlin thought. The only difference was that it mattered far less because he wasn't her parent. She just kept her distance from him, as did most of Nathan's friends and Nathan himself. No one ever went up to the top floor of the house, the fourth floor, which was exclusively his domain.

Evan was the only good thing about being at the mansion, and things between them were going well. Caitlin was so wrapped up in him that she tried hard to ignore most of the other awful aspects of the place. The other guys would tease him and call her his "ball and chain." She could usually laugh it off because she'd been called far worse by Luke.

"You're pussy-whipped, dog," Shep said to Evan right in front of her, a few days after she moved in.

She'd retorted so quickly, it had made Shep's head spin. "First of all," she'd snapped, "Evan hasn't gotten anything from me, so you don't know what you're talking about. And second, you don't have a girlfriend and probably never will—I bet you're still a virgin. And third, you're never going to *get* a girlfriend un-less you have some plastic surgery on your face and lose about twenty pounds, okay? So if you do all that, then you can give me and Evan crap. But not until then."

Everyone had started laughing at Shep—one guy almost fell off the couch he was laughing so hard—so Shep had just said, "Ah, fuck y'all," and stumbled off into another room.

"Thanks for defending my honor," Evan said to Caitlin, chuckling and sipping a beer. She could tell he was deeply amused.

"You should have defended mine," she said, only half kidding.

He smiled. "You got it all covered."

But even though Caitlin could hold her own against the

guys, she couldn't deal with the increasing parental weirdness. As the days passed, Nathan started feuding even more with his father. The tension culminated one hot evening a week after she'd been there, when Nathan's dad stumbled downstairs and picked a fight with his son at the ongoing nightly party.

Caitlin had been sitting at one of the picnic tables on the deck overlooking the ocean, Evan's arm around her shoulders, as she talked to one of the local girls named Vanessa. Despite what Danielle had said, not all the local girls were idiots, although to be fair to Danielle, many of them were—at least the ones who chose to hang out at the mansion. That night there were about thirty kids out on the deck and it was getting dark. Caitlin was wearing one of Evan's large, long-sleeved shirts over hers because of the breeze.

The evening was interrupted when Caitlin heard Nathan and his dad screaming at each other over the loud music. Suddenly the music stopped, and everyone turned to look at what was happening. Nathan's dad stood in the center of the deck, his face red with rage, pointing a finger at his son.

"Don't you dare say that to me!" he yelled.

"Go to hell!" Nathan yelled right back.

"You son of a bitch," his dad rambled angrily. "You cocksucking freeloader! Who woulda thought I'd have a son like this?" He turned around wildly, staring at the kids scattered around the deck. Shocked by his words and attitude, Caitlin pressed herself against Evan. She was having flashbacks to all the awful fights between her and her mom. The deck had become deadly silent.

Nathan's dad spun around again, pointing at everyone gathered there, like his finger was a gun. "My son is a joke!" he said, the words ringing out into the night as he staggered under the burden of anger and alcohol. "A pathetic excuse for a man. And you're all a buncha freeloaders. That means all of you. The whole lot."

"No, we're not," someone said loudly.

"You're drunk, dude," another voice called out from the crowd.

"Who said that?!" Nathan's dad roared. No one said anything in response. Because it was nearly dark, except for the light spilling out of the house and a few candles here and there, he couldn't see the culprits. Caitlin clutched Evan's arm. Even he seemed a little stunned by what was happening. So far, Nathan's dad had seemingly been mostly absent from everyone's lives. Now he was all too present.

"Dad, just shut up and get back in the house," Nathan said, his voice trembling slightly. Caitlin had never seen him this way; usually he was the one who clowned around. "You don't know what you're saying."

"Sure I do. I'm saying you won't amount to a hill of beans. These people are only here because we're giving them a free place to stay. They're after your money, Nathan. That's all they care about."

"That's not true," he said, his voice growing firmer. "I've known most of these guys since first grade. They're my friends."

"So you know the names of all the people here? I doubt it. There are more than your eleven friends from school here. Tell me everyone's names, Nathan. Tell me."

Nathan crossed his arms. "You said it was okay for everyone to come. If you don't like these people being here, then tell them to leave. This is your house—I mean, yours for the moment."

"Never forget it." In the ensuing silence, his dad said to the crowd, "Party's over. I'm going to save my son a lot of heartache right now—just watch. Nathan's obviously not smart enough to know who's genuine and who's phony, so I have to do the thinking for him . . ."

As Caitlin listened to Nathan's dad taunt his son, she thought about her mom and Bill, as well. All three of the adults were deranged. *It's like living in backwards world,* she thought. *The adults are more screwed-up than the kids.* But there was nothing she could do about it. It was just the way things seemed to be. It was reality.

She leaned into Evan and said, "Do we need to leave?"

"No," he whispered back, transfixed by the spectacle of Nathan and his father. "We're cool. His dad will go upstairs and sleep it off."

"Has this happened before?"

"I've seen Nathan's dad blow his top, yeah." He paused and whispered more softly, "I've also seen Nathan's dad hit him a couple times before, back in Richmond . . ."

Just as Caitlin was absorbing that information, Nathan's dad lunged forward at his son, grabbing him by the collar. Nathan had his hands up, trying to push his father away, and was saying, "Okay, okay, just calm down, Dad."

Unfortunately, his dad wasn't listening.

The instant he put his hands on Nathan, a couple of the guys moved forward to intervene, but he was too quick. "Stay the hell away from me!" Nathan's dad sneered, pushing his son toward the edge of the deck. He was so filled with violent, negative energy that no one knew what to do. Caitlin could feel Evan start to stand up, but she held onto his arm, not wanting him to get hurt if a brawl broke out. She'd never actually witnessed a physical fight between guys before, mostly because the guys she knew in California were too laid-back to fight one another. And she'd certainly never seen a father fight his own son.

A few of the local girls and their guys had slipped away, off the edge of the deck opposite Nathan and his dad, or back into the house. Caitlin wondered if she and Evan should do the same. Before she could suggest the idea, she heard Nathan yelp in pain as his dad pressed him up against the wooden railings, forcing his son's upper body painfully backward.

"Dad, Jesus, fucking stop—" Nathan said.

His dad was relentless. "I'll stop when I want to."

Nathan struggled against him for a moment, and then his dad overpowered him, forcing him sideways. He slid along the railings until he reached the gap where the stairs were. Flailing at air, he fell backward and tumbled off the deck, down the short flight of stairs onto the sand.

Caitlin heard several people in the crowd gasp, and a girl somewhere started crying noisily.

"I don't believe this," Evan said. He tore out of Caitlin's grasp before she could stop him and, with three other guys, raced past Nathan's dad, who wobbled at the head of the stairs, and down the steps to help Nathan. Caitlin looked at Nathan's dad, wondering how a parent could be so evil. *He's making my mom look like a saint,* she thought, appalled. To add insult to injury, he didn't look concerned about what he'd just done. Instead, he had a sneer on his sweat-glazed face as he gazed at the shocked crowd.

"Don't like what you see?" he jeered. "Then leave. If not, who wants to be next? I'll take on any of you. All of you, if you want."

"You're an asshole," Evan yelled up at him. He was still crouching on the sand, next to Nathan, who was struggling to get up.

Evan, no, don't say anything! Caitlin prayed. Evan was a big guy, but Nathan's dad was mean. Mean enough to really hurt someone.

Luckily, Nathan's dad ignored Evan. "Go on, get out of here!" he said to everyone watching. "You want an instant replay? Send me over another ass to beat some sense into."

The crowd began to disperse. As Nathan's dad turned his back, Caitlin slipped past him and down the steps to Evan's side. Nathan was crawling away on his hands and knees through the sand. He seemed dazed, but unhurt. Caitlin noticed he'd started to cry. His friends were trying to help him, but he was striking out at them, trying to keep everyone away.

"It's okay," one of the guys said as Nathan finally got up and limped around the side of the house, out of view. Caitlin guessed Nathan was trying to get back inside without having people see that he was crying. Fortunately, his dad had disappeared somewhere off the deck.

"Evan, we have to do something about Nathan," Caitlin said, kneeling there. "Right?"

Evan nodded. "He's probably headed up to his room."

"Then let's go up there and see if he's okay."

Evan agreed. The two of them got to their feet and slowly sneaked back into the house, through the French doors. Most of the people had scattered, and Caitlin was afraid she and Evan would run into Nathan's dad. Fortunately, there wasn't any sign of him.

They climbed the stairs up to Nathan's room, and found, unsurprisingly, that the door was locked. Music was blasting from inside—Caitlin recognized it as Black Sabbath because Luke listened to metal sometimes. She knew, instinctively and from her own experience, that Nathan had it on to cover the sound of his crying.

"Yo, Nathan," Evan yelled, banging on the door. "You in there?"

It was pretty obvious he was, but Caitlin didn't bother pointing that out.

Evan banged again, this time harder. "Let us in. It's just me and Caitlin. No one else."

"It's okay, Nathan," Caitlin called out, in what she hoped was a soothing voice. She wasn't sure he could hear them over the music. They stood there for a few seconds and the door didn't open.

"He's not going to answer," Evan said, turning toward her.

"Try again?"

Evan pounded on the door one final time. "Yo, Nathan!" Still no response. He shrugged. "You know where to find us if you need us," he called out to the locked door. "We'll be in my room, okay?" Nothing.

"Are you sure he's going to be okay?" Caitlin asked Evan. "He didn't get hurt, right? His dad could have really injured him."

"I don't think so. He landed on the sand. I've seen him take worse falls playing Ultimate."

"I hope you're right."

As they headed back to Evan's room, Caitlin wondered if

it was safe to stay at the mansion. *First Bill, now this.* For once she decided to sleep in Evan's room, because she didn't want to be alone.

Later that night, lying on Evan's bed and talking, Caitlin told him she was worried about Nathan and the abuse. She didn't know why it upset her so much, other than the shock of seeing something like that. She guessed the whole "crazy parent" issue struck too close to home because of her mom. The mansion was supposed to have been a refuge from her real life, but it had turned out to be a very present reminder.

"Don't stress about it too much," Evan told her. "It'll be okay. Things always work out for the best."

"That's a pretty optimistic attitude." *Maybe a deluded one, too.*

"Hey, I'm an optimistic guy. Besides, Nathan and his dad have been at each other's throats for years. Nothing's going to change that now."

"You said he hits him?"

"I've seen it once or twice. Nathan's dad is hardcore."

"I just feel bad for Nathan," Caitlin said, replaying the moment over in her mind when his dad had shoved him down the steps.

"Nathan'll be fine," Evan insisted. "I feel sorry for him too, but what can we do? He just wants to be left alone. I'd feel the same way."

She turned over. "You should talk to Nathan and find out how you can help, and be there for him."

Evan rolled his eyes. "Guys aren't like chicks, Caitlin. We don't sit around and moan and bitch about our feelings."

"Is that what you think girls do all the time?"

"No, just some of the time."

Caitlin hoped Evan was kidding. They were holding hands, so she squeezed his and he squeezed back. "Maybe that's better than beating each other up."

"Maybe you're right."

A brief silence fell. "Why'd you come here for the summer?" Caitlin asked. She realized that although they'd talked about so many things, she'd never asked him that question.

He responded thoughtfully. "Free stay at the beach with my friends, I guess? I don't know. It was just kind of assumed I was going once Nathan told me about the mansion. We tend to stick together."

"You guys are the popular clique at school, am I right?"

"I guess so. Aren't you popular?"

"Maybe." She paused. "There wasn't anything else you wanted to do with your summer?"

"No. Just hang out and blow off steam. I know that sounds lame, but school is intense, and next year's going to be crazy with all the college stuff." He paused. "My parents are strict, too, like I said, so this is a good chance to get out and do stuff without them breathing down my neck all the time."

Caitlin understood. "Is the summer working out like you hoped?"

"Yeah." He rubbed a hand up and down her lower back, something between a massage and a caress. "Especially since I met you. There's only so much beer drinking and jet skiing a person can do before they get bored."

"Thanks," Caitlin said, curling up against him, hoping she

meant more to him than an antidote for boredom. "When my mom said we were going to Danbroke, I thought my summer was going to be unbearable, but it didn't turn out that way."

He put his arm all the way around her and gave her a tight squeeze.

"Wanna fool around?" he asked in a mock-playful voice, but she could tell he was serious because his hand was creeping toward her left breast. It puzzled her that he could turn so quickly from a serious discussion to wanting to make out.

"No offense, but I'm not in the mood after what happened tonight. My nerves are still fried. We're going to have to do something to help Nathan."

"I guess so." He pulled her tighter to him. "Let's worry about it tomorrow, okay?"

"Sure," Caitlin said, nodding in superficial agreement. What she was really thinking was: *I need to talk to someone about all of this, someone who I trust and who isn't directly involved.* The urge was sudden, and she wasn't sure why she felt that way. It wasn't so much about Nathan, but about all her own issues and insecurities that the situation had stirred up. With cell-phone service increasingly spotty for some reason, she doubted she'd get hold of Alison, and she'd prefer to talk to someone in person. She realized there was only one person who fit the bill, even if that person wouldn't want to see her.

I need to talk to Danielle, Caitlin thought. *She'll know what to do.* Yet she knew it wouldn't be easy to reconnect with the girl. She decided to bike over to Danielle's place tomorrow and see if she could find her. She didn't expect that Danielle would be happy to see her, but she knew she had to try. They barely talked at the Stop anymore except to exchange superficial pleasantries. In fact, Caitlin had blown off a few days of work recently and wondered if she'd get fired.

Danielle is worth making the effort for, Caitlin told herself, trying to psyche herself up. As she warmed herself in Evan's embrace, she vowed she'd try to patch things up with her friend as soon as possible.

19
on the beach

The next evening, Caitlin rode her bike through town and across the island to Danielle's place. The closer Caitlin got to the trailer, the more nervous she started to feel. The sun had just set, and the sky was growing dark. She hadn't been able to get away from the mansion until much later than she'd hoped. She also realized that maybe, on some level, she'd been putting it off. She'd told Evan she was just going to have a "girls' night out" with Danielle, which was mostly true.

Caitlin had a knot in her belly, and she could feel her heart racing. *It's no big deal,* she told herself, trying to stay calm. As she rode her bike down the path, the island breeze tugged at her clothes. *Danielle's not going to be mad. We never even had a big fight or anything.* But Caitlin wasn't a hundred percent sure of that.

Apologizing wasn't something Caitlin was used to, nor was admitting that she'd been wrong. If she pissed someone off, she usually just tried to stay out of their way until they cooled down. But Danielle was different. Danielle had been her friend when she first came to the island, and Caitlin felt like she owed her. *I guess I let a boy come between us,* she thought, *and that's not the kind of person I want to be.* Caitlin was certain she never would have treated Alison that way back home, so Danielle had a right to be irritated. Caitlin just hoped it wasn't too late to undo the damage.

She took a deep breath as the rusty fence and tangle of underbrush surrounding the trailer came into view, and slowed down on her bike. She looked around as she cruised to a stop, suddenly feeling hot. Trying to stay focused and not chicken out, she got off her bike and leaned it against the fence, near the gate. As usual, the gate was wide open, and she walked through it, rubbing her palms on her shorts.

The ten-second walk across the weed-ravaged front yard to the door of the trailer felt like it took an hour to Caitlin. She was sick of fighting—there'd been enough of it in her life so far: with her mom, with Luke, and with other supposed friends along the way. And after last night, watching Nathan and his dad go at it, she never wanted to see a fight again.

Caitlin climbed the three metal steps to the door and knocked, before she could change her mind. There wasn't any answer at first, so Caitlin waited awkwardly on the narrow steps. *I'll give it another ten seconds and then I'm out of here,* she thought.

But a moment later, she heard noises from inside: the sound of a door opening and then loud music spilling out. The metal blinds were shut on all the windows, but she guessed it was Danielle emerging from her bedroom. Suddenly there was a noise at the door, and the blinds were shoved back. Caitlin saw Danielle standing there, looking back at her through the glass, the surprise evident on her face. In that split second, Caitlin didn't know what to do. She awkwardly raised her hand and gave Danielle a small wave. "It's me," she said.

To her relief, Danielle didn't look angry. She took hold of the door and opened it, so that only the screen door was between them. "Missed you at work."

"I know. I got . . . distracted."

"You'd better come inside." Danielle opened the flimsy screen door, and Caitlin stepped into the interior of the trailer. It smelled like cinnamon.

"I'm so sorry—" she began, as soon as she'd got her bearings, but Danielle cut her off.

"Don't." She turned around slowly, her back to Caitlin, and headed down the narrow hall toward her bedroom. Not knowing what else to do, Caitlin followed her. The Smiths were blaring from Danielle's stereo. When Caitlin reached the bedroom, Danielle was already sitting on the bed. She leaned over, turned the music down, and then she looked at Caitlin. "Why'd you come here?"

"Please, let me explain," Caitlin said, clearing a space in the clutter of CDs and books on the floor, and sitting down across from her. "I know you're probably pissed off at me. I haven't kept in touch. I haven't shown up at work. I don't know what's got into me . . ."

"Evan, perhaps?" Danielle muttered. "Anyway, it doesn't matter. You just moved on and found the so-called cool kids to play with."

So she *was* mad. "It's not like that."

"Sure it is." Danielle looked away in the brief silence between songs. "You think Evan and Nathan are better than me, don't you? That you're better than me. Just because all of you have money." She sounded resigned.

"I fucked up." Caitlin leaned back against a poster for AFI tacked onto the wall, feeling a hitch in her throat. "I'm really, really sorry, Danielle." She looked over at her. "Just because I'm going out with Evan now doesn't mean I don't have time to hang out with you. I just got caught up in the moment."

Danielle stared back. "When I first met you, I thought you were probably a typical rich kid—and for a while, you were proving me wrong. But as soon as Evan and the others came on the scene, you split."

"That's not completely true," Caitlin said. "You were the one who didn't want to hang out with them. You said they were posers."

"Was I right?"

"Not about all of them. Not about Evan." Caitlin sighed. "I don't want to fight. I want to be friends." She smiled ruefully. "God, that sounds stupid, like we're little kids or something. But you know what I mean."

"Sure I do," Danielle said. "We're supposed to kiss and make up, or however you do it in California. But I don't have to forgive you, Caitlin. We're *not* little kids. We haven't even known each other too long."

"I know." *Maybe I shouldn't have come here at all,* Caitlin was thinking.

"When this summer is over, you'll get to go back to your little *O.C.* world, but I'll still be stuck in this dump, living here with Grandma." She gestured around her tiny room. "There's nothing for me on this island. I'm just counting down the days until college. I bet you wouldn't want to trade places with me, am I right?"

Caitlin didn't say anything. *It would be easier if Danielle were yelling at me,* she realized suddenly.

"Seriously, we don't have much in common and we never did," Danielle continued. "I doubt we could have been real friends anyway, at least for long. You belong with Evan and those guys, not here with me."

Caitlin knew she had to disagree, but couldn't find the words. Before she could think up a response, Danielle abruptly stood up.

"Listen, no hard feelings. I don't hold grudges. But it's late, and I have to do the dishes before Rinita and Luke get back from the mainland with some groceries and stuff, so you should probably go."

Was that it? Caitlin looked up at her. "If that's what you want."

Danielle nodded. "It is. Thanks for coming. I appreciate the gesture."

Caitlin stood up slowly and walked over to the door. The trailer was so cramped, Danielle had to press herself against the wall so Caitlin could get past her. *Boy, I really fucked this one up,* she thought to herself. Caitlin stood at the doorway to Danielle's room for a moment and then decided there was no point staying where she wasn't wanted. She felt frustrated, with both herself and with Danielle. She walked to the entrance of the trailer and Danielle followed her.

"See you around, Caitlin," she said softly, as Caitlin opened the door and stepped outside. "Oh, and one more thing. Curtis said don't bother coming back to work at the Stop . . ."

"Great." So she had been fired. Caitlin turned around one last time and looked at Danielle through the screen. "Listen, if you change your mind and want to get coffee and talk, you know where to find me."

"Sure."

Feeling awkward and exposed, Caitlin turned around and walked down the steps and across the yard to her waiting bicycle. It had grown much darker in just those few minutes, the moon rising above her in the night sky. She knew her friendship with Danielle was over—and that it had mostly been her fault.

Caitlin got back on her bike, wishing she could have done things differently. She decided to take the bike path near the ocean back down the island to Evan and the mansion. She was hoping that the ocean breeze and the night air would clear her head a little.

She cycled down the empty street, over cracked pavement, and through the rusted gates that led to the asphalt bike trail running along the top of a sand dune between the forest and the beach. On her right was a verdant wall of trees; on her left stretched the long expanse of beach and ocean. Now that it was dark, the beach had a spooky quality. Caitlin could hear the crashing sound of waves breaking in the ocean, as well as the thrum of the insects that were so omnipresent on Danbroke.

As she rode her bike, her hair blew back behind her in the wind. It had picked up a little, and by the sound of it, the waves had grown larger, too.

At such a late hour, the island seemed completely desolate, and Caitlin felt very alone as she cycled. Under the moonlight, the beach was deserted and no one else passed her on the trail.

The mansion was a good twenty minutes away by bike, and she couldn't even see it down the beach from here.

Then, as she cycled, she saw a strange set of lights on the flat expanse of sand to her left. It was far enough away that she couldn't quite make it out, even under the illumination of the full moon. But as she neared, she suddenly realized it was a car parked on the beach down by the water. While it wasn't strange to see cars on the beach on Danbroke, usually she only saw SUVs and Jeeps parked there, and mostly in the daytime. This car was much smaller, however, and as she got closer, she realized it was a vehicle she knew well.

She wasn't sure how it had gotten there, but it was the red Mercedes that belonged to Nathan's dad. She slowed down a little on her bike, uncertain why the car was parked on the beach, facing the water. She was still a good distance from it, but now she could make out two figures standing behind the car, lit by the red glow of the taillights. At first she was excited because she thought it might be some of the guys out joyriding, and she could burn a ride. But as she continued down the path, she was able to hear voices over the waves and realized it was Nathan and his dad. Fortunately for her, in addition to being elevated by the dunes, the bike path was dark and overhung with tree branches, so she didn't think either one could see her. She'd feel embarrassed if she stumbled across another vicious fight between the two of them. *And afraid.*

She got closer, trying to be quiet and hoping she could cycle past them without being noticed. Still, curiosity got the better of her and she couldn't help overhearing some of what they were saying. She slowed down even more, until she was barely moving, and put her feet on the ground.

Not surprisingly, Nathan and his dad weren't having an amicable conversation. She could hear Nathan's dad screaming in his usual deranged fashion. As she sat there, she could discern almost every word as she listened to him cursing out Nathan.

"You're going to end up just like your mother! You must have inherited her genes for stupid, because everything you do is ass-backwards. This shit with the car is no exception—what were you thinking?! You're as dumb as that idiot Evan. You did it just to piss me off, I know it. You're mad at me for busting up your little party yesterday."

"Dad— Stop— Listen to me."

But Nathan's dad wasn't listening. He was in full rampage mode. Caitlin saw him take a step closer to Nathan. Although the two of them were close in height, Nathan's dad seemed so much larger.

"I don't have to listen to you tell me jack shit!" Nathan's dad barked. "You can't even do the simplest thing right, and your so-called friends know it, too. Why are you always such a screwup? And why don't you ever have a girlfriend? Are you a homo?" He spat on the sand. "I never thought I'd have a son like you."

Caitlin wanted to turn away from the scene, but like a car wreck, it held a grisly fascination for her. She felt sorry for Nathan no matter what he'd done, if anything. Nathan's dad was probably just drunk again. Caitlin could see a bottle of something sitting on the roof of the car.

"I'm not a loser, Dad," Nathan said, looking down. Caitlin hoped he wouldn't look up at the trail and see her, where she remained, transfixed.

His dad laughed. "Sure you are." Nathan didn't say anything in response, which only inflamed his dad more. "You're weak, just like your mom," he continued. "You don't have direction in life, and you never will. You don't know what it means to be a man." He took another step closer to Nathan. Even from her distance, Caitlin could sense the tension and hostility, ready to explode into physical violence at any second. *I should just get the hell out of here.*

"You're right, Dad," Nathan replied. "Whatever you say."

"Damn straight." As Caitlin watched, Nathan's dad suddenly shoved him hard in the chest, and Nathan took a stumbling step backward. "See? You won't do anything. You won't even defend yourself. You're a whipped dog." Nathan's dad stepped forward and shoved him a second time.

"Stop it!" Nathan said, trying to recover his balance. "Don't make me do something I'll regret."

"That's a laugh! I'd love to see the day that happens. But I know whatever I do, you're just going to stand there and take it . . ."

Caitlin stifled a gasp as Nathan's dad suddenly lashed out and punched Nathan right in the face. There was no way Nathan could have seen it coming.

Oh my God, Nathan's dad is a genuine lunatic, Caitlin thought. *As if I'd needed any more proof . . .*

Nathan was so stunned by the blow that he fell to the sand on one knee, the red taillights casting his shadow down the beach. Caitlin couldn't bear to stay there any longer and watch Nathan get beat up. She was just about to yell at Nathan's dad to stop, hoping it would distract him and give Nathan a chance to get away. But right then she saw an object in Nathan's hand. It took Caitlin a second to realize what she was seeing and even when she did, she couldn't believe it. Nathan was clutching a small silver handgun, one that he'd removed from the waist-band of his jeans. He wiped his nose, which was leaking blood. Caitlin covered her mouth with one hand as Nathan slowly got to his feet. Nathan pointed the gun at his dad's chest, and his dad backed away.

"I told you not to fuck with me!" Nathan said, his voice high and frightened. "Now get away from me, or I swear to God I'll shoot you, and then I'll shoot myself." He started crying big hysterical sobs that shook his whole body. "Swear to God!"

20

man down

Caitlin wanted to yell out, "Don't do it!" but she was paralyzed by fear. She prayed that Nathan would just put the gun down. *Maybe it isn't a real gun,* she thought, *and he's just trying to scare his dad.* Yet in her heart, she knew that wasn't the case. The gun was all too real, and from Nathan's tone, she could tell he was completely serious.

"What the hell are you doing?" Nathan's dad said angrily. "Are you crazy? Put that thing down."

"No!" Nathan screamed, on the verge of madness, crying raggedly. He lunged forward with the gun. "Stop talking! I'm going to teach *you* a lesson. About respect."

"I don't respect you," his dad pronounced grimly, like a verdict. "I never will, especially after this. A gun doesn't make you a man."

"I know that, Dad. But nothing's going to make me a man in your eyes, so I might as well not care."

"Nathan, you're acting like an idiot—no surprise there!" his dad abruptly barked. *Doesn't he realize the danger he's in?* Caitlin wondered. "Give me the gun, before I take it away from you. You stole it from my bedroom, didn't you?"

"Yeah, I did. What are you going to do about it? Nothing! Now shut up before you make me use it." In Nathan's rage, his voice even sounded different, like a stranger had taken over his body. He sounded nothing like the guy who'd once leaned out a car window and hit on Caitlin and Danielle.

Caitlin wanted to make it all stop, but she was powerless to do anything but watch. She knew she should probably run and get help, but she was too scared to make a sound in case Nathan heard her. Nathan's father was either too drunk, or too incensed, to understand that Nathan was unhinged enough to actually pull the trigger.

His dad took a step toward him and said, "If you don't give me that gun, I'm going to bust your head open."

Nathan's hand was shaking as he said, "You're not taking it. You're never going to take anything away from me again."

Nathan's dad took another step, his face twisted into a forbidding scowl. "I'm warning you one last time . . ." he said, as if he were the one with the weapon.

Nathan struggled to hold the gun steady. Caitlin felt like she was going to throw up. *I need to get help!* her mind screamed, but her body still refused to move. Although she'd seen a million guns in movies and on TV, she'd never actually seen a gun pointed at someone in real life. It wasn't dramatic or exciting—it was just scary.

"You can shove your warnings up your ass and keep them there," Nathan yelled.

"You arrogant son of bitch!" His father advanced, and Nathan took a faltering step back, surprised by his dad's vehemence.

"That's right," his dad said, "just give up! Give me the gun. You know you're no match for me. Give it up, Nathan. Right now. Give it to me." The words formed a creepy, hypnotic mantra. Nathan's dad looked like a monster, a fat gargoyle stuffed into a dress shirt and slacks, half bent forward as he stalked his son.

As Nathan wiped tears out of his eyes with his free hand, his father made a sudden, ill-advised move toward him, cursing and grappling for the gun.

Caitlin gasped loudly in surprise, but neither Nathan nor his dad heard her. His dad grabbed hold of Nathan's arms and the two of them tumbled to the sand, rolling around, fighting each other like animals. Nathan was screaming, but his father was completely silent. Whatever bonds they'd once shared as father and son had been completely obliterated. To Caitlin they just looked like two guys struggling to beat their opponent and stay alive.

Nathan's dad got hold of his son's shirt and held it tight, trying to wrap it around Nathan's neck. Nathan writhed and struck out with the gun, hitting his dad in the mouth. Caitlin heard the sound of teeth breaking, but still his dad was silent, which made it all the more frightening. His dad began punching Nathan in the side, right in the kidneys, and Nathan yelped in pain and fear. Still, neither of them let the other go, as they rolled around, getting sand in their eyes and mouths, coughing and choking.

What happened next wasn't entirely unexpected. Caitlin

heard the sudden, muffled crack of a gunshot echo across the beach and up to the dune, and her heart froze in her chest, her breathing temporarily stilled.

It was clear that the gun had been fired.

Oh, God— No! she thought desperately. She was crouched low on the ground now, flattened against the bike path so that no one could see her. The bike was lying next to her, and she worried that it might reflect the moonlight and give her away.

She thought for a second that the bullet had just gone into the air, and hoped that the sound of the gunshot would bring Nathan and his dad to their senses. But as she watched, Nathan's father rolled off his son and onto his back, his limbs jerking and flailing like he was having a seizure. A black stain was quickly growing on his chest, over his heart.

Nathan didn't seem to understand what had happened at first, as though his mind was shutting down. He still held the pistol in his hand, as he staggered to his feet, lurching away from his dad. His dad was completely still, and Caitlin tried to see if he were breathing or not. She didn't think he was. All she knew was that someone should get help, if it wasn't already too late. But she was too afraid Nathan might shoot her, or himself, if she revealed herself, so she stayed hidden.

"Dad?" Nathan called out, looking down at his dad's silent body.

I think he's dead, Caitlin thought, with true dread. At that moment, she wished someone was there with her, but she was terrifyingly alone.

As Caitlin watched, Nathan leaned in closer to his father. "Dad, are you okay?" There was still no response from the silent body on the sand. Nathan knelt down and put a hand over his father's chest in a futile effort to stop the bleeding. To Caitlin, it looked like Nathan was going into shock himself because he was shaking. "Dad, I didn't mean it," he moaned, the words barely audible over the sound of the surf.

Holy shit, Nathan's dad is really dead, Caitlin thought as she stared at the body. It had been too long since he'd moved, and blood continued to sluice onto the sand. *I'm looking at a corpse,* she thought. She almost felt like she was having an out-of-body experience. She wondered if there were any way she could be dreaming all of this, but it was too real and visceral to be a dream.

"Dad, get up, okay? It's going to be alright . . ." When there was no answer, Nathan's tears increased. Caitlin felt something on her own face and when she put her hand up to touch it, she realized she was crying silently, out of fear and frustration.

Nathan's legs buckled, and he collapsed down in the sand next to his dad's body. He didn't make any effort to do the things Caitlin would have done, like check if his dad was still breathing or try to staunch the flow of blood again. He buried his face in his hands. Caitlin kept a careful eye on Nathan's gun, which was now in his lap. If it wasn't for the gun, she would have run down there and risked everything to try to help.

I wish Evan were here, she thought desperately. *If only I hadn't gone to Danielle's tonight, I'd be safe at the mansion with him.* Struck by the sudden fear that in Nathan's hyper-paranoid state his senses might be sharpened, Caitlin tried not to even breathe. *Keep quiet, don't move, and get out of here as soon as there's a chance,* she told herself.

Nathan stood up again slowly, using his arms to push himself off the sand. He staggered around in a tiny circle, like he was so confused he couldn't think straight. Caitlin could see his lips moving and knew he was muttering things to himself, but she couldn't hear the words.

As she watched, Nathan walked to the end of his father's body and bent down, clasping his dad's ankles with both hands. Caitlin didn't understand what he was doing. She wanted to yell, *Don't move him!* because she knew it was a mistake to move the victim of a gunshot. But Nathan either didn't know or didn't care. He picked up his dad's legs and began slowly dragging the body across the sand.

It took Caitlin several seconds to realize exactly where he was taking it—and when she did, it took all her energy to stop from screaming. *He can't really be headed where I think he's going!* She'd assumed he'd get help. Yet her worst fears were soon confirmed: Nathan was dragging his father's body directly into the ocean.

Nathan continued to cry and talk to himself, or maybe to the body, as he struggled with it. It took him a long time to drag it all the way down the beach and into the shallows. She could see him struggling with it at the water's edge. The light of the moon glanced off the churning surface, illuminating everything, as did the headlights of the car. Nathan waded into the water up to his knees.

Through all of this, Caitlin could have easily slipped back onto her bike and rode away. Or she could have ditched the bike and headed into the sheltering forest on foot. But she was held back by the thought that someone had to stay there to witness what Nathan was doing. She was also frozen by the fear that if she tried to run, Nathan would catch the movement and see her. So she stared outward into the darkness as Nathan finally reemerged from the water, his jeans soaking. There was no trace of his father.

Dear God, Caitlin prayed, *please give me the strength to get through this, and to get out of this situation alive. I don't want to die here.*

Nathan looked up and down the beach as he got back onto dry land. He rubbed a hand over his eyes, and then again, harder, as if trying to blot out the memory of what he'd done. An imprint of the fight was visible on the sand, along with the bloodstain and the long trail of blood where Nathan had dragged the body into the water.

Caitlin was struck by the horrible thought that maybe Nathan's dad hadn't really been dead, just unconscious or dying. Maybe her own failure to act had contributed to his death. *It was very possible.* She was pretty sure his dad had been dead, but there was no way to tell for sure. Either way, what Nathan had done had sealed his father's fate and was a worse crime than the shooting itself.

As Caitlin watched, Nathan began trying to cover up the evidence of the fight and the killing. Looking around nervously and constantly, but seeming not to spot Caitlin, he knelt and began digging up sand to cover the large patch of blood. Within a minute or two it was all gone, and he smoothed fresh sand over it. To Caitlin, it looked like the tide was coming in, which meant this area of beach would probably be cleansed by the ocean within an hour or two. Nathan methodically began smoothing over the pathway down to the water, where he'd dragged the body. Soon there were only patterns in the sand left—the stain of blood had been removed.

The car was a little different, though. Caitlin could see Nathan pacing back and forth, trying to figure out what to do. Clearly, when Nathan drove away, the car would leave tracks on the sand. The water would wash most of them away, but they'd be visible until then. It was doubtful anyone would come down to the beach and find them on an island this isolated, but Nathan couldn't know for sure. Caitlin thought he might just leave the car there, but with a final backward glance down the beach, he took out the keys and got inside, slipping the gun back in his pants.

Caitlin realized she'd been holding her breath, and she let it out in a long, slow exhalation. *I can't afford to lose my head,* she vowed. *I need to stay calm.* The worst seemed to be over, but now she'd have to figure out what to do next and who to tell. She felt trapped in some kind of nightmare Hitchcock movie, the kind her dad loved and used to watch all the time. They'd always scared her, and living through one was far worse than watching one.

The Mercedes came to life, and Nathan began backing onto firmer ground. Caitlin wondered what would happen if he got stuck, but luck was on his side. The Mercedes made strange grinding noises, but Nathan managed to get it moving through a flat patch of sand between two low-lying sand dunes. The headlights flared as he slowly pulled the car away from the ocean and toward the beach access road.

Caitlin suddenly realized that she'd stayed too long, and her place on the bike path wasn't safe anymore. On his way to the road, there was a good chance the headlights would shine directly across her and give her away. She scrambled up from the asphalt, with no time to grab the bike, and threw herself into the foliage at the edge of the forest. She burrowed in the damp underbrush, trying to hide.

Just as she'd predicted, a split second after she made her move, the headlights of the Mercedes swung slowly toward the place she'd been hiding, illuminating the bike and making a long shadow splay out behind it on the path.

Shit! She bit her lip with fear as she lay there. *There's no way Nathan can miss seeing the bike.* She didn't know if he could tell it was hers or not, or if he'd waste time trying to find out. There were a bunch of mountain bikes at the house and they got used interchangeably. Caitlin prayed the car would just keep driving and that the headlights would move on. But that didn't happen.

She flinched when she heard the car door opening and realized that Nathan was getting out to investigate. She couldn't just sit around and wait for Nathan to find her, so she started backing away on her hands and knees into the darkness of the forest. By the time Nathan got out of the car and walked to the bike on the path, she was well hidden about forty feet into the woods. From a vantage point behind a clump of vines, she could see him illuminated by the headlights of the Mercedes, but he couldn't see her.

"Hello?" he yelled into the blackness, standing there unsure. "Is anyone out there?"

Caitlin didn't answer, remaining shrouded in the shadows and the foliage. She scrunched down to make herself smaller. It was dense enough that there was no way for him to spot her— unless he waded into the forest. He didn't have time to do that, and he knew it. She saw him glance down at the bike. She thought he might pick it up and take it with him, but he didn't.

He just looked around a few more times, panic-stricken, and then turned and headed swiftly back to the car.

That was too fucking close, Caitlin thought, listening to him get back inside. It was only after Caitlin heard the car pull away, and saw its lights recede, that she dared sneak back onto the bike path. Even then, she was afraid of every noise and shadow, afraid that Nathan had returned. She didn't know where to go or what to do. Clearly, she couldn't go back to the mansion because Nathan might be headed there himself.

Caitlin knew she needed to talk to Evan right away, and to the police, as well. *Damn this fucking island,* she swore inwardly, as she wondered how any place in America could exist with no police department. There was no question of trying to tell her mom about it. After what happened with Bill, she could imagine her mom refusing to believe her, or even refusing to talk to her at all. And because of bad service on the island, her cellphone had been out most of the day, which meant everyone she knew and trusted was off-limits for now.

That left only Danielle. Things had gone so horribly just a while earlier, but she intrinsically knew that Danielle would believe her. *That is, if Danielle will listen. I have to go back and tell her right away.* She got back on the bike, her head reeling with shock, and began the return journey to Danielle's trailer.

21

sanctuary

When she got to the trailer, Danielle refused to answer. Caitlin could see a light on in her room at first, and guessed she was home, but Danielle didn't come out. Rinita and Luke were nowhere to be seen; Caitlin wondered if maybe they'd ended up spending the night on the mainland because of some problem with the ferry. The wind had picked up recently, and the waves were choppier because a storm was coming to the island—at least according to reports Caitlin had seen on TV at the mansion.

Caitlin tried everything to get Danielle out, including banging on the front door and her window, as well as yelling her name, but nothing worked. The whole time she kept looking over her shoulder out of fear. Caitlin finally had to concede that Danielle really wasn't there. *Maybe she went somewhere with Luke and Rinita,* Caitlin thought. No matter what the reason, Caitlin realized she wasn't going to be able to talk to her, so she'd have to find a working payphone to call Evan. *Maybe I can get him to meet me somewhere.* She knew she wasn't thinking too clearly, but she was upset and shaken to her core. She felt a sense of numbness, coupled with relief to be alive and rolling anxiety at not being able to share her secret with anyone.

To find a pay phone, Caitlin would have to go into town, and she didn't want to risk doing that yet. She could picture the red Mercedes cruising up and down the streets, looking for her. *Why had Nathan done it?* she wondered. The shooting appeared to be an accident, but by dragging the body into the ocean, he'd implicated himself as a cold-blooded murderer.

Caitlin decided she'd wait for Danielle, or Rinita and Luke if they came back, but not out in the open, where she could be seen by a car. She went around the back of the trailer and hid herself and the bike in the woods, sitting at the base of a tree. It was shocking to realize that she'd gone from once living in a hilltop mansion in La Jolla to being basically homeless.

I have nothing.

She felt like crying again, except she was too scared and worried to waste any time on tears. She was sure tears would come later, when she replayed the murder over and over in her mind.

This island is evil, she thought. *I knew it from the start.* She didn't feel like things could get any worse, but she knew that they always could.

* * *

Caitlin ended up spending the entire night outside, hiding and waiting for someone to come back. But no one did. It crossed her mind many times during the night that maybe something bad had happened to Danielle, Luke, and Rinita, but it seemed unlikely. They were probably just stuck because of the ferry and the worsening weather. It had rained on and off in the night, and Caitlin's clothes were damp. Her body was stiff and sore. She'd fallen asleep for minutes at a time, but had spent most of the night listening to the sounds around her.

Daybreak came and everything grew slightly less scary, but the sun never really appeared. Instead a gray wall of clouds seemed to cover the whole sky. Caitlin staggered up from the forest and out onto the road in front of the trailer. She knew she had to be careful. Evan would be wondering where she'd gone and was probably concerned about her. She hoped he was safe. Without any sign of Danielle, her options were limited. She figured she had to get into town and call the police, and then Evan after that.

Slowly, her limbs aching, she climbed on the bike and began the journey into town. She soon discovered not too many people were up and about except for a few fishermen, but she remained terrified she was going to run into Nathan. At the same time, she was hoping Evan might be out looking for her, and she might run across him.

Neither happened, however, and when she got into town, the island's few stores were still closed, and the single pay phone still broken. She didn't know where to go until she remembered Joe at Buckley's Pizza. She knew he opened up early in the week to serve breakfast because Danielle had mentioned it once. She prayed he was open today—it wasn't even 6:00 A.M. yet. Of course, the restaurant was near the Pirate's Lodge, but she guessed neither her mom nor Bill would be up early, so she wouldn't be in danger of seeing them.

Caitlin knew it wasn't smart to be seen with the bike, but without it, it would take too long to get there. So she biked all the way to Buckley's as fast as she could, the breath caught in her chest. When it came into view, to Caitlin's relief, she saw that the neon OPEN sign was turned on and a couple of old-timers were sitting outside smoking. They both glared at her as she parked her bike and raced inside. Joe was behind the counter, frying up some omelets, a cigarette stuck behind his ear like someone from the 1950s. The Rolling Stones' "Brown Sugar" played from a tiny transistor radio next to the cash register. No one else was in the restaurant.

Joe heard her come in and turned toward her, smiling. "Hey there. Caitlin, right? Danielle's friend." She nodded, and he must have realized by her grim face that something was wrong. "You okay?"

"Joe, I need to use your phone. It's an emergency. Do you have one?"

"A phone? Of course." He walked over to the register and picked up a cordless phone, handing it to her over the counter. "Hope it's a local call. Mind telling me what it's for? You look a little freaked-out, if you don't mind me saying."

For some reason, Caitlin couldn't tell him. Maybe she was just nervous after the whole Bill thing, but she couldn't face explaining it to Joe. She'd then have to face her own guilt about not doing anything to help. "I saw something last night on the beach," was all she said, "and I need to report it to the police."

"Lots of things happen on the beach here."

"This is serious."

He seemed to understand, and said, "Fair enough."

Caitlin took a deep breath, and then, steeling her nerves, dialed 911. To her surprise, nothing happened. There was just silence on the other end of the line. Joe was still watching her and had seen the number she'd dialed.

"There's no nine-one-one on Danbroke," he explained.

"What?" Caitlin thought 911 was a universal phenomenon, or at least something that existed everywhere in America. "Why?"

"It wouldn't make sense. No one could get here fast in an emergency, anyway. The world doesn't care about an island this small."

"Then who do I call?"

Joe gave her a number from memory. "I got it stuck in my head because Buckley's was vandalized last year. It's the number for the station near Hatteras, the closest one."

"Thanks." She dialed the number as he repeated it, and then she waited for someone to pick up. After six rings, an automated voice came on telling her that either all the circuits were busy or no one was available. *How can no one be there?!* she wanted to yell. In La Jolla, the police could arrive on the scene of a crime within three minutes. She looked at Joe and said, "No one's there."

"Stay on the line. Someone'll pick up." He turned back to tend to the omelets.

Caitlin waited, preparing the words she'd say in her head. She knew Joe would overhear her, but it would be okay, because she'd be telling the police and they'd know what to do. It was ironic, and tragic, to think that her own mother was only a short walk away, down the road, but that she was too drug-addled and untrustworthy to be of any help.

Caitlin continued to wait as Joe scooped the eggs off the blackened grill and onto two plates, adding slices of soggy toast.

She kept waiting, even as he took them outside to the fishermen and came back in, pouring himself a cup of sludgy coffee. Caitlin looked up at the old-fashioned clock on the wall and saw that now it was almost 6:30. She kept waiting and waiting and still no one picked up. There wasn't even a chance to leave a message. She was on permanent hold.

"No one's answering," Caitlin said, the desperation evident in her voice.

"They can be kind of flaky," Joe commiserated.

"That's not too reassuring." In frustration, she clicked off the phone. Then she said hopelessly, "I guess I'll try again later?"

Joe scratched his nose. "Now that I think about it, they might be busy helping prepare the Outer Banks. We're supposed to get a doozy of a storm."

"Storm?" Caitlin echoed, still thinking about the murder.

"Didn't you hear? We're supposed to get hit by the edge of Hurricane Ivy."

If she could have felt any further degree of despair, she would have. "Are you serious? A hurricane?" *I've been so out of it,* she thought. *Too wrapped up in Evan and life at the mansion to follow what's been happening around me.* She'd known a storm was coming, but missed the part about a hurricane.

"Tell me more," she said tensely. She didn't understand how anyone could be blasé about something like this. *First a murder, now a hurricane,* she thought. *Could this island get any fucking worse without being certified as one of the circles of hell?*

"It's not a bad hurricane," Joe hastened to add, "and it's a ways from here, tickling eastern Florida. It's supposed to drift up from the Atlantic and graze us."

"What does 'graze' mean?"

"It's a degree worse than 'tickle.' " He took a sip of coffee. "What it means is the weather isn't going to be so nice from now on. High winds, big surf, lots of rain. Best to stay inside. Big storms can be fierce here on the Banks. I'll probably close up Buckley's later today, maybe board the windows if it gets bad enough. Ivy's only a category one, so we should be okay."

Great. Still holding the phone, Caitlin said, "I need to try calling my friend Evan."

"You want anything to drink or eat, by the way? As a friend of Danielle's, you can pay me back later, if you're strapped for cash again." Caitlin could tell he was being nice to her because she was upset. Her stomach was too clenched up to eat.

"I'm fine," she said.

"You don't sound fine. Six years behind this counter have made me a pretty good judge of character. Maybe a cup of coffee would help—free of charge."

"Sure. Yeah. That would be great." In that instant, she just wanted Joe to stop talking, as much as she appreciated his kindness.

She picked up the phone again, and she dialed the number for the mansion, hoping she'd get Evan, but fearing it would be Nathan. Luckily, she heard Evan's concerned voice answer after only two rings, like a lifeline to sanity.

"Evan, it's me," Caitlin said in a breathless rush. "Thank God you're home."

"Caitlin! Where the hell were you all night—"

She cut him off. "Don't worry. I'm okay. I'll explain everything as soon as I see you. Can you come get me?"

"Where are you?" He didn't sound mad, just worried. "Are you alright?"

"Yes. I'm at Buckley's Pizza down at the other end of the island."

"Did you go visit your mom or something?"

"No, I'm here because Buckley's is the only place that's open, and because it's far away from everything else." She paused. Joe had his back to her, rummaging underneath the counter. She knew she probably wasn't making much sense to Evan. "Listen, is Nathan at the house?"

"Nathan?" He sounded surprised she was asking. "I don't know. He's probably sleeping. I'm only up this early because you didn't come back last night. I was just about to go look for you at Danielle's."

"Have you seen Nathan today? Or last night?"

"I don't know what he's been up to. I'm in my room all alone. Why do you keep asking me about Nathan?"

"No reason," Caitlin hedged, knowing that it sounded like she was lying. *It doesn't matter—Evan will understand things soon enough.*

"Where'd you spend last night?" he asked. "At Danielle's?"

"She wasn't home—" Caitlin broke off. "Listen, can you just get over to Buckley's as soon as possible?"

"Yeah, sure. I'm not dressed all the way, though. Can't you come over here?"

"No." She didn't explain why.

"Okay, give me a few minutes and I'll be there." He paused. "You sure you're okay, Caitlin?"

"Just hurry."

They said their good-byes, and then Caitlin hung up and placed the phone on the counter again. Joe was sitting back there on a stool, flipping through an issue of *Sports Illustrated.*

"Sounds like some drama. Boy trouble?"

Caitlin wished her problems were that simple. She shook her head. "I witnessed a crime last night. I don't really want to talk about it."

"I understand. Some things are best kept private, I guess." He gestured at a fresh cup of coffee he'd put on the counter and said, "That one's yours, if you want it."

She reached over and picked it up, taking a sip, feeling the warm liquid traverse her throat and go down into her stomach. Her whole body was still cold from having spent the night outdoors. The gray weather didn't help. It had started to rain again.

"I'm just going to stay here and wait until Evan comes, if that's okay?"

"I figured out that part from your conversation. No worries." Joe leaned back on the stool, the magazine on his lap. "How's Danielle doing? I haven't seen her for about a week or so."

"She's good," Caitlin lied. She didn't feel in the mood for idle chitchat, so she just took a sip of her coffee. *Maybe I'm making a mistake by not telling Joe about Nathan,* she thought, *but I'd rather wait for Evan.*

"Danielle's a smart cookie. She keeps me on my toes when she comes by."

Caitlin nodded. In her head she was urging Evan to get there as quickly as possible, because every passing second felt like an hour.

Her wishes were granted when Evan turned up several minutes later. She saw a white Ford sedan pull into the parking lot, and she headed for the door right away. *Thank God it's not the Mercedes,* she thought. The sedan belonged to one of the local girls who let the boys at the house use it sometimes.

"Thanks, Joe," she said on her way out of Buckley's.

"Don't mention it," he called back.

Caitlin hit the front door and went out into the rain. Evan got out of the car and came around to give her a hug.

"You're all dirty," he said, tucking her hair behind her ears as he squinted at her. "What's going on?"

"Get in the car and I'll explain."

He opened the passenger door for her and then got in himself on the other side.

"I don't want to go back to the house," she said. "We need someplace private, like one of the beach parking lots."

He nodded, looking confused. Soon they were on the road again, and Caitlin began to tell him the whole horrible saga of what she'd seen on the beach the previous night. She started by saying, "Nathan's dad is dead."

22

let it come down

They pulled off the road at a secluded beach access, and the words continued to tumble out of Caitlin. She explained, in detail, what she'd witnessed. Several times her voice cracked, but she never cried. She had to get it all out of her system at once, like a poison. Evan tried to interrupt twice, but both times she told him to let her finish, so eventually he sat there like stone, listening. She ended by explaining that she'd wanted to call him last night, but had been too scared. Finally she ran out of words, blinking, trying to hold back the tears.

Evan seemed completely stunned. He couldn't even look at her, he just kept staring out the windshield at the increasing rain.

"So that's what happened," Caitlin said, wanting him to speak. "I know it's crazy, but it's the truth. We have to get to the police and tell them as soon as possible. I guess we should take the ferry?"

Evan still didn't respond. Caitlin put a hand on his arm,

thinking maybe he was going into shock, too. "Evan? Did you hear me?"

Slowly, he pivoted his head toward her. "I heard you," he finally managed. But that was all he said, so Caitlin stared back into his eyes, waiting for him to say more.

When he didn't, she prompted, "And?!" She was puzzled by his strange demeanor.

He rubbed his face, hiding it from view for a second. When he looked at her again, his expression had reconfigured into something cold and unfamiliar. "Get out of here," he finally muttered.

Caitlin didn't understand what was going on. "What?"

"Get out of here with your bullshit," he repeated louder. His eyes were narrowing to hostile-looking slits. Caitlin never would have believed that Evan could look this way. And she never would have predicted that he, of all people, would react in this manner.

"Evan, please, don't—" she began, but he cut her off.

"I don't believe you." He turned away from her again, straight ahead at the rain coursing down the windshield. "This is some weird-ass bullshit you're trying to pull. What a dumb story."

"It's not a story," she begged. Now the tears were trying to come full force, and she wiped one away. "Evan, it's me," she tried again. "You know I'd never lie to you. Don't act this way."

"I don't know you at all," he practically snarled, his fingers gripping the steering wheel like he wanted to hit something. "I've known Nathan my whole life. He's like a brother to me.

You know that." He looked at her with eyes clouded with anger and fear. "He'd never do anything like what you're saying. Of course his dad is an asshole, but Nathan's not capable of killing someone . . ."

"It was an accident. Like I said, I don't think he meant to. The gun just went off—" Any hope Caitlin had that Evan would cool down evaporated when he interrupted her again.

"Bullshit," he swore, literally stamping one of his feet in anger. "You're as crazy as these local bitches. I should have known someone from California would turn out to be insane." He made a swirling motion with one finger at his temple. "You need help." He looked back out at the ocean. "You're sick."

Caitlin felt too emotionally devastated to be angry. Evan had been everything she ever thought she wanted in a guy; now, he was a total stranger. She began to cry, despite herself.

"Evan, don't do this," she implored. "You know I'm not lying. Why would I make up such a crazy story? I don't have anything to gain." She wiped her nose on the back of her arm. "I know what I saw."

"Nathan's like my brother," Evan repeated. "I'd trust him with my life. I don't know shit about you, Caitlin. Hell, we've only known each other a few weeks. There's no way I'm going to the police with some story about Nathan you invented."

"You know Nathan's unstable," Caitlin pleaded. "His dad pushed him off the deck! They hated each other. It's not a story . . ."

"Sure it is." His mind was made up.

This can't be happening to me, Caitlin thought. It was like a repeat of the Bill situation with her mom. "If you won't help me, then I'll find the police myself," she said, wiping her eyes.

"They'll laugh at you."

"Maybe they will, but I can prove it. Did you see Nathan last night? Did you see his dad? What about the red Mercedes? I can take the police to the exact spot where the shooting happened on the beach."

"It doesn't matter if I saw them or not, and it doesn't matter what you say. I'm never going to believe your story."

"Is it really that implausible?"

He pretended to laugh. "It's a total joke."

Caitlin felt like she was trapped in a bad dream she couldn't wake up from. For all she knew, maybe Evan already knew everything and was protecting Nathan. Some very paranoid part of her mind even thought, *Maybe they're in on it together . . .*

"Bro's before ho's, huh," she muttered bitterly. "Now I know exactly what you meant by those words."

"Everything would have been cool if you hadn't made up this lie. But telling me one of my best friends is a murderer is just ridiculous. You're been watching too much TV." He scrutinized her face, like he was trying to puzzle something out. "Hey, is this some kind of scam? To extort money from Nathan and his dad somehow?"

Caitlin slapped him. She just couldn't help herself. She didn't hit him hard, but it was enough to startle him and make his head jerk back.

"Jesus!" he yelped. "What the fuck was that?!"

"You deserved it," she hissed as she opened the door of the car, letting in the rain. "You're a piece of shit, Evan. I'll be sure to tell the police how you wouldn't help me and tried to cover up for your friend."

"Whatever, Caitlin. I knew you were crazy, and the slap proves it," he said angrily, still rubbing his face.

"I was crazy to have trusted you," she retorted.

"If you were a guy, I'd hit you back."

"I'm sure you would."

She started getting out of the car and Evan yelled after her, "If I tell Nathan and his dad the lies you're spreading about them, you'll be the one getting arrested. No wonder your mom kicked you out of the house!"

She felt a surge of fear. If he told Nathan, then she'd be in serious danger. Yet she knew it was pointless to plead with him. Ignoring him completely, she stepped out and started walking away in the rain, feeling the rising wind whip at her hair. Her still-damp clothes got soaked again in an instant. She heard the engine roar to life, and the car pull back onto the road behind her. She didn't turn around to look. She couldn't face it.

"Crazy bitch!" Evan yelled one last time as he drove away wildly, nearly skidding on the wet pavement.

How could I have been so wrong about you? she thought. She felt a sense of despair and depression that she'd never known before, almost worse than the fear. Because Evan was good-looking and fun to hang out with, it had obviously blinded her to his real personality.

Danielle had been right all along, she thought. She realized she had to find Danielle and Luke and get to the police station on Hatteras. She knew the approaching hurricane would keep her prisoner on the island if she didn't get off it soon.

It took Caitlin fifteen minutes to walk back up to Buckley's, the rain turning her hair into thick, wet strands. She got on her bike and rode quickly back to Danielle's, hoping that now the girl would be there. She didn't know what else to do. As she rode, the rain came down harder, fat droplets pelting her head, mingling with the tears that continued to fall. But despite the tears, there was a fierce determination in her to get the truth out, no matter what. She'd failed to do herself justice when Bill had attacked her, but she wouldn't fail now. The fact that almost no one had believed her, or taken her seriously, just fueled her desire to do everything she could to fix the situation.

She rode through town, which looked even more barren than usual because of the heavy rain, and then to Danielle's trailer. Her heart lifted when she saw lights on in the front and realized that someone had come home. She hauled her bike through the gate and up to the front door.

It only took a second or two of pounding on it before Danielle came out, looking sleepy. Danielle could tell right away that something was really wrong, and as she swung open the door, she asked, "Caitlin? What the hell happened to you?"

"Danielle," Caitlin said. "Where were you? I came back last night and no one was here . . ." She walked into the dry warmth of the trailer, shaking.

"Oh God, I *was* here," Danielle said. "I had my headphones on. Rinita and Luke just got back this morning because the ferry wasn't running last night—"

"Danielle, I'm so sorry," Caitlin said. "I need to talk to you again, and not about us. You were right about everything, especially about Evan being an asshole. I should have listened to you! But I saw something terrible last night, riding back to the mansion, and we need to get the police."

Danielle could tell she wasn't messing around. Even though Caitlin was drenched, Danielle put her arms around her. "We need to get you a towel and some dry clothes. You look like you've seen a ghost or something."

"Almost."

Luke and Rinita were in Rinita's room watching a soap opera, so the two girls managed to sneak past them back to Danielle's room. Caitlin didn't want Luke to hear anything yet, in case it put him in danger.

Once they were in Danielle's room, Danielle shut the door and found a towel for Caitlin. Caitlin sat down on the edge of the bed and told the whole story, this time crying. She told her how Evan hadn't believed her, too. When she was done, she knew that Danielle could tell the story was true.

"That's some serious shit," Danielle said, shaking her head. "You're right, we have to get help. Do you think Evan will tell Nathan that you know?"

"God, I hope not or I'm screwed."

"Does Evan know where you are?"

Caitlin stood up, feeling agitated. "No . . . at least I don't think so."

"Then you're safe here for now. But it's a small island, and we don't want Nathan to come looking for you."

Caitlin shuddered at the thought. She didn't want to put Danielle, Rinita, or her own brother in danger. *Maybe I shouldn't be here,* she thought. Outside, the rain started drumming on the metal roof of the trailer with a feverish intensity, and the trees rustled their branches in the wind.

"I tried calling the police earlier," Caitlin explained. "At Buckley's. I should have told Joe, but I was too afraid. The police didn't answer, I guess because of the storm."

"I know. It's getting bad. Rinita said the ferry master told

them it was the last ferry unless the weather lightened up for a
bit. The police are probably busy trying to evacuate people from
the bigger islands. No one cares about Danbroke, of course. The
storm's just supposed to get worse and worse. I think we're going
to be trapped."

"With no police? Shit." She wished that she hadn't told Evan
anything because now she'd given it all away. She understood it
was possible he'd driven straight back to the mansion and told
Nathan the details of their conversation—which meant Nathan
would know she'd seen him. *He won't hurt me,* she tried to tell
herself. *He's not a psycho, right? Just some screwed-up kid from
Richmond whose dad abused him.* But the thoughts did little to
calm her down.

"Should we tell Rinita?" Caitlin asked, but Danielle shook
her head.

"It'll just upset her. She won't understand. We need the police." Danielle reached for the phone. "I'll call." Caitlin sat
down again on the bed, her head in her hands, waiting expec-
tantly. But when Danielle put it to her ear she frowned and lowered it slowly. "No dial tone."

"Fuck."

"Must be the storm," Danielle muttered. It was dark outside
even though it was still morning. "It happens around here."

Caitlin was glad Danielle sounded sort of calm, because her
heart was pounding madly in her chest. "What do we do now?"

"We all need to get on the first ferry out of here, if there is
one. If we do that, then everything will be okay. We can get to
Hatteras and get help."

"I have to try to find my mom," Caitlin added. "Not that I
really want to, but we can't leave her here. If Evan tells Nathan

what I said, then she might be in danger, too. Nathan could go looking for me at the Pirate's Lodge."

Danielle nodded. "Agreed. We can go by there on the way to the ferry station."

"What about the ferry master?" Caitlin asked, suddenly thinking he could help them. "He's almost like the police, right? Can we tell him about Nathan?"

"He's older than Rinita and he doesn't carry a gun. There's not much he can do." She took a deep breath. "I don't know, though. Maybe he could radio for help . . ."

"It's worth a try. Let's go get my mom first, though."

Caitlin hadn't been back to the Pirate's Lodge since the day Bill tried to kiss her, and she didn't want to return now. But she didn't feel as scared about going to the hotel and braving Bill if she'd be accompanied by Danielle, Luke, and Rinita. *Surely that'll prevent Bill from doing anything crazy,* she thought. To be honest, she was less frightened of Bill now that she'd seen a murder—an event that had been a thousand times worse.

"So let's do it," Danielle said nervously. "That's our plan."

Caitlin suddenly paused. There was something very important she had to say before they could proceed, and she swallowed hard. "Danielle, I just want to say I'm sorry I ran off with Evan and didn't hang out with you. It was really fucking stupid and lame of me. I hope you forgive me . . ."

Danielle gave her a quick smile. It was small, but genuine. "Don't sweat it. Everything's cool, okay? We've got worse problems now."

"No kidding." Caitlin took out a cigarette and tried to light it, but it was too wet. "What do we tell Rinita and Luke about what we're doing? They're going to think we're acting weird."

"We just tell them we need to get off the island because of the storm. Rinita will haggle with us, especially since they just got back. She hates to leave when the weather gets bad, but we can talk her into it." She pulled back her hair. "We'll tell them we're going to get your mom on the way, because we want to rescue her from the hurricane, basically."

"I hope it works."

Danielle looked grim again. "We don't have a choice. It has to. We'll do whatever it takes."

Caitlin nodded, her throat tight with fear. *Whatever it takes.* Together, Danielle and Caitlin got up and left the room, as the noise of the storm wailed outside, growing louder.

23
the abandoned hotel

After some skillful persuading by Danielle and Caitlin, Rinita and Luke grudgingly agreed to go to the ferry. Luke was surprised to see Caitlin again, but he seemed remarkably sullen and uninterested in her. Caitlin felt guilty about abandoning him.

"They've already started evacuating people from Danbroke," Danielle lied to her grandmother. "So we better go. Now." When Rinita protested, arguing with her granddaughter in Spanish, Caitlin stepped in.

"I'll pay for the hotel on the mainland," Caitlin insisted to Rinita. "We'll get somewhere nice for a couple days until the storm passes. That's the least I can do to pay you back for looking after Luke, and for letting us stay here."

"Run back to your boyfriend and leave us alone," Luke interrupted, seemingly just interested in making the argument worse. "I want to stay and see the storm! You haven't been around in forever, Caitlin. I'm not going anywhere with you."

"Yes, you are," Caitlin and Danielle said at about the same

moment. Caitlin wished she could think of a good bribe for Luke, like the four-wheeler, but nothing came to mind.

Neither Rinita nor Luke liked the idea of leaving very much, but Caitlin knew there was no time to waste. The storm was gathering strength, and they had to get off the island. *I don't want to get stuck here with a murderer,* Caitlin thought.

So Caitlin and Danielle finally hustled Rinita and Luke into Rinita's beat-up beige station wagon. With Danielle at the wheel, they pulled out of the gravel driveway and onto the road. The rain came down noisily on the roof as they drove. The windshield wipers were old and ineffective, so the windshield became a smeary mess. Caitlin was next to Danielle in the passenger seat, and Luke and Rinita sat together in the back. Luke kept kicking the back of Caitlin's seat. She knew he could sense that something was really wrong, but he didn't know what, and she wasn't about to enlighten him.

"Luke, stop kicking," Caitlin warned. The last thing she was in the mood for was her brother's attitude.

"This sucks!" he yelled. "I want to be here for the hurricane. It'll be cool."

"No, it won't," Caitlin said absently. Danielle's eyes were fixed ahead on the road, trying to see despite the miserable weather.

"Where's your lover boy?" Luke taunted Caitlin. "What are you even doing here with us? Shouldn't you be off banging him somewhere?"

Rinita said something to Luke in Spanish, sharply, and Luke said, "Sí, bueno." Caitlin was shocked. *Since when does Luke know any Spanish?* she wondered. *Rinita must have worked some kind of spell on him.* Indeed, Rinita's words seemed to calm him down, because he stopped kicking her seat. Unfortunately, he didn't stop talking.

"Mom doesn't care about us," he said. "She only wants to be with Bill. She'll be fine at the stupid hotel, Caitlin. Why do we need to get her?"

"We just *have to*," she replied. "She's our mom. We can't leave the island without telling her. It'd be wrong."

"No, it wouldn't," Luke argued. "I bet we could fly all the way back home to La Jolla and she wouldn't even notice."

"Luke, that's probably true, but now's not the time for this conversation. Just stay—" Her words were interrupted by a nearly simultaneous burst of lightning and a crash of thunder. Caitlin let out a startled yelp. "God, that was close."

"Shit," Danielle muttered, as the thunder rolled off into the distance. "There's no way the ferry's going to be running in this weather. No fucking way. The ferry master won't even be there."

"I know," Caitlin replied dismally. "What do we do?"

"We need to get off the road and find somewhere safe."

Caitlin gazed out the window at the storm. "Let's just try to get to the Pirate's Lodge, okay?"

"We should have stayed put," Luke told them, leaning forward between the seats. Caitlin had been hoping the peal of thunder had shut him up, but he didn't seem too bothered by the weather. "Driving around in a storm this big was a really smart idea, Caitlin. Good thinking."

"Look on the bright side, Luke," she snapped. "Maybe a tidal wave will come and drown all of us. That'd be cool, huh? Huh?"

"At least it wouldn't be boring like you are."

"There it is," Danielle suddenly said, pointing at the looming structure rising up from the sand in the distance on their left. "The lodge." Just looking at the hotel gave Caitlin the creeps. She didn't want to deal with Bill, or Mom. *And who knows, there's always a chance Nathan's already there—waiting for me.* It was a thought too scary to voice.

Another clap of thunder came, and the rain intensified even more. Leaves and tiny bits of debris swept across the windshield as the wind picked up. The storm had gone from bad to unbelievably severe in just the past few minutes. Caitlin hoped it only seemed that way because the hotel was closer to the ocean than Danielle's place. Even Luke was silent for a moment as Danielle drove up the winding road to the hotel's entrance. Water was running down one side of the road in a black river. Caitlin tried to ignore the weather and prepare herself for the inevitable confrontation with her mom. She told herself that she'd try everything she could to get her mother to leave, but she was willing to concede that her mom might not want to come. *Hell, she might be too drugged-up to even open her eyes,* Caitlin thought. *What do I do then?*

Danielle brought the car up to the front of the desolate hotel. There were no other cars around and no sign that the hotel had any occupants. Caitlin wondered if it were possible that her mom and Bill were already off the island and had simply abandoned her and Luke. Prior to this summer, it would have seemed unthinkable. Now, it was all too possible. Still, Caitlin wanted to believe that her mom wouldn't have stranded her. *Of course, Bill might have talked her into it,* she thought. Bill had obviously been a terrible influence on her mom.

Danielle parked the car and turned to look at Caitlin. The sky outside looked dark as night. "If the lines aren't dead, we can make calls from the hotel. We can get the number for a different police station or the Coast Guard, or something." She paused. Rinita was saying something to Luke, which was helping keep him occupied. "We might have to stay at the hotel for a while, if we can't call anyone."

"Call who?" Luke suddenly asked over the rain. It was drumming on the roof so loudly, it made Caitlin feel like she was inside a car wash. "What are you two talking about?" Rinita tried to settle him down again, while Caitlin and Danielle just ignored him.

Caitlin nodded at her friend. "I don't want to be left alone with Bill." She hoped there was safety in numbers. Luke started kicking the back of her seat again. "We need to bring Rinita and Luke inside with us."

"I don't want to get wet," Luke complained.

Caitlin turned around and glared at him. "Too fucking bad."

Luke looked like he wanted to argue, but Rinita smiled and patted his arm. "Listen to your sister," she said, and then she nodded at Caitlin.

"Whatever," Luke said grudgingly.

Caitlin looked at Danielle and said, "Let's go. Count of three." Moments later, they flung open their doors and rushed out into the gray downpour, the wind blasting Caitlin in the face. It was worse than she thought it would be. Sand got in her eyes, and she could feel grit in her mouth. Trying to shield her face with her hands, she glanced back to make sure the others were following her. They were, and as a ragged group they struggled up the steps to the front of the hotel. Rinita had some trouble moving fast, but they helped her along.

Soon Caitlin was standing under one of the awnings, with Danielle, Rinita, and an extremely disgruntled Luke. She knew Danielle could tell she was nervous about stepping back into the building where Bill had tried to assault her. Although they were under the awning, the rain was still coming in from all directions.

"It'll be okay, Caitlin," Danielle said. "We'll find your mom and make some calls and then get the hell out of this place."

I hope so, Caitlin thought. Yet she knew Bill well enough to know he was unpredictable, and that made her scared. Danielle took hold of the front door and pulled it open, and Caitlin followed, trailed by Luke and Rinita. All of them were soaking and cold, Caitlin's T-shirt sticking uncomfortably to her body. As she peered around, she tried to wring some of the water out of it onto the marble floor.

The first thing that struck Caitlin was the unearthly silence and darkness inside the massive lobby of the Pirate's Lodge. The chandeliers were turned off, as were all the other lamps. It took her a moment to realize that the hotel must have lost power in the storm. It was creepy inside, like being in a forgotten crypt, and the small amount of light that filtered through the windows was gray and gauzy. With the doors shut behind them, even the noise of the storm got muffled.

"Man, this place is weird," Luke said, eyeing the shadowy interior. Even he looked a bit unnerved to Caitlin, and it took a lot to rattle him because he was so desensitized by all his violent movies. Caitlin was glad she'd told him about Bill because now he'd know enough to be wary of him.

All four of them stood close to the front doors, looking around.

"Hello?" Rinita called out loudly, startling Caitlin. "Anybody home?"

"Doesn't seem to be," Danielle replied.

"There's a guy named Michael who works here," Caitlin said. "Maybe he's around somewhere." Yet she saw no sign of anyone at all. The front desk was unmanned. It was like the entire hotel had been abandoned—or maybe evacuated. If that were the case, Caitlin thought it was pretty curious that the front doors had been left unlocked.

"Where do you think they all went?" Caitlin asked.

"Doesn't matter," Danielle answered after a pause. She took a step forward into the gloom, the wet soles of her boots squeaking on the floor. "If we can't find your mom, we just need to find a phone. If they're still working, that is."

Outside, the storm continued to howl and wail, the wind rattling the windows and making some of the old shutters slap against them. Caitlin wondered if the storm was powerful enough to break the glass. *Probably.* Luke walked away from the group and tried to peer outside. "I bet there's some killer surf out there," he said, like he wanted to put on a wet suit and leap in the water.

"Yeah, real killer," Caitlin muttered. She wondered what Nathan was doing right at that moment. Or Evan. Then she tried to put them both out of her mind.

Danielle walked over to the front desk, and Caitlin followed her. There was hardly enough light to see. Danielle went around the counter and picked up the phone. She held it to her ear for a moment before lowering her arm. "Dead," she said, handing it over to Caitlin.

It wasn't much of a surprise. *So much for that stupid plan,* Caitlin thought.

A flash of lightning made Luke back away from the window. "Are you going to call Dad?" he asked her.

"No. The phone doesn't work." She put it down on the counter.

"Did Bill do something else to you?" Luke asked. "Is that why we're leaving?"

Caitlin shook her head. "We wouldn't be here if that was the case, would we? Just don't worry about it." She wished Rinita would step in again and take care of Luke because Rinita was the only person he listened to. But Rinita was preoccupied, looking out at the storm.

Danielle picked up another phone she'd found under the counter. It, too, was completely silent. "What room is your mom in?" Danielle asked.

"She was in suite two-twelve, unless she's staying in Bill's suite now." Caitlin listened closely because she thought she heard a noise, but it was just the ominous creaking of the hotel.

"I guess we have to go find her," Danielle said. She didn't sound too happy.

"I guess we do." Outside the wall of glass windows, Caitlin saw a streak of lightning come down from the roiling clouds and hit somewhere beyond the dunes. *This is getting really scary,* she thought, but she tried to stay calm. Her chest felt tight with anxiety.

"Luke, stay close to me," Caitlin instructed. Shockingly, for once he actually did what she said. They began walking down the long hall and up the stairs to the second floor. It got darker as they traveled because there were only a few small windows in the stairway. With every step, Caitlin felt more afraid.

When they got to the second floor, they went down the hallway until they came to her mother's suite. A thin stream of water was leaking down the wall at the far end of the hall, buckling the wallpaper. Caitlin stood at the door nervously, the other three looking at her in expectation.

"I guess I should knock," she finally said, getting up her courage. She drew back her hand and tapped on the door twice, in quick succession. They stood there waiting, but there was no answer. Caitlin knocked again and got no response. "She's not here," she muttered.

Luke stepped forward, nearly shoving her out of the way, and kicked the door as hard as he could. It was so loud and sudden, it made everyone jump.

"Jesus, Luke!" Caitlin said. "Take it easy."

"Mom, it's us!" Luke yelled, ignoring her. "Open up!"

Danielle still looked startled. Rinita just sighed. Worst of all, Luke's action also received no response from within the room.

Then Danielle reached forward and tried the doorknob, which was smart because the door turned out to be open. It swung wide, revealing the dingy living room. "That was easy."

"Thanks, Danielle," Caitlin murmured as she stepped into the suite, right behind Danielle. She heard Luke and Rinita following. *What must Rinita think about this whole mess?* she wondered, but Danielle's grandmother seemed to be remarkably sedate about everything.

"Nobody's home," Danielle said as they stood and looked around the room. The curtains were open, and dim light suffused the room, making everything look grimy and dark. There was a half-eaten croissant sandwich on the table, along with scattered bottles of wine on the floor and bottles of pills on the counter. Dirty clothes and newspapers were strewn all over the couch. It looked like a junkie's den.

Mom's really sick, Caitlin thought. *Bill has clearly enabled all her problems and made everything worse.*

Just then, Luke said, "Is Mom a total slob or what? This place needs some maid service pronto." Caitlin wondered if he realized the depths of their mother's problems.

"Is that room part of the suite?" Danielle asked, pointing at a closed door to their left.

"Yeah," Caitlin replied. "I think it's the bedroom." She wasn't exactly sure where things were, because the rooms were all small and labyrinthine. She didn't really want anyone to open that closed door, but she knew they had to, just in case her mom was passed out on the bed. She walked across the room, avoiding the wine bottles and other refuse, over to Danielle's side. "Here goes nothing." She gripped the handle and then opened the door, revealing a narrow hallway. On the left-hand side, one door down, she saw that a door was open. Strange sounds were coming from within.

Frightened, Caitlin took another tentative step forward, thinking, *What the hell?* She heard a low moaning voice, followed by a familiar husky voice, and then she realized exactly what she'd stumbled upon. *I'm going to throw up,* she thought. Her face started turning red as she spun around and said, "Luke, go down and wait in the lobby."

"You said we need to stick together—" he began, but then the unmistakable noises got louder and Rinita heard them, too. She grabbed Luke's arm and latched onto him.

"This way, young man," she said. "Not for your ears." She led him firmly out of the suite and back into the hall, as he protested all the way.

Caitlin was too embarrassed to look at Danielle. *My mom is having sex with Bill,* she thought, her stomach churning. *Drunk and on drugs, in this pigsty, not caring that there's a hurricane nearby, or that her kids are in danger.* It was pathetic and tawdry, and it made Caitlin feel disgusting herself, like she was tainted. Her fear of Bill, and of Nathan, slipped her mind for an instant, overpowered by revulsion.

Unable to take the feeling anymore, she banged on the wall of the hallway and yelled, "Mom! It's me! We've come to find you."

She heard Bill swear, "Son of a bitch!" and then her mother gasp. There was a thrashing noise, like bed covers being pulled back, and then the heavy sound of someone stepping onto the floor.

"Why are they here?" she heard her mother whine in a slow, hazy way that let Caitlin know her mom was far from sober.

Caitlin clenched her fists, trying to keep the hatred of her mom under control. *My mom has an addiction,* she told herself. *She can't help what she's doing or how she's living.* She looked at Danielle. Danielle was doing a good job of pretending not to understand exactly what was happening.

"I'll be in the living room," Caitlin called out to her mom through clenched teeth.

A moment later, Bill stumbled out and stood there in his jeans, sweaty and bloated, his potbelly hanging over the front of his belt. He didn't seem embarrassed like he should have been;

he looked swaggering and proud. He smelled like he'd been on a week-long bender, the alcohol seeping out of his pores.

Jesus, I'm glad Luke isn't seeing this, Caitlin thought to herself, knowing it would probably traumatize him for life. *Just like it's traumatizing me!*

"Hey there, girls," he said mockingly to Caitlin and Danielle. "Long time no see."

"I'm not here to see you. I'm here to see my mom," Caitlin said.

"Haven't you heard of knocking?"

"We did knock."

He looked like he didn't believe her. "Sure you did." He wiped his thin, sweaty hair back from his forehead. "This isn't your home, Caitlin. I own this hotel. You need to learn some manners. You're not back in pretty little California. You're on Danbroke."

"I have nothing to say to you, Bill. I just want to see my mom, understand?"

"So you can tell her more lies about me?" He chuckled. "I don't think so."

So she'd told him, Caitlin thought. That made the situation even worse. She could only guess what kind of stories he'd fed her mom. "You and I both know I haven't told any lies, only the truth." She peered behind him in the darkness, trying to see. "Mom?" she called out. "Can you get out here? It's an emergency."

"She doesn't have to do what you tell her," Bill said loudly. He took a step toward her and Caitlin fought the urge to run. If Danielle hadn't been there by her side, she definitely would have. She hoped that Luke wasn't hearing the conversation from the hall, but knew he probably was.

Caitlin's mother staggered out of the bedroom right at that moment, emerging behind Bill. She was wearing gray sweatpants and a pink blouse ruined with stains. She looked terrible, like she hadn't bathed in days, and her skin was yellow-gray. Her eyes struggled to focus when she looked at Caitlin.

"Where have you been?" she asked, sounding almost quizzical as she came farther into the room. "I went looking for you . . . Bill said—" She fell silent.

"Mom, don't you remember? We had a big fight and I moved out."

She shook her head slowly. "I remember." Then she said something that almost made Caitlin laugh it was so completely absurd: "Is everything okay?"

"Things are far from okay. We need to get out of here right away. There's a hurricane coming, and I need to get to the police because I saw a crime being committed, a really bad one, last night . . ." She didn't want to use the word "murder" because it sounded preposterous.

"Imagining things again, are we?" Bill asked. Caitlin wished she didn't have to keep staring at his bare, hairy chest. "What kind of crime?" She detected a sliver of worry cross his features. She realized he was afraid she was going to report him to the police.

"Yeah, what are you talking about, Caitlin?" her mom asked, sounding tired. She moved next to Bill, holding onto his arm woozily. "And where have you and Luke been living?"

"They've been with me," Danielle spoke up. "I can vouch for

them. My grandma and Luke are here too, waiting outside in the hall."

Caitlin's mom continued clinging to Bill. He patted her on the head, like she was a faithful dog.

"You can't call the police," Bill said, sounding almost gleeful. "The phones are out. The power, too—in case you didn't notice. It always happens when a storm this bad hits. I've been through six hurricanes, one of them a category three, so this is nothing." He reiterated the word for emphasis: *"Nothing."*

"That's great, Bill. Then you can stay right here and enjoy it," Caitlin said. "But *we* need to go someplace where there *is* a phone. And we need to take my mom with us."

"The phones are out everywhere by now." He sounded so sure of himself, but Caitlin guessed he couldn't be telling the truth. *Or could he?* "And Kathryn's not going anywhere without me."

Bill stared Caitlin down, and she didn't know what to do. She looked to Danielle for help, and then to her mom, who was just staring at the floor in a tranquilized daze. Bill continued to leer at Caitlin, a smirk growing on his face.

"Did I ruin your plans?" he asked. "Have you and your friend been playing Nancy Drew? You two should go back to whatever rock—or trailer—you've been hiding under and leave us grown-ups alone."

Caitlin was about to respond, but it was then that she heard Luke and Rinita start screaming.

24

prey

Luke raced into the room and yelled, "Holy shit, Caitlin! Some guy with a gun just came into the hotel! He's down in the lobby right now looking whacked!"

Caitlin knew exactly who he was talking about before he said another word, but he added, "It's that guy from the mansion— one of Evan's friends. I've seen him before—"

Time seemed to slow down as Caitlin spun around to Danielle. "It's Nathan!" she hissed. "We have to get out of here!"

"Oh my God." Danielle looked around wildly. It was like she hadn't believed this could really happen to them until now. Her face bore a look of pure panic.

Caitlin's mom and Bill just stood there, confused. Rinita came tumbling into the room, moving as fast as she could for an old woman, and slammed the door behind her, locking it.

"What is this, a goddamn trailer party?" Bill asked when he saw her. "I need a drink."

"Did Nathan see you?" Caitlin asked Luke, the feeling of

stark terror rising. "Tell me what happened." *He came for me after all,* was all she could think. *Nathan knows I saw what he did on the beach, and now he's going to try to kill me. He must have completely flipped out and lost his mind, worse than Bill.*

"He didn't see me or Rinita," Luke said, out of breath. "At least I don't think he did. We went down to the lobby. We were trying the phone again, when we saw him coming up the driveway in the rain. Right before he got inside, we ran to get you guys." He paused, staring out at the storm raging behind them outside. "I heard him come in the doors right when we got up to the second level. He was yelling his head off, Caitlin. What's wrong with him?"

"What the hell are you even talking about?" Bill asked as Caitlin tried not to pass out from fear. "Someone has a gun and they're in my hotel? Are you kidding me?"

Luke glared at him. "Did I stutter, motherfucker?" Caitlin recognized it as a line from *Pulp Fiction*, but Bill just looked incensed, and his face started turning purple.

"I'm going to teach you some—" Bill began, but Danielle started talking over him.

"Shut up, you freak," she snapped at Bill. "Caitlin told me about you, and what you tried to do to her. If you tried that with me, I would have kicked your balls up your ass, you fucking grotesque pig. I've always thought you were scum. I might live in a trailer, but at least I have morals."

"Danielle, stop—we need to think," Caitlin said, panicking. She was glad Danielle was giving Bill the abuse he deserved, but it wasn't the right time for it. They were safe for the moment, but it wouldn't take Nathan very long to figure out where they were. The door was locked, but she doubted it would stop a bullet. She knew he could easily blow out the lock if he fired directly at it, and then he'd be in the room. "What do we do?"

"We have to get out of here somehow," Danielle replied, as she looked around the tight confines of the suite.

"It's easy to get out," Bill snapped. "You just open the door and walk right out, the same way you came in. And that's what I'm going to do, to get to the bottom of this." He started walking to the front door of the suite.

"Aren't you listening?" Caitlin said. "There's a guy with a gun out there!"

"Luke's lying," Bill replied. "I'll bet he has an overactive imagination. Like you, Caitlin."

"No!" Caitlin said. "He's telling the truth." She figured it didn't matter anymore if she told everyone about what she'd seen on the beach. "The guy's name is Nathan Lowry and he's from Richmond. He's staying at a mansion on the other end of the island." She took a deep breath. "I saw him shoot his father last night on the beach when they got in a fight. It was an accident, I think. No one else was there, but I was hiding on the bike path, and now Nathan's come to get me—"

Inexplicably, Bill started laughing, so Caitlin stopped talking. "You are so full of crap, I'm surprised it's not oozing out your ears. You're doing this to get back at me and your mom, aren't you? You're jealous of us. You think I'm stupid?"

Realizing that she wasn't going to get anywhere with Bill, Caitlin decided to ignore him. She focused on her mom, addressing her like she would a child. "Mom, we have to leave this place. It's not safe for us anymore. You need to come with me, so you don't get hurt, okay?" She still hadn't figured out how they'd escape, with a potential madman roaming the halls.

"She's not going anywhere," Bill said, not even letting her mom speak. *Not that Mom seems capable of saying much,* Caitlin thought, given her mom's muddied eyes and expression.

Caitlin thought she heard a sound outside the room and froze. *Am I imagining things?* She wondered if Nathan were already on the second floor. Danielle seemed to have heard something, too, because she raced over to the window and looked down.

"Is this the only way out of here?" she asked Bill urgently, who paused to look at her.

He nodded grudgingly. "Other than the front door, I suppose so."

Caitlin went over to Danielle's side and Luke followed. The adults stood around behind them, Bill muttering something to himself, as Caitlin, Danielle, and Luke gazed down at the drop from the room's small four-pane window. They were only on the second floor, which meant they weren't too high up, but it would still be a jolt if they jumped. And any mistake might mean they'd twist, or break, an ankle.

Caitlin saw that outside, slightly to the left of the window, were piles of old, bundled cardboard, soaking wet and mostly disintegrating under the force of the storm. Some had blown loose and were being scattered around the trash-strewn yard. They would have to aim for the remaining piles, rather than the concrete patio. It didn't look pretty either way, but they didn't have a choice. Caitlin had no clue how she was going to get her mom or Rinita out the window, if at all.

"Listen," Caitlin said, turning to everyone in the room and

trying to sound convincing. "Nathan's extremely dangerous. He obviously knows I'm onto him, and he wants to keep me from going to the police. We all have to get out this window as soon as possible and away from this place. If we can get to the car, then we can go somewhere else—"

"You've got to be shitting me," Bill said. "Have you lost your ever-loving mind? No one's going out that window. There's nowhere to go in a storm this bad. Everyone's either left the island already or they're holed up someplace safe. You're crazy to go outside . . ."

"You're an idiot to stay," Danielle muttered. "You're going to get shot unless you listen to us. Of course, that might be what you deserve—in which case, don't worry about it." She unlatched the window, grabbed hold of the bottom of the frame, and yanked it up, letting the storm into the room.

Caitlin felt her ears pop, like the pressure change on an airplane, as the noise of the wind overwhelmed her. Rain immediately started blowing into the room through the screen, traveling sideways. The sky was now a peculiar greenish-gray color that looked completely unnatural. Caitlin had never seen anything like it before and thought maybe this was what a hurricane looked like. She wondered exactly how close Hurricane Ivy would come to Danbroke. It looked worse than just a "grazing."

"Fucking hell," Bill swore at Danielle. "Close that window right now before the carpet gets ruined."

"The carpet's already a piece of crap. What does it matter if it gets a little water on it?"

Caitlin couldn't believe they were wasting time arguing about something as mundane as the carpet when Nathan was in the same building as them with a gun. "Hurry up!"

"What's wrong with you kids?" Bill raged. "You need a one-way ticket to reform school. Both of you."

Grim-faced, Danielle stepped back and kicked out the screen with her boot. "Reform school, my ass."

Bill looked startled, but he rallied immediately. "You crazy Mexican bitch!" he began, stepping toward her, his flabby chest bouncing up and down above his belly.

"I'm Filipina!" Danielle yelled against the storm. "Not Mexican. Learn some geography, for fuck's sake."

Bill half raised one of his large hands, like he was thinking about slapping her. "This is *my* hotel, and I'm not going to stand for you trashing it, whatever shitty country you come from."

Caitlin didn't know exactly what Bill was about to do, and she never got a chance to find out. Right then, there was a huge banging sound on the door, and everyone jumped, even Bill. Someone was beating on the door and turning the handle back and forth. It was like a scene out of one of Luke's horror movies, only there was no way to press Pause and make the movie stop.

"Let me in!" a voice roared from the other side of the door, in a frenzy of anguish. Caitlin instantly recognized the voice as Nathan's, only it sounded like a twisted version of the guy she'd first met those weeks before, a deformed version, in which the darkest elements of his personality had taken complete control of him. "Caitlin, you're in there, aren't you?!" he screamed full throttle. "Open up!"

Caitlin didn't reply. She just couldn't. She felt all the blood leaving her head. Rinita hustled off into the dark hallway to the bedroom to hide, her hands over her ears. Bill looked like he was going to have a heart attack; clearly, he hadn't believed anything they'd told him and was now struggling with the realization that it might be true. Bill was a big man, but he wasn't any match for someone with a gun. *And he knew it.*

Caitlin's mother grabbed hold of Bill's arm again and said, as if she'd just woken up, "What's happening, Billy?"

"I don't know," he said, backing away from the door warily, Caitlin's mom clinging to him like an unwanted appendage.

The banging noises continued, as did Nathan's yelling. "Let me in!" he kept screaming over and over. "I have to see you, Caitlin! I have to talk to you!"

Out the window, a flash of lightning came and illuminated everyone in the room for a brief, flickering instant, like a strobe light. It galvanized Caitlin and Danielle into action.

"We're going out the window!" Danielle hissed softly at Caitlin, so Nathan wouldn't hear. "Now! If we get out, we can run into the forest near the beach and hide." Caitlin could tell she was worried about Rinita, but they were out of time.

Danielle put one leg out the window and swung herself over, so she was straddling the window ledge. "Follow me," she mouthed, as she brought her other leg around, the wind trying to push her back into the room. A second later, she launched herself off the ledge and was gone, plummeting down to the ground below. Caitlin didn't even hear her land because the noise of the storm was so loud. She admired Danielle's courage and moved to follow.

Bill and her mom had started arguing. "I'm going to open the door," Bill was blustering. "It's just some punk kid. I can handle him! I can handle anyone."

"No, don't—" her mom was pleading, trying to stop him.

Caitlin turned back to Luke as she reached the window, getting pelted by rain. "Luke, we have to run for it. I'm going to follow Danielle, and then you come right after me, okay? You have to do it. You don't have a choice, and you can't wimp out." The words were as much for her sake as for his.

Luke looked scared, but he was trying to hide it. He nodded in response. Caitlin wanted to send him out the window first, to protect him, but she knew it would be easier if she went out before him, to show him it was okay. If not, he might just stand there arguing, refusing to budge. Acting as quickly as she could, she sat on the ledge, getting doused with facefuls of cold rain, and looked down. The drop seemed more precipitous than it had when she'd been fully inside the room, and she felt a moment of vertigo.

Still, a two-story jump was much less scary than facing Nathan and his gun. Danielle seemed to be fine, crouching down there, looking up at the window into the rain. Her hair was blowing around in the powerful wind.

"Jump! Do it! C'mon!" Danielle was yelling, her words getting whipped away by the noise of the storm. Gusts of wind and rain buffeted her, strong enough to make her stagger against them. With a lot of effort, Danielle managed to hold her ground.

Caitlin took a deep breath, said a silent prayer, and then jumped. She landed on the pile of cardboard two seconds later, sliding sideways and almost cracking the back of her head on the brick wall of the hotel. But within a moment, she was back on her feet, staring up at the window, one of her knees aching, but feeling mostly okay.

The ferocity of the storm was like nothing Caitlin had anticipated. The rain was whipping her face so hard it hurt, and it stung her eyes, making her blink. Gusts seemed to come from every side, and the air was thick with sand and dirt. If this were just the edge of the hurricane, she couldn't imagine what it was like to be directly in its path. She put a hand over her eyes to protect them. The rain was cold, and it felt like it was sucking all the energy out of her, while the wind simultaneously tore the breath from her lungs.

"Luke!" she cried, looking up and shielding her eyes, knowing they didn't have much time. As soon as Nathan figured out they were jumping out the window, he'd just leave the hotel and run around back to hunt them down. "Come on!" she called out desperately. Danielle joined the chorus.

There was no way Caitlin was going to leave her brother behind with an armed maniac. Although she knew she was the person that Nathan wanted, she was pretty sure at this point he might hurt anyone who stood in his way. She wondered what the adults would do. Her mom and Rinita needed to jump out, too, but she didn't know if they could. She didn't care what happened to Bill.

As she stared up at the window, a head finally emerged, but it wasn't Luke's. To her absolute horror, she realized it was Nathan. *He's in the room already!* She screamed involuntarily, and then she felt a hand on her arm, jerking her sideways.

It was Danielle. "Run!" Danielle screamed in her ear, as thunder crashed above them. "It's too late!"

Caitlin screamed her brother's name one last time. Just before she tore her eyes away from the window, she saw the gun in Nathan's outstretched hand. For a horrifying second, she thought he might just start shooting at them right there. But he didn't. *I left Luke, Mom, and Rinita to die,* she thought, in an agonized internal wail, as she ran after Danielle, into the thick foliage behind the hotel that separated it from the sand dunes, the beach, and ultimately the ocean. She didn't know where they were headed; her only hope was that they'd be able to evade Nathan and hide in the underbrush. Now that Nathan was in the room with Luke and Mom, she didn't know what he'd do to them. Maybe Bill could fight Nathan off, but she doubted it. Nathan would just shoot him, too.

Caitlin ran until she and Danielle got into the thin strip of forest, not looking back because she didn't want to slow down for a second. Only when she reached the forest and collapsed did she risk a glance back at the hotel, but the window was obscured from view. Danielle slumped down next to her, both of them gasping for breath.

All Caitlin could think about was Luke and her mom. *I shouldn't have run,* she thought. *I'm the one he wants. Maybe he would have let the others go if I hadn't run. Maybe I could have reasoned with him.* But she'd run out of pure instinct, without time to think it through. And she knew if she'd just stood there, Nathan might have shot her without giving her a chance to reason with him at all.

"I'm scared," Caitlin said, trying to get her breathing normal again. She kept her eyes glued to the wall of trees they'd run through, waiting to see if Nathan would reappear.

"There's no time to be scared," Danielle said, but she sounded as though she was talking to herself.

The trees prevented some of the rain and wind from reaching them, but not much. It seemed like the temperature was plummeting with every passing minute. Caitlin's clothes chafed as the rain continued to fall down on her, and she had to blink every second to clear her eyes.

"Where are we going to go?" Caitlin asked. She was thinking maybe they could just stay outside, but she knew they had to find help.

Danielle was looking around. "There's nowhere to go, no one to call. It's just us."

Right then, fighting back tears of frustration and fear, Caitlin had an idea. She didn't know if it would work, but she realized it was the best chance they had. "Danielle, this is crazy," she yelled over the storm, "but Bill has a yacht. He went sailing with my mom on it, I think. A boat's probably the absolute worst place to hide in a hurricane, but I bet there's some equipment onboard we could use to call for help. It would still have power, maybe."

"Maybe." Danielle thought for a second. "I don't know if we can even get on a boat in this kind of weather. Where is it docked?"

"Unless Bill moved it, it's in the inlet just up the beach, that way." Caitlin pointed to their right. "There's a small pier behind the hotel, and it's the only boat there. Or at least it was."

"It might be better to stay here in the forest . . ." Danielle's words trailed off. "But you're right. We can't just leave Nathan alone with everyone. We have to help." Caitlin knew Danielle was probably terrified about Rinita—who was virtually her only family—but she could see that Danielle was trying to suppress the fear.

Caitlin nodded. She knew they'd be more exposed on the beach if Nathan were already out there with his gun. She also knew the waves would be huge, and possibly flooding the inlet and crashing over the dock and boat, which would make it impossible to get onboard. *And even if we get on the boat, there might be nothing there we can use to call anyone,* she thought. *It could be a complete, stupid folly.*

Despite all of this, she abruptly said, "Let's do it." At least that way they'd be taking action and not just sitting around waiting for Nathan to stalk them like victims.

Danielle looked at her. "We might get hurt, Caitlin. Or worse."

"I know."

"But it's worth it?"

"I think so."

Caitlin slowly stood up, followed by Danielle, brushing leaves and dirt off her knees. They began running through the forest together, in the direction of the inlet and the dock. The thunder and lightning continued above them, nonstop, as the storm raged on.

My idea is either going to help Luke, Mom, and Rinita, or else it's going to get me and Danielle killed, Caitlin thought as she plunged forward through the branches, toward her fate. She'd be saving Nathan the trouble of shooting her if she drowned trying to get on the yacht. Yet she was determined to do whatever it took to save herself, and her family, as well.

I'm not going to give up, she thought. *Until I'm dead . . .*

25

the yacht

When Caitlin and Danielle tumbled out of the forest and onto the dunes, they both froze at the sight of the ocean. What had once been a placid sheet of water, gently lapping at the smooth white beach, was now a roiling mass of turbulent waves. The water was dark, with whitecaps and currents everywhere, and its surface was jagged as continuous sheets of rain lashed it from above. The wind had whipped it into a frenzy, and some of the waves were easily eight feet tall. Caitlin remembered how calm the water had looked her first day on the island and found it hard to believe this was even the same stretch of ocean.

Caitlin looked over at Danielle and could tell that she was thinking the same thing. Without even needing to talk about it, together the two girls retreated back to the edge of the forest, where they knelt at the base of a tree and hid again. Caitlin knew at any moment Nathan might stumble upon them, but she tried to focus on the task at hand. She shielded her eyes from the rain as she stared out at the inlet, which was several hundred yards to their right. The water stretched out on either side of it, crashing onto the shore with resounding force. Caitlin could barely see the dock and Bill's yacht.

"How the hell are we going to make this happen?" Danielle asked desperately, wiping water out of her eyes. "I don't want to go near that thing."

"I know." Caitlin kept her eyes focused on the boat. Bill had obviously underestimated the power of the storm, or didn't care about his yacht, because it was still there, tied to the dock, bobbing up and down violently in the waves. It looked like it might break free at any second, which was a disturbing thought. Still, because the dock was elevated, many of the waves passed underneath it, which meant it was possible—in theory, anyway—to get onboard.

I'm just not sure I want to get onboard, Caitlin thought. She didn't even know exactly what she was hoping to find there because she didn't know anything about boats. She assumed there had to be some kind of communication system that didn't depend on phone lines or power lines. The boat was decent-sized, with a high, covered platform for driving the vessel and a large cabin underneath. She thought at the least, the yacht might be a good hiding place if Nathan came after them. He'd never suspect that they'd seek out the most dangerous spot on the island to hide.

"We can't wait around forever," Danielle said, staring back at the forest behind her, looking for Nathan.

"Should we go for it?" Caitlin asked, swallowing hard. She knew it was a huge risk. "Like we planned?"

"It doesn't look very fucking safe," Danielle said urgently, slicking her wet hair back, "but neither is standing out here. Whatever we do, we need to decide right now."

Caitlin felt like her mind was only half there; the other half kept thinking this was all some sort of delusion. She tried not to think about Luke or her mom and what might be happening up in that room with Nathan.

"I'd rather drown than get shot," Caitlin muttered. She looked at Danielle, and Danielle nodded.

Again, the two of them came out of the forest and began to run down the beach in the direction of the inlet and the dock. The sand was soaked, and it tugged at Caitlin's shoes like mud as she ran. It was impossible to see, and each time a whip crack of lightning came, she was afraid she was going to get hit. She felt completely exposed, at the mercy of the storm and Nathan's madness, too.

The whole time she ran, she kept looking behind her to see if Nathan was following them. She nearly stumbled a few times in the sand, but she kept plunging ahead. She knew she couldn't afford to fall down and waste a second because now they were visible. If Nathan had a view of the beach from wherever he was, he'd know exactly where they were headed.

Finally, after what seemed like an eternity but could have only been a minute or two, Caitlin and Danielle reached the groaning wood dock. Water was spraying over its surface, and for a second, Caitlin was afraid she'd be too scared to even try to get on the boat.

"We have to wait for a break in the waves," she yelled, but as the words left her mouth, she realized there would be no break. The waves were pounding the beach and surging through the inlet one after another, drenching the dock. The water was making a deafening hissing sound, like an army of cicadas. She knew they wouldn't have to go far down the dock, just enough so that they could get onboard and inside. But that was too far.

Shit, how are we even going to get inside anyway? she suddenly wondered. She doubted that Bill had left the keys in the cabin door. The worst would be to get swept overboard into the water while trying to break in. There'd be no way to survive during such a violent storm. If the waves didn't drown her instantly, the currents and riptides would suck her out to sea.

Caitlin and Danielle paused on the beach in front of the dock, both struggling to catch their breath. Caitlin looked behind them into the forest, straining to see through the rain if Nathan was headed their way.

"You see anything?" she screamed over the noise, the fear making her voice break.

Danielle shook her head. "Not yet."

"We have to do it," Caitlin said, trying to muster up her courage. "Right?"

"I think so."

Neither of them wanted to go first, so they went together, holding onto each other for balance as they stepped onto the slippery surface of the dock. The boat was less than fifteen feet ahead of them, grinding and scraping its hull against the pylons as it lurched around. It made a dull, thudding sound that reverberated down the length of the dock, and Caitlin felt it in her feet. As they moved forward, she crouched low to the surface. The dock itself felt like it was moving back and forth in the surging water. Danielle was still right next to her, moving at the same pace, a look of extreme concentration on her face.

"Look out!" Danielle suddenly yelled, clinging to Caitlin tighter as they saw a huge surge approaching the dock just thirty feet out. Caitlin fell to all fours, bracing for the wave and gripping the wooden slats. Danielle did the same. Before Caitlin knew it, a wall of freezing water crashed over her, making her gasp. But she didn't give up her hold on the dock.

When the wave passed, Caitlin looked over at Danielle, who'd been knocked back a few paces. "Are you okay?" she asked. Danielle nodded, shivering. Within a few seconds, they were both moving forward again. The wind kept threatening to knock Caitlin over, so she kept her head down and her eyes half-closed to protect them. *I must be insane,* she thought. But they didn't have another plan.

When Caitlin reached the boat a pace ahead of Danielle, she looked back down the beach and still didn't see anyone there. Caitlin felt sudden exhilaration. It looked like they were going to be able to find temporary refuge in Bill's yacht without Nathan seeing them. The next question would be whether or not they could find a way to call the Coast Guard, or the police, from inside the vessel. *We have to make this work,* Caitlin thought. She was hoping there'd be some kind of emergency distress signal onboard, or flares. *Not that flares could even be seen by anyone in a storm like this.*

The yacht was moving violently, but it was tied so close to the dock that it actually looked possible to climb onto the back of it. The only problem was it looked equally possible to get washed off by a wave, or thrown overboard if the boat lurched sideways unexpectedly. The entire back fishing deck was filled with sloshing seawater that had already washed into the boat.

"How are we going to get onboard?!" Caitlin yelled. The tips of her fingers were starting to feel numb from the cold and the wind. Another wave crested over the dock, spraying her and nearly making her fall. She knew they couldn't stay out in the open much longer.

Danielle didn't even answer Caitlin's question because she was so overwhelmed by the storm. She staggered against one of the pylons that supported the dock, trying to get a moment's respite. Caitlin followed and did the same thing, hugging the wet wood, trying not to let the wind push her off the edge. All around her swirled rain and seawater.

To reach the door of the boat, she saw that they'd have to clamber onboard the back and then try to get through a small metal door to the cabin—a door that was presumably locked. *There has to be a better way,* Caitlin thought. She wondered if they could climb through one of the two windows on the side of the yacht. Of course, that could be even more dangerous, but she thought it might be worth a try. It would mean they wouldn't have to risk standing around on the back of the boat while they struggled with a locked door.

Clearly, Danielle was thinking the same thing, because she moved forward and started kicking at one of the windows with her boot. For a second, Caitlin thought she might succeed in breaking it, but the window didn't give. Danielle geared up for a final kick, but Caitlin was afraid she might slip and fall, so she yelled, "Stop!"

Caitlin walked swiftly up to the other window and put her hand over the abyss between the boat and the dock to touch the glass. The boat was moving up and down, and back and forth, but she managed to grab hold of the window's outside latch. She struggled to keep her grip, even though it tore at her arm as the boat lurched. She supported herself by grasping the edge of a pylon with her other hand while she continued to tug at the latch. As she put all her weight into it, to her surprise and relief, she discovered that the window wasn't locked. She managed to slide it open in one motion, aided by the boat, which plunged forward at precisely the right moment.

"Danielle! Look!" she yelled, motioning to the window. Danielle had been covering her eyes from the blinding rain. "We can get inside now!"

Danielle saw and came over immediately, literally crawling down the dock so she wouldn't fall. Waves continued to spray across them.

Caitlin felt terrified about getting onto the boat, but she knew they had to do it. She looked down at the gap and could see the ocean foaming and boiling below. As the boat moved around, the gap narrowed and widened. Sometimes it was an inch across, sometimes more than two feet. Caitlin was terrified of the gap, afraid that she'd slip into it and get crushed.

Danielle yelled into her ear, "We're going to fall in!"

Caitlin knew it was too late to go back. *Besides, where would we go?* She leaned forward, grabbing onto the edge of the window. She tried to keep her feet stable on the dock, despite the wind, the rain, and the waves. *I need to get through this window,* Caitlin told herself. *That means I need to stay calm and not freak out.* She looked quickly around and made sure there were no large waves approaching. Then she looked back at Danielle. "I'm going for it!" Without allowing herself to think too much, she pushed herself up off the dock and in through the window.

Her head and arms made it, but she didn't have enough forward momentum. She felt herself slipping back into the gap as the boat rose up in the water. She started to panic. Her legs slipped against the slick fiberglass hull of the boat. She felt her stomach clench as she clawed at the inside of the boat, trying to grab onto something. The boat smacked back down on the other side of a wave, and Caitlin scrabbled to get through the tight opening, her legs flailing. For a second, she thought she wouldn't make it and her whole body went ice cold. Then, gasping for air, she finally tumbled into the dark interior of Bill's yacht.

She fell onto a sharp object that dug into her back, and she screamed, trying to get her balance. She rolled over, and managed to push herself up against the inside wall of the cabin. As she got to her feet and looked back through the window, she saw Danielle following directly after her. As Danielle jumped, she grabbed the girl's hands and helped pull her through the window. Danielle sprawled onto the floor next to her. Soon they were both sitting there, holding on to whatever they could so they didn't get tossed around.

"That was way too fucking close," Caitlin said, shaking. The contents of the boat were scattered all over the floor like rubble, and her legs were scratched and bloody. But for the first time in a while, they were out of the rain, and hopefully hidden from Nathan.

Danielle got on her knees and Caitlin saw she had a deep cut on her arm. "I'm okay," Danielle said, as she moved over and shut the window. The noise of the storm receded to a dull roar.

The boat was moving around so much, it was hard to think. The cabin was cramped, and Caitlin crawled forward on her knees, with Danielle, over to the small, rectangular, rain-splattered front windows facing the beach. From her vantage point, she could see that the beach was still deserted, with no sign that Nathan had followed them.

Danielle started rummaging around right behind her, looking for any equipment that would let them send out a call for help. "I don't see anything yet," she said. Caitlin turned away from the windows and joined in the search, thinking, *There has to be something we can use. Boats send out SOS signals all the time!* She saw an array of buttons and switches, but they looked like navigation tools to Caitlin—not that she knew the first thing about how to operate a yacht like this.

"What's this thing?" she asked Danielle, pointing to an electronic-looking black box.

Danielle shook her head. "Something to do with the engine. I think."

Caitlin continued searching as she cursed herself inwardly for being so stupid. She couldn't see anything that resembled a communication device—no phones, no CB radio, no computer, not even a walkie-talkie. *Nothing.* She felt a numbing sense of despair because obviously coming on the boat was a bad idea. They'd put their own lives at risk while still failing to save their families. Caitlin felt terrible that she'd dragged Danielle down with her into this awful situation as well.

If only I'd listened to her at the start, we wouldn't be here right now and Luke and Mom would be safe, Caitlin thought. But Caitlin knew she couldn't go back and undo her past mistakes. She told herself she had to persevere and hope that somehow they'd find a way to send for help, while keeping themselves alive.

"There's nothing here!" Danielle said, wading unsteadily through the rubble on the floor. "We're fucked!"

Caitlin was about to respond that maybe they should get the hell out of there, but then the boat slammed against the dock and knocked her forward, making her gasp. She was afraid the boat might start disintegrating. As she got her breath back, something caught her eye. Out of the rain-soaked front windows, she thought she saw a distant figure moving on the beach. She froze, her pulse skyrocketing. *It couldn't be.* She hoped it was an illusion.

"Danielle!" she hissed. "I think I see someone."

Danielle stopped moving and stood up, clutching the side of an open cabinet, trying to keep her balance. "Where?"

Caitlin pointed out the window. "On the beach."

Danielle squinted. It was difficult to make the person out because of the rain, but Caitlin could definitely see a dark figure moving across the windswept landscape. It looked like its head was down, against the wind and rain, as it walked across the beach, parallel to the water. It was moving very fast and very purposefully.

"Someone's really out there," Caitlin said, because that much was obvious. She felt like she was choking on her words. "Is it Nathan?"

"I can't tell," Danielle replied. "Let's hope it's some other crazy local . . ." Caitlin and Danielle stood there, gripping some cabinets as the boat moved, both trying to figure out who they were looking at.

Could it really be anyone other than Nathan? Caitlin wondered. She hoped fervently that it was someone who'd help them, but rationally she knew it wasn't. No one else would be crazy enough to come anywhere near the beach as a hurricane was passing by, not even all the misfits who called Danbroke home. *It has to be Nathan.* Caitlin wondered if that meant her brother, her mom, and Rinita were dead now—or if it meant Nathan had let them go. She was almost too burned-out to feel anything, except sick and disoriented from the reeling of the boat.

Neither Caitlin nor Danielle moved or made a sound as they watched the dark figure. The storm continued to rage above them, water gushing down from the top canopy of the boat and making the windows even more difficult to see through. Caitlin didn't know if Nathan would be able to figure out where they were. The boat was the only hiding place down by the water, but she hoped Nathan would underestimate them and think they'd stayed hidden in the forest. *But then why would he be on the beach?*

A sudden flash of lightning illuminated the beach for a second, but it was still too hard to see who the person was. Caitlin tried to see if he had a gun in his hand. She didn't know what they'd do if Nathan figured out they were on the boat. *Die, perhaps,* she thought bleakly.

Danielle turned toward her and began to whisper something, but Caitlin grabbed her and brought a finger to her lips. She'd been watching the person on the beach, and something truly terrifying had happened. The figure had stopped moving and was looking straight in their direction. Slowly, it raised an arm and pointed at them.

26
life and death

"He's seen us," Caitlin said. She knew it was true, even though she didn't know how it happened, because it would be impossible for someone outside to see into the boat. Yet she felt the knowledge blossom inside her: Nathan was pointing right at them, he knew where they were, and he was going to come after them with his gun.

"Are you sure?" Danielle asked, grabbing Caitlin's hand as she watched the figure stare back at them. "It's dark in here."

"But he's pointing . . ." Caitlin didn't want to take her eyes off that dreadful figure on the beach. Despite the gusts of wind and the torrential rain, the figure stood its ground.

"We're stuck in here," Danielle said, followed by something in Spanish that might have been either a curse or a prayer. *Either way, it won't help us,* Caitlin thought. She felt they were beyond the help of any religion now. She didn't even want to blink in case she missed the moment when the figure started moving again. *Or shooting at us.* She was desperately hoping that somehow she was wrong, and it would just turn around and walk back into the forest, or continue its deranged journey down the beach.

She knew that wouldn't be the case, though, and it wasn't. The figure took a slow step down the beach, straight toward the dock. Thunder crashed, and Caitlin and Danielle flinched, but the nightmare figure continued its inexorable journey toward them, seemingly unfazed by the storm around it.

Caitlin knew they didn't have time to get off the boat and run, and she knew that the boat—with its multiple windows—made them easy targets for a killer. Nathan had already killed at least one person, so she guessed it would be even easier for him to kill again. He'd had a psychotic break, she figured, like one of those crazy kids who goes to the mall and starts a shooting spree. *And now, even though we don't deserve it, we're going to be his random victims,* Caitlin thought.

Danielle was rigid with fear next to her. "He's coming our way," she managed to say.

Caitlin nodded. There was no time to look for a weapon, barely time to hide themselves somewhere in the small vessel. It was impossible to move quickly enough, like being in a nightmare where everything slows down.

Just as Caitlin was about to tear her eyes away from the approaching figure, which had just reached the wooden dock, she suddenly realized something. The figure looked too large to be Nathan. It had a height he didn't possess.

Her thoughts racing, she blurted out, "Danielle, look! I don't think it's him!"

"What?"

"Look closer." Granted, it was hard to gauge a person's size on the massive beach, especially when the waves were moving the boat constantly, but there was something about the approaching figure that struck a familiar chord in Caitlin. She realized, with a rush of knowledge, that it wasn't Nathan at all headed their way, but Bill Collins.

She exhaled a huge breath of air. "Jesus fucking Christ, it's not Nathan! Danielle, it's not him." She felt her tensed shoulders start to relax. Bill was bad, but he wasn't as bad as Nathan.

Danielle looked at her with large eyes in the dim light. "If it's not him, then who is it?"

"Bill."

Danielle squinted. "God," she whispered. "You're right."

Caitlin knew Bill was a complete monster, and that what he'd done to her was unforgivable, but she had to admit she felt nothing but relief to see him headed their way. It meant that Nathan wasn't about to murder them in cold blood, and that Bill, and presumably the others in the hotel room, had somehow survived. She speculated that maybe he'd been able to overpower Nathan and get the gun away from him. Bill was an unlikely hero, if that word could even be used to describe him, but Caitlin was ecstatic to see him approaching instead of Nathan.

Bill was close enough now so that when lightning struck nearby, it lit up his features, and both Caitlin and Danielle could recognize him for sure. *No wonder he doesn't seem scared by the storm,* Caitlin thought. *He's been through so many before.*

Bill headed down the dock, as Caitlin and Danielle struggled to open the window and yell for help. They got it open and stuck their arms out. He saw and waved back. Fighting off torrents of water, he managed to reach the first pylon, and then the second, until he was almost at the boat.

"Help us!" Caitlin was yelling as the boat banged against the dock. Both she and Danielle kept waving their arms out the window.

Surprisingly, Bill brushed past them and leapt onto the back of the vessel, fumbling with a set of keys to unlock the door to the cabin. A moment later, the door flung open, bringing with it a huge gust of wind and ocean spray as he stumbled inside. Because of his height he had to stoop as he entered.

"Thank God you found us," Caitlin said, reluctantly eyeing their savior. "We were hiding from Nathan. Is everyone okay? What happened to Luke and my mom?"

Bill shut the door behind him, fighting against the wind, and then turned back around. His arms were stretched out on either side of him for balance, so he was blocking the exit. "Shut that window," he commanded in a less-than-friendly voice. The dim light made it hard to see the expression on his face.

His attitude disturbed Caitlin, but then again, he'd always been creepy, so why should he be any different now? Danielle slid the window shut, muffling the storm again, and stared back at him, looking puzzled.

"What's the deal?" she asked him.

Although Caitlin figured Bill was there to rescue them, she was starting to get an uneasy feeling in her stomach. *There's no way Bill would be insane enough not to help us, right?* she wondered. *Not after everything we've been through with Nathan. Surely one madman is enough . . .*

But when Bill started speaking, Caitlin got the answer to her question. "You're on my boat," he snarled. "This is my property. What the hell are you doing here?"

Was he fucking kidding? Caitlin wondered, as she tried to

think of an appropriate response. "There was no place else to go," she said defiantly, trying to stay calm even as the boat heaved up and down over another wave. "There's a hurricane out there, or haven't you noticed? We thought Nathan was chasing us."

"We didn't want to get shot," Danielle added.

"You two thought wrong. Nathan's still back at the hotel." Bill's words were curt and aggressive.

"We didn't know that," Danielle replied. "Nathan came after Caitlin because of what she saw him do, so we figured he chased us outside—"

"Nathan's a pussy," Bill interrupted. He unzipped his soaking jacket, staggering a little, revealing a black T-shirt. "Want to know why Nathan was looking for you, Caitlin?" Caitlin shook her head yes. "He wanted to confess his sins. He knew you saw him shoot his dad, but he just wanted to talk."

Caitlin was confused. "But he had a gun . . ."

"He's such a moron, he didn't know what he was doing. I think he wanted to give the gun to you. He's planning on turning himself into the police after the storm dies down, but he wanted you to corroborate his story—that it was all an accident. He's afraid they'd call it murder. Afraid of facing justice. He needed you to explain things, to help him out." Bill paused for a peal of thunder. "Guess he just went about it the wrong way. Killing a man isn't for everyone, you know. It addled his mind." Bill grinned, a sickening kind of smile that distorted his features. "There was no need to run anywhere, you stupid girls. Understand? You put your lives in danger for no reason at all."

Caitlin felt like she'd been slapped, and she gripped the

countertop. She couldn't believe the things that Bill was saying, or the way he was saying them.

"You don't have to worry about Nathan, and you never did," Bill continued, still grinning and sounding almost proud of himself as he looked back and forth from Caitlin to Danielle. "He's up there in suite two-twelve, sobbing his guts out to that old Mexican woman and Kathryn right now." He spat onto the already wet floor. "Pathetic."

"Bill, please, we need to get help, don't you see that?" Caitlin begged. "Is there a way to radio the Coast Guard from here?" She'd decided to pretend that everything was okay, because she didn't know what else to do.

Bill leered at her. "Sure there's a way, but we don't need them. This boat and me have been through a lot together, including storms worse than this one. We'll be fine. You two girls need to do what I say, though . . . if you don't want to get hurt."

Caitlin got the sense that he was talking about more than getting hurt by the storm. "What do you mean?" she asked hesitatingly.

"I mean, you need to do *exactly* what I say." He wiped a hand over his eyes, getting the water out of them. "Note for note."

"Listen, if Nathan isn't a problem, then we need to get the hell out of here, because it's not safe," Danielle said, trying to reason with him. "I want to see my grandma. There's nothing keeping us here anymore."

"Is that what you think?" he retorted mockingly.

"Yeah, what are we waiting for?"

He stood there, swaying and grinning, like he was toying with them.

"What the fuck is your deal, Bill?" Danielle snapped. "Am I missing something?"

He swung his head to glare at her. "You're missing the fact that this is my yacht, Danielle. My little piece of the island. I make the rules here. Just like at the Pirate's Lodge."

"Caitlin told me what you did to her there," Danielle spat, as Caitlin felt a rising sensation of despair. "She told me everything—all the details. If you don't help us get out of here, then I'm going to tell everyone. You'll get arrested and charged with assault."

"Danbroke is the wild west, girl. You should know that by now. Good luck getting anyone to listen to whatever you say. You live in a trailer. I own the largest hotel on the island."

"A shitty hotel," Danielle said, refusing to back down. "I won't stop until someone believes me."

"Your threats don't scare me," he said, glaring down at her. He took a step forward, still using his gangly arms for balance, but neither Caitlin nor Danielle budged. This was mainly because the cabin was so small that they had no choice. "Want to know why?"

"Why?" Danielle asked, before Caitlin could intervene.

"Because you have to be conscious to talk!" Faster than Caitlin thought a man his size could move, Bill lunged forward and hit Danielle square in the chest, knocking her backward against the cabinets. Her head hit a metal shelf sticking out of the wall, and Caitlin heard a nasty cracking sound, even over the noise of the storm. There was no way she could have stopped Bill, because it happened so fast. In an instant, Danielle went from standing next to her to lying in a crumpled, silent pile on the floor. As the boat listed to the left, Danielle's body slid in the rubble and banged into the wall.

Caitlin watched in disbelief as Bill started to chuckle to himself. *I wish I could just make this all disappear,* Caitlin thought. While keeping her eyes glued to the maniac just a few feet in front of her, she knelt down in the rocking boat, trying to keep her balance as she reached out and felt for Danielle.

Danielle looked like she was completely knocked out. *She hit her head hard enough to get a concussion,* Caitlin thought, *or worse.* She tried to figure out what she should do next, how to fight the monster. She wanted to look around for a weapon, but she was too scared to take her eyes off Bill.

"Your friend had it coming," Bill intoned blandly.

Caitlin was terrified he'd walk forward and start attacking her, but instead he did the opposite. He took two small steps backward, giving her room. She felt relieved at first, but then realized he'd only done it because he was confident he had her cornered.

"I never liked that girl much," Bill said, as though he were talking to himself. It was like he didn't realize they were on a boat in the water, in a dangerous storm. He seemed to be living in some interior fantasy world that bore no relation to reality. "Danielle didn't belong here. Never did, never will. Not like you, Caitlin. You belong here: both you and Kathryn . . . you even more than her."

Caitlin wanted to tell him what a psycho he was, but she knew she couldn't afford to provoke him. She'd have to measure her words and actions carefully if she wanted to get to shore safely with Danielle still alive.

"Bill, why are you doing this to me?" she asked. A roll of thunder passed overhead. "I think we should both go back to the hotel and take Danielle with us. I won't say anything—we can just say she slipped and hit her head. It's fine with me. I just want to be out of the storm and safe again." That was a lie, of course, because she was never going to let Bill get away with what he'd done—and Bill knew it.

"Nice try," Bill said, chuckling again. "But I don't believe you."

The boat lurched as a wave pounded it, and both Caitlin and Bill were temporarily knocked off balance. The boat tilted perilously to one side before recovering. Caitlin noticed that because of his size, it took Bill a little longer than her to get to his feet. She thought maybe that knowledge would come in handy; she just didn't know how yet.

Bill kept his eyes on her. "Now that your friend's out of commission, we get to be alone for a spell. That's all I've wanted, Caitlin, since I first saw you." Bill paused, putting an arm out to steady himself. "As soon as we met, I knew that I had to have you, that it would be like the old days with Kathryn. The best times of my life. I was young then, and strong, and I could think straight." He furrowed his brow. "I was confident. My mind wasn't clouded. I'd do anything to get those days back, and I mean it—*anything*. I've been waiting for my chance all these weeks. Did you get that photo I left for you in the bathroom stall?"

She didn't answer, but he continued anyway.

"I've been following you, Caitlin. Watching you. I've seen you and that boy tongue kissing on the beach. I can teach you things you've only dreamed about. The photo was my way of letting you know that you were never alone. I've got so many more of them back at the lodge . . ."

Caitlin couldn't keep the revulsion from her face, even as she struggled to maintain a neutral expression.

Bill noticed, but apparently he didn't care. "I know what you think of me. It doesn't matter. All I can see when I look at you is Kathryn, and that's what counts: What I see, what I feel. What I *need*." He took a step forward, like he was playing a game. "Have you ever been touched by a real man?" She shuddered, as he added, "Kathryn told me that you're still a virgin."

If only he'd stop smiling, Caitlin thought, filled with hatred. The smile made his actions so much worse, because it signified to her that he was beyond both reason and redemption.

"You're no match for me, Caitlin," Bill continued. "And there's nowhere to run anymore. Prayers are wasted breath. You might as well give in."

"Give in to what, Bill?" She suddenly thought that if she could keep him talking, it might prolong the inevitable.

"My desires, of course. What the hell do you think we're talking about?" He took another step toward her, and reached into his back pocket. He took out a dive knife with a serrated blade and pointed the tip in her direction. If she could have gotten even more scared, she would have, but she was already barely hanging on to her sanity. She didn't know if he wanted to cut her up or rape her, or what. *Maybe both.* She only knew that seconds were slipping away, and soon it would be too late to avoid whatever awful things he had in store for her.

The knife was unsteady because of the boat. Caitlin glanced at Danielle, who was still motionless, and then back at the knife. "Bill, what are you doing with that thing? You don't want to hurt me."

"I'm not going to hurt you. The knife is just an incentive for you to obey me. If you do, then you might live." He paused. "If not, then I'll slice you up like a Thanksgiving turkey and toss the pieces overboard." He shrugged. Caitlin pressed herself against the hull, her mind blank. "It's easy to die in a storm out here. Happens all the time . . ."

As he approached slowly, Caitlin recoiled in horror. It was then that her luck finally turned: the boat gave a gigantic heave and spun sideways, breaking free from the dock.

Caitlin felt a moment of weightlessness, as the boat plunged into the water and went up again. Then gravity came crashing back in, tossing her against the wall. Bill fared even worse and got thrown backward onto the rubble pile, hitting his head hard on the way down. Caitlin couldn't tell if he'd lost his knife or not, and she didn't want to find out. She struggled to her feet as Bill writhed on the floor, trying to get up.

In that split second, Caitlin had to make a tough decision. If she ran out of the cabin, she knew that she'd risk leaving Danielle with Bill. But she was pretty certain that Bill would come after her and leave Danielle alone. *He's only interested in me,* she thought. She knew she had to take the risk, because it was her sole chance to escape and get help for both of them. The only way out, of course, was to go directly past Bill and through the door of the cabin. She didn't have time to climb through the window again.

Without thinking, she ran forward and literally scrabbled over his back, as he squirmed in the muck at the bottom of the boat. He tried to grab her ankle, but his hand slipped, his fingernails gouging her flesh, as she reached the door. She grabbed the handle and turned it, pressing against the door with all her might. The door opened, and immediately the wind and rain battered her face, temporarily blinding her. The roar of the storm was so loud it was completely deafening. She crawled on her hands and knees through the door and onto the slippery deck, trying not to slide back into the cabin.

"Come back here, you bitch!" Bill yelled, as she escaped into the downpour. Panicking, she tried standing up, but skidded on the slick surface, almost falling over the edge and into the churning water. She barely managed to stay onboard by grabbing a coil of rope tied down to the deck. As the yacht bucked and heaved in the waves, she gripped the rope as tightly as she could, knowing it was her only lifeline.

The boat had become completely unmoored by the force of the storm, and was now drifting in the inlet, toward the open sea. Massive waves as tall as the boat were cascading toward the inlet under the sickly gray sky. Caitlin realized it was likely that she and Danielle were both going to die violent, senseless deaths in a place they hated. She felt nothing but rage and an almost unbearable desire to live against the odds. Gripping the rope, she turned around to face her tormentor, just in time.

"I'm going to kill you!" she heard Bill roar, as he burst out of the door behind her. Blood was running down his neck and was splattered on one of his hands. It looked like he'd cut himself with his own knife in the fall. He was clutching the knife in his other hand, bearing down toward her with the passionate zeal of someone who'd lost his mind—but didn't care. Caitlin threw her arms up in front of her face to protect herself from the blows, and began to pray.

A split second before the blade sliced into her, through her hands she saw something strange happen to the side of Bill's head. A bright pink mist exploded out of it, into the wind and rain. At the same moment, one of his eyes disappeared into a pool of red mush and pulp. His remaining eye glazed over and he toppled onto her, his limbs thrashing against her body. The knife skittered away into the water. His mouth was open, like he was trying to scream, but he wasn't making any sound.

Caitlin didn't know what had happened to him. She struggled against his weight, trying to get out from under him, as yet another wave poured down on them. His warm blood jetted onto her face as she finally kicked him aside. He landed facedown on the deck, still writhing.

Caitlin slumped against the bulkhead, knotting the rope around her hands to keep from being tossed overboard. As she watched, she saw blood continue to spurt from Bill's head and mingle with the saltwater and rain pounding the deck. *Did someone shoot him?* Caitlin hadn't heard a gunshot, but realized the storm could have masked it.

She was too terrified to be relieved that Bill was down, no matter what the reason. The boat was being tossed around so wildly, she thought it was just a matter of time before it sank, or she got washed over the edge. Her hands were completely numb from the ropes. She thought of Danielle in the cabin below, probably still unconscious, her body getting battered. She didn't stand a chance.

The sky was darker than ever, and Caitlin realized that even now, with Bill out of the picture, she was going to die anyway. Nature didn't care about her or Danielle, or anyone. The storm was relentless and unforgiving.

She vowed to try to stay alive until the very end. There was no question of giving up. She knotted her arms around the ropes even more. *Maybe the storm will pass,* she thought, but she didn't believe it. *Maybe the water will calm down and I can get back to shore.* It was an alluring fantasy. She choked as water drenched her face, and for a second, she thought the boat might tilt all the way over. If that happened, she'd be trapped underneath. Then it righted itself, the ropes tugging on her arms and making her scream out in pain.

Please God, please God, she silently screamed over and over, praying for her torment to end. But the torment had no end, it went on and on, and each moment that she was strapped to the boat seemed like an hour.

At some point, a huge wave crashed over the deck, so big that she couldn't breathe. *Is this it?* She shut her eyes. She opened them just in time to see Bill's twitching body slide off in the backwash, and into the pounding surf. He left no trace. Even his blood was already gone.

As she started praying again more fervently, she saw a white light suddenly gleam across the water and illuminate her full force in its glow. For a split second, she thought that she was dying. Then she realized, as she struggled to stay conscious, it was another boat. One much larger than hers, bearing down on her through the waves.

The large vessel was headed directly toward the inlet and Bill's yacht, lights sweeping out from it in three directions. Even through the noise of the storm, she heard its massive engines as she struggled to stay upright. Just as she began fading into unconsciousness, there was a lull in the waves, and she saw one of the spotlights sweep the distant beach and illuminate something down at the end of the dock.

It's a person, she realized dully. *Someone smaller than me, too small to be Nathan.* In the second that the light passed over the figure, she thought she saw an object glint in its hand, something that looked like a gun.

Instinctively, she knew who it was, even as the spotlight moved onward, plunging the beach into darkness.

It was Luke.

Caitlin's vision started to swim, and everything gently faded into velvety blackness. The sounds of the ocean and the storm began to diminish, and she felt herself floating away. She wondered if she were going to be rescued now, or if it were too late for that.

Caitlin could no longer feel any sensation in her body, as the water continually washed over her. She wasn't sure if she were alive or dead. Her last thought was the odd realization that she was completely at peace, and that her journey was over.

aitlin Ross sat at the desk in her bedroom in La Jolla, day-dreaming as she stared out the windows at the glittering Pacific Ocean far below. The events of the summer seemed more like a fever dream than reality, and that feeling intensified with every passing day. A little more than six weeks had gone by since Caitlin had nearly died at the hands of Bill Collins. Sometimes she had to remind herself it had all been real.

Caitlin had just gotten off the phone with Danielle. The two of them talked several times each day, and Caitlin knew they would be friends forever, bonded by such an incredible, life-altering experience.

In fact, Danielle would be coming to visit her in three weeks, to spend some time with Caitlin in La Jolla.

"Now I'll finally get to see your place," Danielle had joked, "and it better be nicer than my grandma's trailer, or I'll be really depressed."

Caitlin couldn't wait for Danielle's visit, and for the two of them to be reunited. She had plans to take Danielle to all the cool places in town, and to introduce her to all her other friends. Caitlin no longer thought of La Jolla as boring and awful; she was just glad to be back home.

Caitlin and Danielle had also talked about Luke on the phone.

"Rinita's missing him like crazy," Danielle said. "All she talks about is what a nice boy he is, and that she's worried about him. She wants to make sure he's eating okay and not in any trouble, too."

"Luke's doing fine," Caitlin told her, which was mostly the truth.

One of the things Caitlin and Danielle never talked about that much was their traumatic rescue. Caitlin had been saved that day on Danbroke by a Coast Guard vessel patrolling the shore. Usually no boats would have been out because of the weather, but the Coast Guard was looking for a small airplane that had crashed earlier that day. Instead of finding any trace of the plane, they'd found Caitlin instead. Somehow in her weakened state, she'd managed to tell them that Danielle was injured and down in the yacht's cabin, so they'd rescued her as well.

Caitlin only half remembered being taken onboard the Coast Guard ship, along with Danielle. A bulky man in a wetsuit had hauled her over his shoulder to safety. She'd thrown up saltwater, she remembered that much, as the crew took her onto their boat and tried to help her breathe again. She'd been taken down into the hold and laid on a cot. They'd put heating blankets around her and started an IV line. Their vessel was under siege by the storm, but unlike Bill's, it was large enough to withstand it. At some point Caitlin had passed out again completely.

From Danbroke, Caitlin had been taken back to the mainland, in a route that brought them out from under the shadow of the storm. They'd landed at Pottersville, a small town on the edge of South Carolina. Both she and Danielle had been admitted to a local hospital for treatment. Danielle had a mild concussion and some bruises, but they were both pretty much okay—at least physically. Slowly, from the police who visited her hospital bed, Caitlin learned the truth of what had happened that day on the beach.

Bill had indeed been fatally shot by Luke. Caitlin learned that Luke had grabbed Nathan's gun after Nathan's confession, and had run off to the beach to find her and Danielle. He knew somehow—probably because of what she'd already told him about Bill—that she was in danger. He'd put his own life at risk to save hers. There was no question of the police bringing charges against him once Caitlin and Danielle explained what had happened between them and Bill. The police also found over two hundred photos of her that Bill had secretly taken and hung up in a hidden room at the Pirate's Lodge, like a demented shrine.

Bill's body was never found, although after the hurricane passed, the Coast Guard searched the waters intensively. Luke never spoke to Caitlin about what he'd done. He saved those discussions for his therapist, who he now saw three times a week.

The storm had dissipated up the coast by the time Caitlin saw her family again. Her mother, Rinita, and Luke met her and Danielle at the Pottersville Hospital. After another few days there, Danielle had flown to Toronto with Rinita, to stay with her father for a while because she couldn't face going back to the island. Besides, their trailer had been badly damaged in the storm. Caitlin said a tearful good-bye to her, but knew she'd be seeing the girl again very soon.

Both she and Caitlin would have to go back to the Outer Banks in six weeks to testify on behalf of Nathan at his pretrial hearing. They would go down there after Danielle's visit to La Jolla. Nathan had been held briefly in a North Carolina juvenile detention center on charges of manslaughter, but was now out on bail. Caitlin had been asked by the police to testify about what she'd seen that night, and to confirm that Nathan and his dad had struggled over the gun, that it hadn't been premeditated murder. In the end, it had turned out that Nathan was just a disturbed, abused kid, not the kind of psychopath that Bill had been.

Caitlin never really understood why Bill had come after her. Apparently, he'd been losing money for a long time, and had a drug and alcohol habit as large as her mom's. He and her mom had fed on each other's worst tendencies and had spiraled out of control together. It turned out the reason that most of his staff had left wasn't just the lack of money to pay them. It was also because they were afraid of him and his increasingly strange behavior. It appeared as though he'd been using Caitlin's mom for her money, and had swindled nearly fifty thousand dollars from her before his death. He'd also fed her false information about Caitlin and Luke, pretending to her that he was keeping an eye on them. That was why her mom hadn't come looking for them on Danbroke.

Caitlin's mother underwent the most significant change after what had happened on Danbroke. It was a like a mental switch had been thrown when she realized that Caitlin and Luke had almost died out there on the island. Caitlin had always heard that addicts needed to hit rock bottom before they finally sought help—so maybe it had taken something this terrifying to make her mom understand she had a problem.

In any case, her mom had begun an intensive outpatient drug rehab program in San Diego less than a week after they got back. To Caitlin's knowledge, she had stopped taking pills for the time being. Caitlin knew addicts often relapsed, but she hoped that her mom would stay the course. It was the first time she could remember since her parents divorced that her mom was completely sober.

"I'm so sorry," her mom had told her, tears in her eyes. "From now on, everything will be different."

Caitlin only hoped it was the truth and promised to do whatever she could to help her mother make it through.

When Caitlin first returned to La Jolla, she barely left her room for two weeks; she just talked to her mom and to Danielle on the phone as she tried to recover. She only allowed Alison to see her. Caitlin's dad was remarkably absent from the proceedings. He'd flown out to visit her and Luke for a week with The Model, but there was no offer for them to come and stay with him. Caitlin realized that he had his own life now, and if the role he wanted to play in hers was merely tangential, then she'd have to accept that.

I'd rather know where I stand than pine for something that doesn't exist anymore, Caitlin thought. As much as she hated her mother, it was her mom who, in a weird way, had stood by her in the end—by getting the treatment she needed.

Caitlin had eventually reunited with her old friends, at a huge party Alison and Alison's mom had thrown for her. They hadn't invited Ian, which suited her just fine. She was glad to be back home, but she felt a slight sense of dislocation. She knew her friends in La Jolla could never comprehend what she'd been through, as much as she still loved all of them. She could also tell some of them were a little nervous around her, like they didn't know what to say. Caitlin understood, and it was something she talked about a lot with Danielle.

Hell, I'd feel exactly the same way if I knew someone who almost died. It was just freaky it had happened to her. Caitlin knew she wasn't the only one who felt different after Danbroke, because Luke had changed, too.

In some ways, he was the same obnoxious brother he'd always been, except he looked a little older to her, his eyes a little more hooded and serious. She noticed that while he still played video games all the time, he'd retired his collection of paintball guns. There was no need to ask why. He had killed a man for her, to save her, and she knew he'd carry that burden for the rest of his life. She hoped that one day in the future, when he was older, they could talk about it together and she could tell him how grateful she was.

So things were going well, and Caitlin and her family were on track to not only recover from Danbroke, but to be in better shape than before.

And yet . . .

There would always be an "and yet" from now on, Caitlin realized. Although they were happier on the surface, and getting better with every passing day, the trauma of Danbroke would never leave them. Caitlin knew she'd never be able to forget the things that had happened there, from the isolation, to the betrayal of Evan, to Nathan and the murder. *And worst of all, Bill Collins.* She would carry those scars for the rest of her life, even if they made her stronger.

With time, she hoped the memories would fade a little, and become bearable—if frightening—reminders of her lost summer. She wanted to get on with her life and not be a prisoner to any lingering fears. *I don't want to be a weak person.*

Caitlin stared out the windows of her room again, down at the deceptively peaceful ocean and the sunbathers cluttering the expanse of beach. Absently, she ran her fingers over the old cigarette burn on the oak desk. She remembered when she used to think La Jolla was the worst place on earth, an attitude that now seemed incredibly naïve. She knew she'd learned a lot about herself on Danbroke, although her newfound wisdom had come at a cost.

Will I really be able to forget and move on? she wondered. Not enough time had passed yet for her to know how the experience would truly affect her. Her therapist, who she now saw twice a week to help her deal, had repeatedly said that time, distance, and perspective would fix things. Caitlin wasn't so sure. Luke was seeing a different therapist, as was her mom, and Caitlin often wondered what kinds of things they talked about. They didn't share those details with each other because they were just too private, the traumatic experiences of the island still fresh and raw, like wounds.

Caitlin stood up and prepared to head downstairs to see her mom and Luke, to continue the process of rebuilding their family. It wasn't going to be easy for any of them. On the way out of her room, she pulled her blinds shut so she wouldn't have to see the ocean when she came back in.

Caitlin walked down the hallway, trying to think happy thoughts. *There's so much to look forward to, I should just focus on the positive,* she thought. School would be starting in a while and would hopefully bring some welcome distractions, as would Danielle's visit.

Caitlin got downstairs and went out the back door of the house to the pool, where Luke was lounging on a deckchair, sunglasses on.

"What's up, sis?" he asked, turning to look in her direction.

She noted the use of "sis" instead of "bitch," or any of his usual derogatory terms, and thought that was a good sign.

"Not much," she replied.

Luke's response was a burp.

Caitlin sighed, sinking into a chaise lounge and staring up at the blue sky she'd gazed at so many times before. It would be easy to pretend that things were the same as always, yet she knew there would be no uncomplicated happy ending for her. She guessed that on some deep, emotional level, no matter how many years passed, it would be impossible to forget the summer that had changed her life forever . . . and could have ended it for good.

Acknowledgments

Huge thanks to my incredible agent (and music consultant) David Dunton at Harvey Klinger Inc., my fantastic editors Lauren McKenna and Megan McKeever at MTV Books/Pocket Books, and my beautiful and talented wife, Elizabeth McAulay (aka Lisa).

Big thanks also to Nikki Van De Car at Harvey Klinger, Erica Feldon at Pocket, Shari Smiley at CAA, Matt O'Keefe, Leah Stewart, Bobby & Sarah McCain, Pam Cooper, M. Kalvakota, William Sleator, John & Lisa Ware, John Paul Jones, and everyone who liked my first novel, *Bad Girls*.

Much love to my wife, our two cats, Ishmael & Bronwyn, my parents-in-law, and, as always, my mom, Carol-Julia, and my dad, Alastair.

Visit www.alexmcaulay.com for more information about *Lost Summer* and *Bad Girls*.

As many as 1 in 3 Americans
have HIV and don't know it.

TAKE CONTROL.
KNOW YOUR STATUS.
GET TESTED.

To learn more about HIV testing,
or get a free guide to HIV and
other sexually transmitted diseases.

www.knowhivaids.org
1-866-344-KNOW

09620